The Economic REACTOR

The
Economic
REACTOR

Creating Growth and Prosperity

RAJIV BAHL

RUPA

Published by
Rupa Publications India Pvt. Ltd 2016
7/16, Ansari Road, Daryaganj
New Delhi 110002

Sales Centres:
Allahabad Bengaluru Chennai
Hyderabad Jaipur Kathmandu
Kolkata Mumbai

Copyright © Rajiv Bahl 2014, 2016

The views and opinions expressed in this book are the author's own and the facts are as reported by him which have been verified to the extent possible, and the publishers are not in any way liable for the same.

All rights reserved.
No part of this publication may be reproduced, transmitted, or stored in a retrieval system, in any form or by any means, electronic, mechanical, photocopying, recording or otherwise, without the prior permission of the publisher.

ISBN: 978-81-291-3978-8

First impression 2016

10 9 8 7 6 5 4 3 2 1

The moral right of the author has been asserted.

This book is sold subject to the condition that it shall not, by way of trade or otherwise, be lent, resold, hired out, or otherwise circulated, without the publisher's prior consent, in any form of binding or cover other than that in which it is published.

CONTENTS

Preface	*vii*
Introduction	1
1. The Nuclear Reactor	13
2. Interacting Minds and Their Ideas	18
3. Control Rods—The Brakes on the Idea Reactor	47
4. The Coolant and the Pipeline—Tapping the Idea Reactor	76
5. The Heat Exchanger—The Riches of the Marketplace	151
6. Letting It All Happen—Culture Matters	210
7. Happiness	262
In Conclusion	283
Acknowledgements	291

PREFACE

I went out to sea on merchant ships in the mid-1960s when I was a boy not yet 16 years of age. Those were the days before cargo containers and container ships. Port stays were measured in days and not hours. A port stay of a week or two was the norm, affording ample opportunity to see a place close up. General cargo ships sailed on liner routes, calling at many ports along a fixed route.

The world in those days did not have the sameness it does now. The same fast food chains and luxury brands did not stare you in the face no matter where you went. The differences between places were more pronounced, at times startlingly so, even between neighbouring countries. I will never forget my surprise upon visiting Taiwanese ports shortly after seeing ports in the mainland of then communist China. In China everyone, both men and women, was dressed in drab Mao suits and went about their work with a perceptible sullenness. In Taiwan, the dockside was flush with motorcycles. The sullenness had been replaced by an easy banter among the stevedores.

In the heyday of the British Empire, Aden, Rangoon, Singapore and Hong Kong were thriving port cities. Later, their economic policies changed. Hong Kong and Singapore encouraged enterprise and continued to thrive. The situation in Aden and

Rangoon, on the other hand, deteriorated to the extent that in 1970 it was difficult to buy a tube of toothpaste in Rangoon because it was rationed and in short supply. I remember that in 1980 my wife, who was sailing with me on the ship I worked on, and I walked into an empty restaurant on the main street of Aden and could not be served as we had not booked a table in advance. The reason we needed to book and order in advance at an empty restaurant was to give them time to buy meat and vegetables. The economy of this once-thriving port city had become such that a restaurant could no longer expect an occasional walk-in customer.

It seems that sensible economic policies contribute more to material well-being and happiness than political diversity or even independence. Singapore was not politically diverse, the opposition having little space in it. Hong Kong was not independent, being administered by the UK. Both Aden and Rangoon belonged to independent countries—Aden in South Yemen was ruled by a leftist government and Rangoon in Burma by a military junta. India had been independent since 1947 and had a very diverse polity, but until 1991 it had anything but a sensible economic policy. The difference in growth and general well-being between the pre-1991 period and the post-1991 period, when some constraints on doing busines were removed, can be seen in a multitude of statistics, chiefly GDP growth rates which doubled in a few years.

Income levels for the same jobs can vary startlingly across countries. In 1970, when my ship culled at Tacoma, Washington State, USA, I became friendly with a young, longshoreman named Vern Parrot. He was kind enough to invite me over. He lived in a fine stand-alone house, drove a convertible and had a boat on a trailer parked in his front lawn, which he liked to take on weekends to the Juan de Fucca Strait. His Indian counterpart, who loaded and unloaded the same ships in India, earned perhaps a tenth of what Vern did, probably lived in a one- or two-room shanty and had only a few basic clothes to his name. His personal transport, if he had any, was likely to be a bicycle. The difference in material wealth between countries manifested itself in funny ways. On entering even a modest bar or restaurant, in many parts of the world, you were encouraged to take away a nicely printed matchbox with the name and phone number of the establishment, by way of advertisement. In Africa, on the other hand in the 1970s I saw customers painstakingly counting the number of matchsticks in a matchbox to ensure that none had been pilfered.

It is difficult to understand the incongruity of economic situations across the world. Natural resources and the climate do not account for the differences. Sub-Saharan Africa has more natural resources than South East Asia and a similar climate, yet there are no African tiger economies. Similarly, back then, America, the USSR and Western Europe were comparable in size, population and natural resources, but the economic development of the USSR lagged far behind that of the other two. The conditions prevailing in each of these countries varied considerably, yet there was a degree of predictability in the differences. When visiting a port for the first time, we were able to predict with some accuracy the kind of place it was, having considered the economic orientation of the country, whether it was open to private enterprise, if it was insular and planned, whether it treated its women as equals, and whether it was fair and open in its dealings with strangers like ourselves. If a society subscribed to free trade and enterprise, if it was open to interacting with strangers and if it was fair in its dealings with outsiders as well as its own members, it was likely to be a prosperous and happy place.

Culture, it seemed, to my shipmates and me, was as important as economic policy in determining the economic well-being and happiness of a place. I dare say our assessment of the culture of a place was different from that of a diplomat or a visiting professor or expert. A diplomat's interactions are mostly with the crème de la crème of society, whereas ours as sailors were on waterfronts which the elite seldom visited and where the similarities and dissimilarities between people were far more pronounced.

Later, after hanging up my sea boots, I started a small business in India and experienced first-hand the travails of doing business in a difficult place. India ranks near the bottom of the ease of doing business index and I was fast made aware of the many ways in which businesses could be prevented from starting or growing. This awareness, along with what I had seen in different parts of the world, prompted me to start reading about economic matters in an attempt to understand what I had seen and was experiencing and place it in a larger economic picture.

Eventually, I began to perceive the economy of a country as an engine with many different parts, all of which had to function satisfactorily for the economy to perform to its full potential. It did not help if some parts functioned superlatively while others did not function at all.

As a clearer picture of the economic engine formed in my mind, I decided to try and put it down on paper and contemplated writing a book about it. I must confess I started this book with extreme trepidation. Not being an economist, I questioned my credentials for writing about economics and found them wanting. For ten years I procrastinated. However, at the end of all the self-doubt and procrastination, the book in my mind still seemed to make sense. I had to write it if only to see whether it made sense to other people too, the idea that a definite economic engine existed, the model of which could help identify malfunctioning parts of any economy. In retrospect, perhaps a trained economist, steeped in a particular school of economic thought, might not have been able to write a book based largely on first principles, the findings of which have gone against many accepted practices.

INTRODUCTION

We live in a world where countries are at very different levels of economic well-being. In these countries, we see the extremes of human existence. On the one hand, we find conditions of material plenty, contentment and general happiness that have rarely been achieved in history except by the ruling elite of any country. On the other, we witness poverty, hunger, human degradation and despair. Most countries lie somewhere between these two extremes. At any given time, not all countries are seen to be moving towards a better tomorrow. Some are improving their lot while others appear to be slipping behind. The economies of the world are, in short, in disarray.

It is difficult to visualize the two extremes of existence and, at the same time hold in our minds the concept of the world as a global village. No village can harbour both extremes and continue to exist. In a world that is constantly shrinking and becoming more interconnected, the two extremes should not coexist. Many countries that are not doing well economically blame their poor performance on past misfortunes, such as periods under colonial rule, wars or internal strife. If we accept that some countries that are not doing well were indeed handicapped by a legacy of history and assuming that we have by now figured out how to manage the economic fortunes of any country, we would expect to see the same nations, now that their unfortunate past is behind them, improving their performance and catching up with the rest of the world in leaps and bounds. But such instances are rare. Very few third world countries, as they were once called, have managed to post sterling growth.

And it's not just the developing countries that have failed to grow satisfactorily. Developed countries too have shown patchy and uneven growth. Starting from 1950, Japan's real GDP growth averaged 9 per cent for two and a half decades, for the next one and a half decades it averaged 4 per cent and since the 1990s, it has been struggling to grow at all.[1] The American growth story too has been quite inconsistent. Between 1950 and 2013, American growth was over 6 per cent in eight non-consecutive years and negative in nine years.[2] Japan and America are not the only countries to have experienced erratic growth; most countries have experienced the same.

Naturally, the periods of low or negative growth are not planned but occur despite every effort to prevent them. The tools used by governments and central banks to prevent or reverse a stalling economy are monetary policy and at times protectionist measures such as restricting imports and banning immigrant workers in order to try and protect local jobs.

Monetary policy is the process by which authorities control the supply of money and interest rates. An expansionary monetary policy increases the supply of money and lowers interest rates. It is an attempt to combat slowing growth and employment in a recession. By increasing money supply and lowering interest rates, it is hoped that easy credit will entice customers to spend and allow businesses to expand, employing more people. A contractionary monetary policy is one that reduces money supply and increases interest rates. It is used to combat inflation. Using monetary policy and protectionist measures such as curtailing imports, as the only tools to rectify the ailments of any economy is like taking your modern car, which is a fairly complex system, to a mechanic who only knows how to tinker with the fuel pump.

The economy of any country is a vastly more complex system than a modern car. The complexity of a system depends on the number of parts comprising the system and the number of ways in which the parts interact with each other. The greater the complexity, the larger the number of perturbations generated in the system. The economy of any country where there are millions of free acting agents interacting with each other is an extremely complex system. It would be strange indeed to expect that all the disturbances that arise in such a complex system will arise at one single point and be resolved by tinkering with just that one part of the system, namely, money supply controlled by monetary policy.

In an attempt to set right a malfunctioning economy, monetary policy has often been used extravagantly. The US Federal funds' rate is the benchmark interest rate, influencing all other interest rates, and not just in America. It is determined by the US Fed through its Federal Open Market Committee, which also makes key decisions about the growth of money supply. Starting from 1950, when the rate was below 5 per cent, it followed an uptrend up to 1980 when it peaked at 20 per cent and then began a downtrend; now in 2016 it is near 0 per cent levels, where it has been steady for the past few years.

The year 1980 must have been a confusing one for the US Fed. In that year, the Fed raised the rate to 20 per cent, lowered it to 10 per cent and then raised it again to 20 per cent.[3] To me, this looks like confusion bordering on panic, and is a clear indication that not all ailments of an economic system can be set right by monetary policy.

There have been some notable exceptions to the general practice of countries trying to achieve growth largely through monetary stimulus. China and India are two fine examples. China started growing in the 1980s and has had high uninterrupted growth for over three decades. India started growing in the 1990s and has enjoyed reasonably high uninterrupted growth for over two decades. Earlier, the economies of both countries were moribund. Before the 1980s, China followed traditional communist practices and almost all enterprise and industry belonged to the state. Once individuals and private companies were allowed to conduct business, and had at least limited property rights, the floodgates to private enterprise were opened, resulting in unprecedented growth. In India the initial situation was marginally better. While individuals had property rights, in practice their enterprise was stunted because of the plethora of permits and clearances required from multiple government departments for starting even a small business venture. When some of these constraints were removed, the economy responded immediately and began to grow at unprecedented rates.

The steps that China and India took to spur growth had little to do with monetary policy. Any monetary stimulus provided was peripheral to the main steps taken to encourage private enterprise. Whether wittingly or unwittingly, both China and India took steps that addressed the deficiencies in their economic engines. Had China and India merely tried to stimulate growth by increasing liquidity, it is unlikely that they would have achieved the growth rates they did; further, it is highly probable that they would have spurred inflation.

In hindsight, the steps that China and India took to grow their economies appear obvious. However, from the time the two countries became independent, it took China 30-odd years to act and India 40-odd years to act. It is possible that had there been a better understanding of how an economic engine works, and of its parts and how they interact, it may not have taken so long. Hundreds of millions of people would have escaped poverty decades earlier.

Just as the underperformance of an economy is sought to be blamed on its history, various reasons have been put forth for the good performance of other economies. However, none of these reasons passes muster consistently. Natural resources have at times been held as the key to economic success, but several countries have achieved economic success with few natural resources. Japan, South Korea, Taiwan and Singapore are perfect examples. Technology, the talisman of our times, is often believed to be crucial to economic success. However, a lot of work goes into developing technology, and even if a high degree of technological prowess is achieved, it does not always translate into economic success. The erstwhile Soviet Union possessed both immense natural resources and technological competence, as evidenced by its success in the space and the arms race, where it competed with the best in the world. Vast natural resources and technological prowess were not enough to get its economy going.

There is yet another popular explanation for the reason behind dismally performing societies, although it is not clearly articulated in this age of political correctness. It is that the people of economically healthy nations are somehow intrinsically superior—perhaps they are more hard-working, or more disciplined, more honest, or have a stronger work ethic, or are even more intelligent. Sadly, with all their psychologically debilitating effects, these views also have adherents in the economically poorly performing nations. The experience of the diaspora from myriad third world countries that have settled in richer countries points in the opposite direction, however. Most of these immigrants have achieved far more in their new homes than they could have done in their own countries, not just as better-paid labour, but also by running their own businesses and holding responsible, decision-making positions in their jobs.

The success of the Indian and Chinese diaspora is apparent, perhaps because they are larger in number and more easily recognizable. While in the last few decades both China and India have done well economically, prior to this both countries could be held up as examples of how not to run economies. Yet it is the people from these very countries who settled down in other countries and did quite well in their new homes.

If no consistent reasons for a country's well-being come to mind, does something like a universal economic engine really exist, with all its parts meshing together to produce economic growth and human well-being, with consistent and predictable results? I strongly believe it does, and that it is possible to analyse any working economy with accuracy and pinpoint its strengths and weaknesses and thereby initiate remedial action. This economic engine is no creation of mine. It exists and it works. I am only an observer trying to see the working of the complete machine. Sometimes I think of it as one of those pictures that are completely unintelligible until they have been stared at for a length of time, when suddenly the picture starts coming together.

The economic engine is a complex machine comprising many parts linked together. Like any chain, the strength of any economic engine is only as much as its weakest link. A weakness in any one area cannot be compensated by strengthening another area. In a malfunctioning engine, remedial action must be taken at the point or points of weakness and not any other point, simply because it is easy or convenient to address that point. Economic well-being and growth are the result of many factors, which this book tries to understand. It is essential to understand each of these factors. Loose monetary and fiscal policies have only a limited and temporary impact on growth and employment. Growth and employment depend far more on the generation, release and implementation of new ideas and the existence of an efficient marketplace with low transactional costs that lets these ideas be put to the test.

Before I proceed to describe this economic engine, I seek the reader's indulgence in permitting me a small detour on the subject of systems.

The world is full of systems or sets of rules covering just about everything that's ever been observed or invented. The number of all these observed or invented things is almost infinite. However, the systems or sets of rules governing all the different phenomena are often quite similar to those for many other such phenomena in apparently unrelated areas. The number of systems or sets of rules, as against the different observable phenomena, is considerably less than infinite. In other words, there are just so many ways in which things are put together and function.

Giant metrological systems—such as cyclonic storms which can affect a quarter of a million square kilometres and release energy at a rate 200 times the worldwide electricity generating capacity, or as much as a 10 megaton nuclear bomb exploding every twenty minutes—and the engine of my small car are both heat engines and follow the same principles. Heat input comes from burning gasoline in a car and from the sun-heated upper layers of ocean waters in the case of a cyclone. The heat energy moves to a heat sump, the cooling from the radiator in the case of the car and the cold upper regions of the atmosphere in the case of the cyclone. The release of energy in the car is converted into motion and in the storm it is converted to gale force winds and storm surges. The point to note is that though these two mechanisms are very different in size and structure, both are heat engines and follow the same set of rules for their functioning.[4] There are other striking similarities across systems.

I first encountered the concept of 'half life' in high school physics while studying the decay of radioactive elements. It was counter-intuitive. If half the atoms of a given radioactive material decay in, say, one year, then the remaining half ought to decay in another year. However, only half the remaining atoms decay in the second year and half of those still remaining in the third year, and so on indefinitely. I assumed this to be a peculiarity of the subatomic world and left it at that.

Later when I started a food processing business and while studying food preservation and sterilization I was surprised that the half-life rule was applicable to living organisms. This was even more counter-intuitive. If half the living organisms could be killed in the torture chamber of an autoclave in, say, 10 minutes, surely it should require only a little more time to kill the rest. These were, after all, living organisms and could endure only so much punishment before dying. Again, my intuition was wrong. Living organisms follow the same set of rules as inanimate atoms. Only half the microorganisms are killed in the next 10 minutes and half of those remaining in the next 10, and so on until all the microorganisms are killed and the food is sterile.

And this is not just true of microorganisms. Insurance companies using reams of statistics to calculate their premiums know that a given percentage of people in any age group will die in any year and that almost exactly the same percentage of the remaining will die the following year.

Microorganisms are millions of times larger and more complex than atomic nuclei and human beings are millions of times larger and more complex than microorganisms. Why should the attrition rates of all three follow the same pattern? It does not seem to matter that atoms are inanimate, microorganisms among the simplest of life forms and human beings complex multicellular life forms. They all perish following the same rules.

There are often surprising similarities in quite unrelated areas. Does anything strike you as common between a river delta system, a bolt of lightning striking the earth, a tree quietly growing its branches and the organizational chart of an expanding corporate or government organization? Little, other than that it is difficult to tell apart aerial photographs of delta systems, lightning bolts, autumnal pictures of branched-out trees, and the organizational charts of bureaucracies. All these phenomena conform to fractal geometry and closely resemble computer models based on fractal geometry.

Is this coincidental or does it mean that this model is the best way for any entity that needs to cover a growing space?[5,6] Assuming the latter and looking for more examples, we find a hierarchy of tubular membranes and air passages branching out from the largest bronchial tubes to the tiniest alveoli in our lungs. We also find the branches of every artery and capillary in our circulatory system conforming to the same pattern. Does this tell us something useful? That if our intention is to prune government or corporate bureaucracy, it is no use trimming the end branches of the system, which will over time grow back in far greater numbers than before, but to aim instead for major branches which are perhaps more dispensable now, for any reason, than they were earlier?

The force of gravity and electromagnetic radiation are two of the four primal forces. (The other two are the weak nuclear force and the strong nuclear force and both are perceivable only in the nuclei of atoms.) These two forces are fundamentally different, as theorists who have been trying for decades to meld them into a unified field theory will no doubt endorse. However, they both diminish with distance and their strength reduces by the square of the distance from the source.

Some similarities are more intractable than others and often require a touch of genius to spot them. It took Pythagoras, who solved right-angle triangles and their ratios, to notice that harmonious notes were emitted by a set of hammers striking iron if the hammer weights had a simple mathematical relationship with each other and that their weights were simple ratios or fractions of one another. That is, hammers half, a third or a quarter of the weight of a particular hammer would all generate harmonious sounds. A hammer that bore no such relationship with the other hammers would strike a discordant note.

Pythagoras applied his discovery to lyre strings. By fixing a single lyre string and plucking it, a standard note is produced by the entire length of the vibrating string. By fixing the string at particular points along its length, it is possible to generate other vibrations and notes. Crucially, harmonious notes occur at very specific points. For example, plucking the string at a point exactly halfway along it generates a sound one octave higher and in harmony with the original note. Similarly, by fixing the string at points that are exactly a third, a quarter or a fifth of the way along it, other harmonious notes are produced. However, fixing the string at a point that is not a simple fraction of the length of the whole string creates a sound that is not in harmony with the others.[7]

There are explanations for why the hammer weights and lyre string lengths produce similar results, but why should the human ear and human mind find these sounds harmonious? What is it about whole numbers and their fractions that hammer weights, string lengths, human ears and human minds all resonate to the same symphony?

The number π is the ratio of the circumference of a circle and its diameter. It is approximately equal to 3.143 and is true for circles of all sizes. There is no answering the why of it. It is just the way circles are. However, circles aren't the only place where we find π. Under ideal conditions, the ratio of the actual length of a river and its distance in a straight line from source to mouth tends to approach π. It took an Albert Einstein to understand why this happened. That is not all. π appears routinely in equations describing the fundamental principles of the universe. It is found in the equations for Heisenberg's uncertainty principle, Einstein's field equation of general relativity, Coulomb's law for electrical force and Kepler's third law constant. It also shows up in formulae for distributions in probability and statistics.[8]

This detour was not about the ubiquity of π, fractals, numbers and their fractions, musical notes or tropical storms. It was about getting the reader accustomed to the idea that there is often great similarity in seemingly unconnected phenomena. Things can be put together in just so many ways and function. Having hopefully achieved my limited goal, I can now proceed further. Before I do so, however, I must confess to my initial discomfort at the idea of a limited number of somehow preordained systems in operation. It is like trying to limit a limitless universe. Then came the realization that the universe is in reality limited by universal constants, such as the speed of light, the Newtonian constant of gravity, the Planck constant, the electromagnetic constants, the atomic and nuclear constants and the physico-chemical constants. It is also limited by what is mathematically possible. We may not yet understand everything in the universe but that does not imply that the universe is free to do magic and not act within the constraints of what is possible. In this light, it is easier to accept the similarities we see across systems.

I wonder if there is a way of propounding an outlandish idea in a manner that makes it seem less outlandish. Being unable to find one, I must state my idea outright: the workings of an economic engine are for almost all purposes identical to the workings of a nuclear fission reactor. All the components of a nuclear fission reactor, including fissile material, emitted neutrons, striking more fissile atoms, control rods, coolant, piping system and heat exchangers have their counterparts in the economic engine. But why is this observation even important? Is it simply a matter of idle curiosity or can the realization of this similarity benefit us? On examining the workings of a nuclear fission reactor and an ideal economic engine, if we are convinced that there is indeed a striking resemblance between the two, the workings of a nuclear fission power plant can serve as a tool for us to understand various aspects of the omnipresent economic engine as it functions around us.

An ideally functioning economic engine is in fact a far more complicated machine than a nuclear fission reactor. With its relative simplicity, a nuclear reactor is far easier to understand. By understanding the one and comparing it with the other, we may well be able to detect and point to those parts of the economic engine that might require some adjustment.

REFERENCES

1. http://socialdemocracy21stcentury.blogspot.in/2013/01/japanese-real-gdp-growth-19252001.html. Accessed on 25 April 2016
2. http://useconomy.about.com/od/GDP-by-Year/a/US-GDP-History.html. Accessed on 25 April 2016
3. http://useconomy.about.com/od/monetarypolicy/p/Past_Fed_Funds.html. Accessed on 25 April 2016
4. http://en.wikipedia.org/wiki/Tropical_cyclone. Accessed on 25 April 2016
5. http://en.wikipedia.org/wiki/Benoit_Mandelbrot. Accessed on 25 April 2016
6. http://www.amherst.edu/~rloldershaw/nature.html. Accessed on 25 April 2016
7. Fermat's Last Theorem—Simon Singh—Fourth Estate, 1997
8. http://en.wikipedia.org/wiki/Pi. Accessed on 25 April 2016

1

THE NUCLEAR REACTOR

NUCLEAR REACTORS CAN BE DIVIDED INTO A FEW TYPES DEPENDING mainly upon the fuel they use. Their internal logic and essentials, however, remain the same.

The starting point of all reactors is the fuel, which is a fissile isotope of uranium, plutonium or thorium, or a mixture of all three. A fissile material spontaneously emits neutrons. Scientists cannot change the inherent ability of fissile materials to emit neutrons at the rate at which they normally do. Emitting neutrons at a predetermined rate is just something fissile materials do. This process is called radioactive decay and has been going on since before the earth was formed.

A neutron emitted by an atom of a fissile material travels at a high speed and has the potential to strike and be absorbed by another of the same material, causing that atom to split and release two or three fresh neutrons, depending upon the fuel, and a lot of heat energy. These newly emitted neutrons have the same potential to strike other fissile atoms, splitting them and releasing more neutrons and more energy. A nuclear reactor is said to have gone critical, or in other words, become self-sustaining, when every splitting atom causes at least one more atom to split.

If an emitted neutron fails to interact with another fissile atom, that neutron travelling at millions of miles per hour is lost to the reactor forever.

Although nuclear physicists have been unable to control spontaneously emitted neutrons, they have managed to increase the chances of an emitted neutron's absorption by another fissile atom and are thereby able to get a sustained reaction going inside the nuclear reactor, harnessing the energy released by the splitting atoms. Before we look at how they do it, let's talk a little bit about uranium, the most common nuclear fuel.

About ninety-nine per cent of uranium found in nature is Uranium-238 and just 0.7 per cent is the fissile isotope of Uranium-235. The numbers at the end are the sum total of neutrons and protons in each isotope. All uranium isotopes have 92 protons and the balance are neutrons. Uranium as it exists in nature has almost no chance of going critical as it contains too little of the fissile isotope and the emitted neutrons travel too fast to be captured by other fissile atoms. Also, the bits of Uranium-235 in nature are too far separated from each other to enable emitted neutrons to strike other fissile atoms in sizeable numbers and be absorbed by them.

In order to ensure a sustained nuclear reaction, nuclear scientists have done three things: first, they have enriched Uranium-235 from 0.7 per cent to about 2–3 per cent, making it three or four times the original concentration. Second, they have closely packed the fuel in the shape of rods, increasing the probability of emitted neutrons interacting with other atoms. Finally, they have surrounded the fuel rods with a moderator that greatly slows the emitted neutrons, further increasing the chances of other atoms capturing the neutrons. Sometimes the moderator could simply be pressurized water, hence we have a pressurized water reactor.

Further, if the moderator is changed from water to heavy water, that is, water made with deuterium, another isotope of hydrogen, the movement of the emitted neutrons slows down to the extent that it is no longer necessary to enrich the Uranium-235 in order to achieve criticality. Hence the term heavy water reactor.

There is also a bonus of sorts. Uranium-238, which forms 99 per cent of the uranium, is not an idle bystander. When one of the neutrons emitted by an atom of Uranium-235 is captured by an atom of Uranium-238, it transforms it into Plutonium-239. (This is a multistage process, but the steps occur so quickly that for our purpose it may be regarded as a single step.) Plutonium-239 is also a fissile material and when it absorbs another neutron, it in turn splits emitting energy and more neutrons which are able to carry the reaction further.

Having applied these changes, the nuclear reactor is now critical and produces energy in the form of heat, both from the heat energy released when atoms split and neutrons are emitted as well as from the kinetic energy converted to heat energy when they are slowed down by the moderator. The heat energy needs to be siphoned off with a coolant, often water, which is led around the reactor vessel and then to a heat exchanger or steam turbine to convert it to useful electricity. The continuous supply of coolant is extremely important. The energy output in a well-functioning reactor is large and in the event of stoppage or reduction of the coolant supply to the reactor, the energy build-up can be disastrous. The accident at Three Mile Island in Pennsylvania, USA, in 1979 was triggered by the failure of a pump feeding the coolant to the reactor. The accidents at Chernobyl and Fukushima were also caused by coolant failure.

Thus far we have been looking at the necessary steps that must be taken in order to make the reactor critical and attain a self-sustaining chain reaction producing heat energy that can then be led off and used as required.

There is one other major component of the nuclear reactor, which is used to control the rate of fission to prevent overheating or, in the worst-case scenario, a nuclear explosion caused by an uncontrolled chain reaction.

This control is exerted by inserting rods made of a material capable of absorbing the emitted neutrons without its own atoms splitting between the piles of nuclear fuel. In fact, before the reactor is fuelled and started up, the control rods are put in place, and when everything is in order, they are raised very slowly until criticality is achieved. However, if there are too many control rods and the neutrons emitted by the fissile material do not get the opportunity to be absorbed by other fissile atoms, the reactor does not attain criticality and is a non-starter.

Nuclear scientists will no doubt complain that this is an over-simplification of a complex system, and they would be right. Less than a human lifetime ago, some of the greatest scientists of the time were struggling to achieve a self-sustaining nuclear reaction. Having said that, it may come as a surprise that the first achievement of a sustained chain reaction happened not in any fancy laboratory but on a tennis court in Chicago on 2nd December 1942.

The reactor was a pile of uranium and graphite blocks, assembled under the supervision of renowned physicist Enrico Fermi. Fermi himself described the apparatus as 'a crude pile of black bricks and wooden timbers'. Compared to present-day reactors, Fermi's hot pile was a primitive affair, but it must be viewed as a proof-of-concept undertaking. A proof-of-concept undertaking is an experiment or a pilot project to validate a particular concept, in this case the concept was that of a controlled chain reaction. The results of the experiment were a huge success, even if hot piles are relatively easy to achieve.

While the experiment was successful in demonstrating the validity of the concept, it was still a hot pile and not a full-blown nuclear power plant. The energy generated by the experiment was not put to use. There was no coolant and no heat exchanger. Had this been the end goal, it would have been an exercise in futility and merely a curiosity. It is the same with the economic engine. If all the parts of the engine are not there or not functioning, it is not really of much use to anyone.

In the following chapters I will mention each part of the nuclear reactor and examine in detail how the corresponding part of the economic engine works.

2

INTERACTING MINDS AND THEIR IDEAS

In a nuclear reactor, radioactive materials like uranium or thorium are positioned such that their atoms can interact with each other. When an atom spontaneously emits a neutron, that neutron can cause another atom to emit a neutron of its own.

It is the same with human minds and their ideas. An idea released by one person can cause the emergence of another in a second person's mind. Knowledge is increased when minds exchange ideas. It is not only increased in the sense that the same knowledge is held in more minds. Absolute knowledge is also increased with the exchange of ideas, thoughts and concepts.

◆

To demonstrate the inevitability of this process, I ask the reader to let me indulge in a thought experiment. Imagine two communities, somewhere at the dawn of civilization, about 10,000 years ago, living in the same geographical region. One is a community of farmers who have mastered the new science of planting seeds, tending to the plants and harvesting the grain or vegetables. The other is a community of shepherds with accumulated experience of herding and rearing goats and sheep. Both communities are competent. The farmers understand when to plant wheat and when to plant seasonal herbs and vegetables. They understand that they have to let their fields lie fallow at times to prevent them from going barren. They have also grasped the periodicity of long and short days as well as the recurring cycle of rain and dry spells. They take all of this into account when they plan their crops and, by the standards of their time, are quite successful in their endeavours, except perhaps when the weather gods show their displeasure.

The shepherds are good at rearing their flocks. They follow a limited nomadic existence, going up to the highlands in summer and returning to the pastures in the plains in winter. They have acquired an understanding of the seasons and their flocks have rarely been snowbound. They rely on their flocks for meat, milk, from which they also make cheese, and leather, sometimes using the fleece to make clothes. Sheep are not yet bred for fine wool, which will happen more than a thousand years into the future, perhaps when spinners of cotton interact with shepherds.

These two communities have existed in this manner for many years, maybe even several generations. Both communities lead a satisfactory existence and with the passage of time, each has evolved its own customs and folklore. Both communities, being in the same geographical region, are aware of each other. There is only occasional contact with one another, when a little barter trade takes place. The farmers need sheepskin to sew into garments to keep the winter chill at bay, and a sheep or goat now and then for the occasional feast. The shepherds, of course, need grain and vegetables or dried herbs to break the monotony of their limited fare.

Now let us imagine that these two communities, which have

been leading their lives quite isolated from each other, grow closer. It does not matter why or how. It could be a threat of war or an affair of the heart. It could be the drying up of a river or an omen that appeared in the skies. What matters is that the two communities now share the same address, which, from a small hamlet, becomes a village. The farmers and shepherds have their own farms and pastures in the surrounding countryside but live in the same village. The children of the village play together and marriages between the children of farmers and shepherds are not unthinkable.

It is at this point that a major change occurs. They are no longer two communities living close to each other but one community having access to two streams of knowledge. Each member of the enlarged community has access to more knowledge than before. Further, the coming together of the two communities results in knowledge and awareness that was not present in the sum total of the knowledge earlier held by the two separate communities. Concerns and considerations that neither community had harboured before become important now:

Fences become an idea worth delving into to keep the sheep away from the crops.

Legality and ethics come into the picture when considering who will pay for the fences or trampled crops.

Fodder becomes a cropping option.

Animal droppings, which were little more than an eyesore on the pastures, acquire value as fertilizer.

Milk, which has a short shelf life, now becomes a tradable commodity along with concerns as to how much the milk is worth in terms of grain or vegetables.

Land becomes an asset with multiple possible uses. Which use will yield higher returns?

Labour becomes a concept. In which activity will the least labour yield maximum returns?

What has happened here? How did the new awareness and knowledge come about? No new discoveries in animal husbandry or farming techniques have been made, yet the sum total of awareness and knowledge has increased. Prior to their coming together, every member of the farming community knew about the traditional ways of farming and every shepherd knew traditional shepherding practices. It was only when new ideas ricocheted off minds holding different bodies of knowledge that further ideas emerged. It is easy to visualize a farmer learning of the shepherds' need to migrate in search of grass, grasping the value of fodder; or of a shepherd, learning about the necessity of keeping fields fallow, grasping the value of animal droppings as fertilizer. It is also easy to visualize how putting some of these ideas into practice would generate other new ideas.

An idea is not a priori event. It is not without cause. It depends on an existing body of knowledge and experience which, when impacted upon by a new fact, observation or idea, might trigger off new ideas. There is no guarantee that an idea will be triggered off and even if it is, there is no guarantee that it will be a good and desirable idea from any observer's viewpoint. All we can do is try to ensure that ideas keep coming. What is required for ideas to keep emerging is communication between people, education and easy access to knowledge and information.

At the risk of belabouring a point, I feel I must draw attention to the sheer magic of the creation of new ideas through the simple process of increasing the possibilities of communication between people holding different bodies of knowledge. It is not by chance that the vast majority of ideas that have marked our progress since medieval times have been born in cities, which were once home to only a small fraction of the population. Cities permitted communication between people of different trades and interests, following which the creation of new ideas and innovations, whether intentional or otherwise, was a natural and unstoppable consequence.

Economists sometimes explain the economic progress of early cities by the size of the cities which made the division of labour possible, thereby enhancing productivity. This is certainly a factor in the economic growth of cities, but just as important is the fact that the size of the cities and the easy intermingling of people from different trades and backgrounds also facilitated the emergence of ideas.

People coming together to exchange ideas may well have been the single largest factor behind the stupendous growth of the Abbasid Caliphate which, after its victory over the Ummayads in 750 CE, was open to ideas from non-Arab and non-Muslim sources, in sharp contradistinction to the practice of the Umayyed Caliphate which restricted itself to Arab Muslim sources.

A different but equally illuminating example is the mystery of why China did not become the dominant superpower from the early fifteenth century into current times. China was unified into one country during the Qin dynasty in 221 BCE by Qin Shi Huan and with the inputs of a powerful administrative service soon became a huge but steerable power. It was the country where some of the most far-reaching discoveries were made, including printing, paper making, gunpowder, coal burning, the magnetic compass and large shipbuilding. Starting in 1405 CE, Zheng He, an admiral under the Ming government, undertook a series of seven voyages, the last of which was in 1433.[1] His flotilla comprised 28,000 men in 317 ships, many of which were larger than the combined size of the three ships that Columbus commanded when he discovered America. Zheng He undertook voyages to Arabia, Brunei, East Africa, India, the Malay Archipelago and Thailand, and to Hormuz in the Persian Gulf. The size of his fleet was unprecedented. The size of his larger ships would only be surpassed once steel ships had been invented. The size of his armada would only be surpassed in the Second World

War. His voyages began 87 years before those of Christopher Columbus. He reached India 92 years before Vasco da Gama's four small ships reached the same ports. There are speculations that some of Zhenge's ships might have travelled beyond the Cape of Good Hope many decades before Bartolomeu Dias discovered it. Wherever he went, it was with a purpose to awe the local rulers and proclaim the might of the Chinese emperor. He gifted gold, silver, silk and porcelain and took back curiosities like ostriches, zebras, camels, ivory and giraffes. He also brought back with him envoys from thirty states, who travelled to China to pay their respects at the Ming court. The Chinese were certainly aware that their naval might was unsurpassed. And then the Chinese did something inexplicable. They banned all ocean voyages, burned the records of Zheng He's adventures, and scuttled all the ships.

This banning of ocean voyages, along with the building of the Great Wall of China and the tribute system, which ensured that any foreigner wishing to visit China could do so only after offering a suitable tribute, a gift made in order to acknowledge the suzerainty of the Chinese emperor, limited the flow of ideas into China. From a position of overwhelming superiority in the fifteenth century CE, the idea quarantine that China imposed upon itself resulted in a great humbling of China by the European powers and the Japanese in the nineteenth and early twentieth centuries.

Let us go back to our idyllic village of the farmers and shepherds. We left them when the farmer's body of knowledge had started interacting with the shepherd's body of knowledge and they were, together, generating entirely new ideas and knowledge. It was hoped that new ideas would keep cascading and that there would be continued innovation and prosperity all round. It sounds too good to be true. If this is indeed how things happened, we would not find backward communities anywhere. Yet the process seems almost unavoidable. New bits of information interacting with an existing body of knowledge and giving rise to new thoughts is a non-volitional act. Can anything go wrong and halt this process, or even prevent it from starting? In this thought experiment, we have taken the coming together in close proximity of the two communities as a given, but would this have taken place so easily in reality?

The coming together of the two communities would probably be a rare occurrence, fought against, tooth and nail, by many members of both communities. Generations of practising one's own customs and way of life reinforce those customs as the natural way of things and anything different is seen as a deviation, unnatural and not worth emulating. Shepherds are shifty and unreliable, never staying in one place and usually untraceable. Farmers are stodgy and have limited horizons, and their fertility rites are clearly directed towards evil spirits. The leaders of the two groups, their chiefs and shamans, would probably have viewed the coming together of the two communities as a loss of their own power and status and opposed any such merger. Even if such a union were to take place, the practice of their own traditions over many generations would have made the adoption of new practices by both groups difficult. In the absence of writing, the elders in those times were the main repositories of knowledge and tradition. They would have been unlikely to endorse new practices that went against and devalued their store of knowledge. They would tend to negate new ideas. They would, in effect, be acting as control rods in a nuclear reactor. Control rods receive neutrons and absorb them, eliminating them from further participation in any chain reaction.

In the story about the farmers and shepherds we assumed that both groups had existing bodies of knowledge, which when exposed to new information, elicited new ideas. Similarly, in the real world we need to equip our minds with bodies of knowledge. We have known this for a long time and devised education to achieve this goal. Education, however, is a catch-all phrase and encompasses everything, from what we learn at our mother's knee, to what we study at school, to what we learn in the school of hard knocks. Returning to the metaphor of the nuclear reactor, what can we do to make our minds more fissile and able to spontaneously emit ideas? What should we focus on in our education system to bring about an improvement?

What we learn at our mother's knee is from the accumulated knowledge and wisdom of the mother. A mother cannot impart knowledge that she does not possess. The school of hard knocks is, by its very definition, an arena of random events and therefore almost impossible to influence. Regular school, it would appear, is the most appropriate place to intervene.

Before we try and devise an outline for the ideal educational system and syllabi, it is important to understand what we expect from them. I can think of no better way to express what I think education is about than to quote Albert Einstein: 'Education is not the learning of facts but the training of the mind to think.' This is truer today than it was during Einstein's time and will be still truer tomorrow if we can maintain open access to the knowledge highway of the internet. Just as the calculator made learning by rote of multiplication tables redundant, the information available on the internet is making the learning of facts by rote redundant. Today it is meaningless to think of an ideal education system without taking the internet into account. The internet, however, has not obviated our ability to think and to hold in our minds as accurate a depiction of the world as we can.

The education system we devise for our young must be able to implant in their minds as accurate a picture as possible of the world around us, including its history, geography and current understandings. It must enable our young to access information and ideas and most importantly teach them to dispassionately evaluate new information. It must, in other words, enable them to think. It must enable them to put forth their ideas and, being mindful of their rights, share them. It must also impart to them the skills and values that will enable them to work with others to their mutual benefit.

Traditionally, formal education has been broken down into three stages: primary, secondary and tertiary education. The role of primary education is unambiguous. It is supposed to impart the basic skills of reading, writing and arithmetic along with some principles of science and an awareness of our world, including its history and geography. The role of tertiary education is also clear, as it is intended to impart specialized training in a particular field. The role of secondary education, however, is not very clear. What is secondary education expected to impart that should not be covered by primary education in the first place? The immediate response to this question will be that secondary education covers in greater detail subjects mentioned in primary education. This may well be true but that underscores the reality that, by itself, primary education is incomplete and contributes little to enhance understanding. Primary education, as it is now, should not be considered as a target to achieve, not even a midway target. I think the role of primary education needs to be reviewed and enhanced to meet the need of developing thinking minds. Thinking minds cannot be developed in the four to five years of what is now called primary education. Primary education must comprise 10 to 12 years and encompass what are now both primary and secondary education. Once that is achieved, we should move straight to what is now the tertiary stage. Of the two, the primary stage is by far the more important and consequently deserves greater attention.

What passes for primary education in some countries, such as the ability to painstakingly read a few lines, understand road signs and sign one's name, is not an education at all but a skill akin to, say, basket weaving. It helps not a whit in assimilating, generating or implementing ideas. To start with, we need to develop the basic ability of a thinking mind to receive information, evaluate it, integrate it into its existing world picture and then hopefully come up with its own ideas. It is this ability of human minds that drives the entire economic engine upon which the well-being of every member of the community depends. Every society must try and do what it can to ensure that the minds of their young start assimilating and generating ideas. Second, we need to remember that numbers matter. We need to increase the ratio of minds that generate ideas to those that suppress ideas.

What the above requirements point to is free and compulsory universal primary education. This is an observation that not many of us would disagree with. Many countries might feel that they have already achieved this goal and there are many more, encompassing perhaps the majority of humankind, where this has not yet been achieved. The leaders of countries where universal primary education has not been achieved will probably not dispute its necessity and point to their growing literacy numbers as evidence that they are on the way to achieving it. They probably put their dismal situation down to a lack of resources and state that they are aware that education can uplift underprivileged sections of society. This reasoning needs a slight change of nuance.

A good universal primary education will not only uplift the downtrodden, it will uplift us all. A penny spent upon the education of an underprivileged child is also a penny spent on your child and your future. As it goes for a penny, so it goes for a fortune. The idea that set off another which triggered the idea that changed our world a little bit for the better could have come from anyone. The idea that started this chain reaction would have run against a brick wall if it had first encountered minds to which the idea had no meaning. The idea that changed the world would have died at birth. The idea would in effect have struck a control rod that absorbed it but failed to emit another idea in turn.

Uneducated minds act as unwitting control rods by simply receiving ideas and, far from emitting another idea, negate the idea without being able to consider it rationally. Every uneducated child is not only a potential zero in the idea reactor, but a potential minus. This is the strongest argument for universal education. The fewer the number of educated minds in a given population, the greater the number of uneducated minds or control rods. In many societies in the developing world this is applicable especially to women. Women are not only denied a secular education but also schooled, often at home, in the traditions of their societies. These traditions become the lenses through which they view the world around them and with the help of which they evaluate new ideas, normally negating them, for they have been schooled to value traditional over non-traditional. I will examine this in greater detail in the next chapter, which focuses on different kinds of control rods. Here I wish to stress that the lack of a good education can turn a potentially fissile mind that would spontaneously emit ideas into a control rod that acts as a dead end for ideas.

Before proceeding further, let us consider the internet and the flood of information that it has made available. In earlier times, information was precious and difficult to come by. It was dispensed in judicious doses by teachers, textbooks and expensive encyclopaedias, and by parents, assorted elders and other luminaries of society. This information was expected to be accepted as it was given to us. In a sense it was given intravenously without any need of further digestion. Our minds were barely involved in analyzing or evaluating it.

The advent of the internet has changed the scenario. It is now possible to access at the click of a few buttons, information on almost any subject, along with the opinions—often completely contradictory ones—of a myriad other experts.

To deal with this tsunami of often contradictory information, we need to provide ourselves with an effective filtration system to try and separate the gold from the dross.

The role of primary education is to provide the essential tools without which further progress is impossible. These are popularly referred to as the three Rs: Reading, 'Riting and 'Rithmetic'. We now need a fourth R, Reasoning. It is only with this tool that, even if one is not able to clearly categorize a given piece of information as true or false, we can categorize the information into plausible or implausible. This is not a skill set that can be developed in a year or two. Much like arithmetic, it would need to be built up from the rudimentary to the elaborate all through the years of primary education. It is never too early to start teaching children to reason. It should also be pointed out that reason is a tool that can be used in all situations.

Reasoning includes elements of logic and the rules of arguments, the building up of conjectures based upon earlier proven facts or the demolishing of an argument with the method of *reductio ad absurdum*, by reducing an invalid proposition to an absurdity. The art of approximation and cross-referencing can also be useful in spotting a preposterous proposition. Children should be encouraged to develop the ability to choose the least fanciful solution amongst those offered for a given problem. The seeding of clouds and the rain dance are two solutions offered for the same problem. As is to be expected, the two approaches have differing rates of success. These are the skills that would will help in the choosing of valid and relevant information from the information overload that we are now deluged with, as we choose the building blocks that build within our minds a picture of the world approaching reality.

Despite this, there will be times when it is not possible to determine the veracity of a proposition. Students must therefore also gain the ability to live with uncertainty while labelling in their minds the elements of the proposition that are unproven and proceed with the proposition as a working model. The model can be later rectified as per newly discovered facts. Living with uncertainty should not be taken as licence for minds to hold opposite propositions to be true. This is a sure way of damaging the mind's ability to process information. I wonder what mental gymnastics are required just to stay rational, from students in some American states where Intelligent Design and Evolution are taught with equal fervour. I further wonder if it is pointed out to these young minds that these two propositions cannot both be true; at best, only one of them can be.

It would also be helpful if the limits of our current knowledge are acknowledged. To an enquiry about the existence of life in other solar systems, a brief textbook chapter could outline the possibilities of such an occurrence along with the admission that not enough is known currently to answer the question with certainty. Perhaps in time, these will be a more definite answer. However, as per current knowledge, there is a strong likelihood of life existing elsewhere and less likelihood of intelligent life existing elsewhere on the basis that though life has existed on earth for billions of years, intelligent life has existed for less than a million years. Such an admission would reinforce the fact that knowledge is not something handed down from teacher to student or from generation to generation, it is not sacrosanct and is always open to review. Our quest for knowledge is but a search that should continue forever, giving us as a species a clearer picture of our world and our universe.

I hasten to clarify that I am no educationist and don't claim to have the authority to outline the way any subject should be taught. What I am looking at here is how we can help our young to sift through the vast amounts of information available to them and provide them with the tools required. Having admitted to my lack of qualifications to talk about any academic subject, I will go out on a limb and do precisely that and talk about a few subjects, beginning with history.

History, because it is a part of our identity, can try and make us understand why we are where we are. It can remind us of our achievements and our follies. It can tell us about ourselves, our potential for great deeds and our susceptibility to mass brainwashing, where large numbers of us can be made to do things we would normally abhor. It can tell us of our courage when we stand firm against those who oppress us and our cravenness when we meekly succumb to those who trample upon us. Our history is an important part of the edifice of our world, but it must be taught and depicted as a progression of ideas and achievements than the tales of kings and empires.

History as it was taught to me was largely a litany of kings and conquerors, presidents and dictators, wars and battles with very little in the way of the history of the human race. To be sure there was passing mention of the Stone Age, the Copper Age, the Bronze Age and the Iron Age. But it was presented as though it were preordained, like the change from childhood to adolescence and adulthood without mention of the ideas and discoveries that enabled these steps. Nothing about the fortuitous addition of tin ore to copper ore resulting in bronze, a much harder and more useful metal, was mentioned. Nothing about the discovery that a fire made of partly burnt wood, or charcoal, made a much hotter fire than a fire made of plain wood, making it possible to smelt iron and leading to the Iron Age. We were told that democracy started in Athens as if it were lightning striking there. We were not told about the momentous leap of faith the citizens of Athens took when determining that they would not be ruled by a ruler but guide their destiny themselves. We were taught that the Magna Carta was signed in 1215. We were not made to understand the great courage it took to stand up against the king and tell him how the people would be ruled. We were certainly told that the king at the time was King John but the name was hardly of consequence. What was of consequence was the courage it took to stand up against a legal sovereign at a time when the 'divine right to rule' was a universally accepted idea. We were not taught the lesson to be derived from this, namely, if you value your rights and liberty you have to be prepared to fight for your rights or else they will be trampled upon.

I would like to see history starting from our establishment as a species in Africa, our emigration out of Africa and our spread across the globe. Admittedly, little is known about these early years, but much can be fleshed out by conjecture, provided we don't try to pass it off as fact. A bit more is known about the routes taken in our spreading out and some gaps are being filled by comparing the DNAs of native populations. Perhaps we could point to the small changes in the genetic makeup of different populations in response to climatic differences, such as the our skin's need to produce less melanin pigmentation to better absorb vitamin D from the limited sunlight in upper latitudes, resulting in lighter-coloured skin. Or the need to lengthen the nasal passage in more arid climes because the lungs can only use warm-moist air, or the need to retain the epicanthal fold in the eyes, which we all have as foetuses, in response to intense cold, resulting in narrower eyes.

The history we teach our young should enumerate our major achievements and follies with an attempt to understand what led to those events and what their consequences were. The burning of the Library of Alexandria, which was in its time the greatest store of human knowledge, was perhaps the first step into the Dark Ages of Europe. The invention by Johannes Gutenberg in 1455 CE of the moveable type printing press and the ease with which numerous copies could be printed made the future burning of knowledge almost impossible. Cheap and numerous copies of books also made the great spread of education possible.

The stranglehold maintained by the Church over free thought

ushered in the Dark Ages of Europe and remained for nearly a millennium. Copernicus delayed the printing of his book on the heliocentric solar system, which argued that the Earth was not at the centre of the universe, thus going against the scriptures, until the very end of his life. It is believed that the first copy of his book was placed in his hands on the day he died. Subsequently, the Church banned not only the book but all future work on the topic. Galileo Galilei did not take the ban seriously and was placed under house arrest for the rest of his life. Through his immaculate timing, Copernicus had avoided similar or worse treatment.

These are two well-known examples of the Church punishing free thought, but the greatest damage was done to the loss of ideas that did not see the light of day. The fear must have been so palpable that no one dared offend the Church, going so far as to use convoluted reasoning in order not to be even remotely connected to a possible controversy. Girolamo Saccheri (1667–1733) was a mathematician of great potential and was working on proving the redundancy of Euclid's Fifth Postulate, something that mathematicians including Omar Khayyam (better known for his *Rubaiyat*) had been trying to prove for almost two thousand years. His work led him to a non-Euclidean geometry which was internally self-consistent and mathematically valid. 'For a moment, Saccheri hovered on the very brink of mathematical immortality and backed away.'[2] He couldn't! To accept the notion of a non-Euclidean geometry took too much courage. So mistakenly had scholars come to confuse Euclidean geometry with absolute truth that any refutation of Euclid would have roused the deepest stirrings of anxiety in the minds of Europe's intellectuals. To doubt Euclid was to doubt absolute truth and if there was no absolute truth in Euclid, might it not be deduced that there was no absolute truth anywhere? And since the firmest claim to absolute truth came from religion, might not an attack on Euclid be interpreted as an attack on God?

Whether we are educationists, students or ordinary members of society, we must be wary of any restrictions placed upon our fields of enquiry. The real reason for any form of censorship is the perpetuation of the status quo. The best approach to censorship is reflected in a quote by François Marie Arouet, better known as Voltaire, and credited by many as the man who ushered in the Age of Reason: 'I may not agree with what you say but I will defend to the death your right to say it.'

The lists of our achievements and follies are long and beyond the scope of this book. Indeed, it is beyond the scope of my abilities to try and mention them all. A moment's reflection will bring examples of both readily to mind. It should be the endeavour of history books to list our important achievements and follies and to try and understand why these follies were committed and how best to avoid repeating them, and also what led to our achievements and how we might encourage more of them. Lists of kings and the years of their reign and also the territories they captured and the battles they won should be outside the scope of primary education and left to those who wish to make history a career. The lessons of history are more important than the details of history.

There is another subject I would urge educationists to include in the curriculum of primary education: ethics. Our ethics determine how we deal with fellow human beings. Good ethics reduce transaction costs and permit us to be more collaborative. If we have the confidence to believe that the person or persons we are interacting with subscribe to the same set of good ethics we believe in, we will interact more readily and be more forthcoming in sharing our ideas. This helps speed up the progression of ideas. As with reasoning, I believe it is never too early to start acquiring good ethics. To be sure, we are all taught to be good and to do good but the definition of good has always remained a little vague. Most cultures have accumulated their own sets of do's and don'ts, much like the Ten Commandments, and these are good starting points for ethical behaviour. However, we need to go beyond this and study how different patterns of behaviour tend to elicit different responses of behaviour from those we interact with.

It is worth taking into account that what may be considered ethical behaviour from the perspective of an individual and immediate family can be quite different when viewed from the perspective of the community and still different when viewed from the perspective of the nation state. Then there is ethical behaviour as viewed from the perspective of the entire human race, which has begun to be practised by wealthy individuals and countries, who try to address issues of health and education in far-off lands from where they get no immediate returns. Finally, there is ethical behaviour as viewed from the perspective of all life on earth and this is the driving force behind the environmental movements that are slowly coming to occupy centre stage in many parts of the world. It may well be that ethical behaviour, from the perspective of all life, is 'the good in itself' that Immanuel Kant was trying to nail down in his *Critique of Practical Reason*, when he refers to a universal moral law.

I suspect it may have been a general lack of ethics beyond the level of the individual or clan and a fear of plagiarism that held back the sharing of ideas and knowledge in many venerable cultures, preventing them from reaching their true potential. Restricting the flow of knowledge will always prevent knowledge from triggering new ideas and continuing progress. Could it be that the chief reason for ancient cultures like India, China and Egypt not reaching their potential despite many discoveries and achievements was that they failed to evolve patent, copyright or anti-plagiarism laws? The thought is tantalizing. Fortuitously, at the start of the European Renaissance, Florence, England and Venice had the rudiments of patent and intellectual property laws in place.

Yet one more subject that needs to be introduced in primary school, starting perhaps at the age of ten, is economics. I'm not hoping to turn primary school pass-outs into economists, but in today's world, which is increasingly influenced by the economic decisions of governments and large financial institutions, primary school pass-outs must have some awareness of the impact of the policies of the government and the practices of financial institutions. Basic economic truths need to be taught early. Concepts such as 'there is no free lunch' and that the tab for the lunch will eventually have to be picked up by an individual or individuals and not by a disembodied omniscient government will help temper their expectations of freebies. Understanding the laws of supply and demand will help them understand their world better when there are sudden surges or slumps in the prices of any goods. They need to understand the few pros and many cons as their governments step into the minefield of deficit financing. They need to recognize the danger to their savings, when they are older and have savings, if the institutions they have entrusted their money with leverage those savings by lending far more money than they have. They must understand the effects of inflation, which depletes their savings and makes the poor among them poorer. A basic understanding of economics is imperative starting at even such a young age and I am sure economists will have other home truths they would like to impart to young minds.

There is one last addition to the curriculum that I would like to see. It is about making our young aware of the rights they enjoy under the constitution and laws of the country they live in and to teach them that there is nothing wrong in standing up for their rights. There is currently an unsettling trend the world over of laws being enacted to curb individual freedom and of governments arming themselves with the right to intrude upon personal privacy. These laws may have come up as a response to terrorism and some of them may be desirable, but not all of them. Curbing the right to criticize and lampoon the government and bureaucracy of the day is certainly not desirable. Curbing the right to debate existing provisions of the law or even the constitution is not beneficial either. Such curbs act as control rods and impede progress to better systems.

A comparison with the rights enjoyed by citizens of other countries and the consequences thereof, both positive and negative, should be brought to the knowledge of our young, so that when it is their time, they can seek to incorporate some of those rights into the laws of their own countries.

The three Rs of primary education are now five Rs and two Es—Reading, 'Riting, 'Rithmetic, Reasoning, Rights, Ethics and Economics.

Primary education, as I have argued earlier, should be made compulsory and be funded by society. As this effort involves a considerable outlay of money, one must consider carefully how best this may be achieved. Surely, many opinions will be put forward and debated over. I can only share my views and hope this encourages discussions leading to a solution.

The expenditure involved in providing quality primary education is significant and there is also a need for educated manpower. The potential value an effective educational programme has for society is incalculable. With the stakes high in terms of both cost and benefit, we must spare no effort to devise the best system possible for achieving our ends. Many of us already have deep-rooted ideas about what an ideal educational set-up should look like, how it should be operated and funded. Unfortunately, not all of us have the same set of ideas and I urge each of us to contemplate Deng Xiaoping's famous quote: 'It does not matter if the cat is white or black. If it can catch a mouse it is a good cat.'

Our primary education is too large and important a subject to be denied the efficiencies of the marketplace. At the same time, free market forces cannot be given unsupervised access to it. Societal bodies have a distinct role to play, including the running of benchmark quality schools. I am a little unclear as to the distinction between societal, governmental and the state in a democracy, as the same citizens run and represent all three.

I use the term 'societal' as it implies citizens taking responsible collective decisions and this usage hopefully imparts that sense of responsibility to all citizens. The term governmental, on the other hand, takes away the sense of responsibility from citizens, transferring it to a remote entity. The term 'state' is even more remote and inaccessible, for a government may still be voted out of power but a state cannot be voted out. Any statement that says that a particular course of action is to be decided by either the government or the state implies that the interests of the government and the state can differ from those of general society. I am aware that the days of direct democracy are long over, but hope that with the full blooming of the information technology industry, we as a society may be able, in important matters, to take collective decisions quickly and easily.

Once society has decided how much it can spend on primary education, it must calculate the expenditure per child. Vouchers for this amount should be given to the parents of each child to give to the accredited school of their choice.

Let private enterprise invest in schools. To attract the best teachers, investors may need to give sweat equity to teachers with track records of excellent performance. This is to be welcomed as it will give experienced teachers a stake in the long-term imparting of quality education. A total stake of 5–15 per cent for educators with proven track records in educational institutions may even be mandated.

Schools will, of course, try and make profits. This is the only way they can grow. Competition is the one reliable way of curbing excess profits. Unless schools become profitable and valuable, sweat equity given to educationists will be without value.

The accreditation process, after which schools will be able to encash the government vouchers given to them by the parents, must be a transparent process and, particularly for societies with limited resources, unrealistic standards must not be laid down. It is worth keeping in mind that the main purpose of education is to teach minds to think. Facilities like playing fields and swimming pools, no matter how desirable, are not central to the purpose of primary education. Schools that provide extra facilities may, if the competition permits, be able to charge students more than the vouchers given to them. With passing time and greater prosperity and rising standards of living, it is to be expected that society will be able to fund better-appointed educational facilities in a regular, systematic manner. Perfect equality of all schools may be impossible to achieve. However, if some benchmark schools are set up by the state and operate within the voucher amounts paid for each student, it should curb any tendency towards excessive profits and limit the spread of exclusive schools.

There should be external exams every two to three years. This is for the purpose of evaluating schools and teachers so that parents can make informed choices when selecting schools. If through this process students get feedback on their own performance, all the better.

No current thoughts on our educational systems, whether primary or secondary, can be meaningful without considering how information technology may be used as a force multiplier. Society will need its best and most communicative teachers to record lectures which can be shown on screens in classrooms. The teachers, in whose presence those lectures are to be screened, would need only to be trained to take questions for a particular lecture, making the training of these teachers possible in a modular format. This would be of great value to a society wishing to make a period of educational service compulsory for its primary and secondary education graduates, thereby augmenting the supply of teachers competent in their fields.

At the end of primary education, youngsters should be fifteen or sixteen years old, having completed ten or eleven years of largely society-funded education. They should now have a modest but reasonably accurate edifice of their world in their minds, along with the capacity to sift through easily accessible information and add to that edifice at will, in as much detail as they wish to. They would also have the ability to interact with others, look for possible opportunities and make decisions that will hopefully benefit them.

After the setting up of a meaningful primary education system, we need to look at what is now called tertiary education, which is graduate and postgraduate studies. We have seen why primary education needs to be funded by society, to ensure that there are as few as possible potentially non-thinking minds which suppress the flow of ideas. Does society as a whole need to finance higher education too? I think not.

Before I proceed to describe how higher education should be funded, let me point out that I presuppose the existence of a well-functioning judicial system, with emphasis on the speedy adjudication of matters under contract law.

Of all those who finish primary education, most will go on to seek jobs or be apprenticed into various trades. Only a few will go to college for further studies. These few will expect to do better and earn more than those who chose not to study further. Benefiting from the higher studies undertaken will also be those who hope to employ them and gain from the enhanced knowledge garnered during their years of higher studies. It is equitable that the cost of higher education be borne either by the students themselves or by those in trade or industry or research bodies including colleges and universities who wish to benefit from the increased knowledge of the students. Commercial bodies cannot be expected to pay for a student's education without an assurance that the student will work for them for a specified period. This is where contract law comes in.

The same applies to apprentices. People professing their trades are not in the business of free education and would need to be recompensed for their efforts, perhaps by an agreement that once the apprenticeship period is over the apprentice will work in the organization for a specified period. It is to be expected that there would be variations in the contracts agreed to in different trades. It is up to the law of the land to ensure that the guidelines set out to govern these contracts are fair and undue advantage is not taken of young people, who will always be in a weaker position than those providing advanced education and apprenticeships.

This arrangement would have the added advantage of industry bodies, which have more persuasive powers than students do and know their requirements better than educationists do, being able to persuade colleges to continuously upgrade their courses in response to the ever-evolving needs of different trades and vocations.

Alternatively, students not willing to bind themselves to an organization for even a limited period of time should have the option of taking out a loan to fund their further studies, but this once again presupposes the existence of an effective justice delivery system, wherein the lender is sure of getting the loaned money back along with interest.

Having looked at the process in which education makes minds more fissile, there are two more areas we need to look at: communication and the freedom to express unpopular ideas. Let us look at communication first.

Before new ideas can be produced, people need to interact. Interaction can take many forms and happen in many different ways. The earliest human interactions took place with people talking face-to-face. In the beginning, I imagine, when humans roved in small bands as hunters or gatherers, an idea was an ephemeral thing, finding resonance only if it referred to something basic and of immediate import, or thereafter be lost forever. With the invention of writing, ideas acquired more permanency. Any idea that was written down was potentially indefinitely available to anyone, including future generations. The development of cities and universities permitted more people with similar interests to exchange ideas and come up with new ones, speeding up the growth of total human knowledge. This was further enhanced by the invention of moveable type and the mass printing of books.

Though it may appear that with books the transfer of ideas was only unidirectional, from the writer to the reader, in reality a multitude of books and pamphlets was printed and the propagator of a new idea soon obtained feedback in the form of printed acclaim or rebuttal. This process effectively made the exchange of ideas a two-way affair with the added advantage of permitting a far larger number of people to interact in the formulation of ideas than ever before. Further, it gave a sort of permanence to ideas. An idea can often be a very fleeting thing, as we have all at times experienced, when we get an idea and fail to note it down and are then assailed with the niggling feeling of having missed something important.

What the printing of books did for the exchange and propagation of ideas, the internet promises to do many times better, by involving an unprecedented number of people. In order to take full advantage of the information highway on the net, every country must ensure that their citizens can access the internet at as low a price as possible. For ideas to cascade, their communication is as important as education. If we think that education, especially primary education, is important enough to spend tax money on, we must put communication in the same category. Fortunately, the dynamics of setting up cheap access to the information highway are such that it can be self-sustaining, without governments needing to spend tax money on it. Telecommunication companies will willingly invest in setting up the infrastructure, as they are doing currently. Governments will, however, need to support them.

Indeed, the availability of a fast internet connection for all its citizens is one of the most meaningful steps a society can take to speed up the generation and spread of ideas, thereby increasing the potential for quick economic growth. Some societies have realized this. France and Finland are among the first countries to have passed laws that make the access to broadband services a right. It is a legal right for the citizens of Finland and a human right for the citizens of France. Finland has also quantified the minimum speed for internet access. By July 2010, every person in Finland was to have access to a 1 megabyte per second connection, according to their Ministry of Transport and Communications, and by 2015, have access to a 100 megabit per second connection.

There is no getting away from the fact that the radio spectrum is a commodity in limited supply. It needs to be allocated in a manner that yields the best results. In a situation where there are more parties wishing to operate the spectrum than the available bandwidth allows, bidding for the spectrum is almost inevitable. This is what governments do. They auction different parts of the spectrum for huge amounts of money, earning hundreds of billions of dollars. This is counterproductive. We must constantly keep in mind that it is the idea reactor which is the mainspring of all economic growth. Like education, which needs to be funded by society, communication and access to information without which ideas cannot germinate needs at the very least not to have money taken away from it. I am sceptical when governments implicitly claim that they need the additional revenue to better manage their finances. Let us keep in mind that just a few years ago this huge stream of revenue was not available to any government, but we see little improvement in government finances the world over.

If anything, they are a great deal worse than they were before governments started tapping this additional revenue source.

This may not be coincidental. Governments, by tapping this large source of money, may have inadvertently stepped into a Resource Curse[3] area. When a country is blessed with abundant natural resources, it paradoxically experiences a Resource Curse which, among other things, results in lower GDP growth, profligacy in governmental spending leading to increased inflation, lower growth in industry, less competitive products, increased corruption and less responsive governments. None of these is a pleasant outcome of the Resource Curse, but I think there is another outcome which might be far worse. This windfall of money for governments imbues them with a false sense of omnipotence, where they feel they can solve all problems by throwing money at the problems, even those that are caused by excessive liquidity in the first place, like property bubbles and inflation-fuelled food prices.

Getting back to the process of allocating radio spectrum, I do believe that an auctioning procedure is the best and most equitable way of allotment. However, the process should be different from the one now employed, keeping in mind that our objective is to provide the cheapest possible access to the information highway on the internet which has become the cheapest and fastest way to exchange ideas. Instead of auctioning the spectrum to the highest bidder and the money going into government coffers, the government could lay down the minimum services that the winners of the spectrum would have to provide. Anything above the minimum requirements could work to the competitive advantage of one service provider against another and should be encouraged.

The bidding should have three parameters: the first is the lowest price at which the specified services will be provided. The second is the amount a bidder is willing to invest in order to bring its promised services and operations online, along with a business plan showing that the money they plan to invest is more than adequate for their purpose. This amount should be covered by a sizeable earnest money deposit, to prevent frivolous bidding, into an escrow account, from which money can only be withdrawn with the concurrence of the government for specified expenditure, along with credible bank guarantees for the balance amount. On winning the spectrum bid, the entire sum of money or bank guarantees should be put into the escrow account, to be duly audited by government auditors to ensure that there is no bleeding away of the money through unrelated expenses. These steps are needed to prevent the successful bidder from siphoning out money for other purposes, thereby endangering the timely roll-out of the service bid for. The third parameter is the fastest time frame in which the services are to be rolled out after winning the spectrum bid. To prevent unrealistic time projections for the purpose of winning the spectrum, there should be a penalty clause included for overshooting the promised time frame, provided the delay is not caused by any action or inaction on the government's part. To further incentivize the timely roll-out of services, the penalty money could be divided in a rational, pre-specified manner amongst those parties who manage to provide the services ahead of schedule. If there are no parties able to provide the required services ahead of their projected time frames, the penalty money could find its way into government coffers.

Having forgone any income from the sale of spectrum and having enabled the dissemination of knowledge to its citizens at the cheapest possible rates, and also having helped in the rise of hopefully profit-making telecom companies, the government must tax their profits as those of any other income-earning entity. The same is true for entities involved in education. One might argue that since the government is funding primary education by way of issuing education coupons to children in the first place, it makes no sense to tax education-derived profits which would only drive up the costs of delivering the education. However, I feel that if the profits of educational entities are taxed just like those derived from any other activity, it will instil a sense of prudence and greater transparency in the running of the enterprise. Further, it may help drive home the point that all profits, whether generated by industry, endowments or charity, are legitimate income for governments to tax.

The final component of a well-functioning idea reactor is freedom from the fear of punishment for stating ideas that run counter to popular perception. Without this we might well find ourselves in the same situation as Girolamo Saccheri who backed away from contradicting Euclid and what was then considered to be absolute truth. This final component of the idea reactor is so important that I will consider it again in the next chapter.

REFERENCES

1. http://en.wikipedia.org/wiki/Zheng_He. Accessed on 26 April 2016
2. Isaac Asimov, 'The Plane Truth'. In *Left Hand of the Electron* (Panther Books Ltd, 1976)
3. http://en.wikipedia.org/wiki/Resource_curse. Accessed on 26 April 2016

3

CONTROL RODS—THE BRAKES ON THE IDEA REACTOR

IN A NUCLEAR REACTOR, CONTROL RODS SLOW DOWN THE REACTOR. They are a safety measure to prevent the reactor from running out of control and causing a meltdown or worse. Control rods absorb the neutrons emitted by fissile atoms without releasing further neutrons. If there are too many control rods the nuclear reactor will not function. It will be a non-starter.

It is the same with ideas. Ideas are generated and when communicated, they are given new twists. When people receive ideas that have no meaning for them or of which they disapprove, they act as control rods by refusing to pass them on, thereby clamping down on the generation and flow of ideas. If due to certain circumstances an idea is generated but not released, those circumstances also act as control rods. The slowing down of the generation and release of ideas leads to the slowing of economic growth.

◆

In this chapter we will look at how ideas are prevented from emerging and, if they do emerge, how they are prevented from being released.

As I have stated above, an idea that interacts only with a mind to which it has no meaning or of which one disapproves without considering its merits is one that has been stopped in its tracks. This is a straightforward statement and needs no further elaboration. It is self-evident. How, then, do we explain the great progression of ideas at the start of the Scientific Revolution, when only a minuscule percentage of the population was educated and an even smaller number had scientific training? I believe it is because of the setting up of universities across Europe, which permitted a small group of educated and thinking minds to interact and churn out ideas without the presence of control rods amongst them.

It is no coincidence that the exponential growth in the number of universities in Europe coincided with the Scientific Revolution. Prior to 1200 CE there were only two universities in Europe, namely, the universities of Bologna and Modena, both in Italy. Thereafter many universities started being set up in Europe. Eighteen universities opened in the thirteenth century, 23 in the fourteenth, 38 in the 15th and 62 in the sixteenth.[1] By the end of the sixteenth century, the European Renaissance was well under way and the Industrial Revolution was fast approaching. This period also saw a decline in the direct or indirect influence of the Church on universities, freeing up areas of study that had hitherto been frowned upon by the Church. The decline of Church influence was partly because of verfiable scientific discoveries that went against its beliefs. In particular, the stranglehold that Aristotelian thought had on many scientific topics was weakened. Aristotle's writings were regarded by the Church as almost sacrosanct. 'The Renaissance enabled a scientific revolution which let scholars look at the world in a different light. Religion, superstition and fear were replaced by reason and knowledge.'[2]

From the universities emerged thinkers like Nicolas Copernicus (1473–1543), Andreas Vesalius (1514–64), Galileo Galilei (1564–1642), William Harvey (1578–1657), Johannes Kepler (1571–1630), John Napier (1550–1617), Pierre de Fermat (1601–65), Evangelistor Torelli (1607–47), Blasé Pascal (1623–62), Robert Boyle (1627–91), Isaac Newton (1643–1727) and Gottfried Leibniz (1646–1716). These inventors and thinkers, along with many others from university backgrounds, changed forever in the space of about two centuries our understanding of our world and universe.

We will never know what thoughts, what chance remarks set these discoverers off on their quests for knowledge or what valuable feedback helped fine-tune their ideas. To me it is inconceivable that the same people could have made the discoveries they did had they not been in the idea reactors of the universities. Very few discoveries have been made by people sitting by themselves in pastoral settings, which is where the vast majority of the human race then resided.

Universities in those days were not the giant set-ups they often are these days yet they spewed out ideas and discoveries as any well-functioning idea reactor could be expected to. This tells us that size is not the only criterion and there are other important factors.

First, there must be no ban on any area of enquiry in the manner in which the Church banned any study of a heliocentric universe. Second, there must be receptive minds capable of absorbing an enunciated idea and taking it to its conclusion or to the next level or at the very least finding it to be interesting enough to pass the idea along. These conditions were met in the early European universities. Small groups of scholars and professors working in the universities unleashed a flood of ideas and discoveries that led us from the Renaissance to a scientific age and the Industrial Revolution.

In the case of nuclear reactors there are small reactors and large reactors. The basic science behind both is the same. I am sure there are major technological difficulties in scaling up to a large reactor if one's previous experience is only with small reactors, but the logic of their functioning does not change. The same is true of idea reactors.

The concept of setting up small idea reactors is fairly common, with governments and industries setting up think tanks with limited mandates to come up with a better policy or a specific new product or marketing strategy. The process is straightforward. A group of people with experience in the required and peripheral subjects are made to work together for the desired objective. These people bounce ideas off each other, and since they are all experienced in the subject, their ideas are not unintelligible to each other. In effect there are no control rods in operation and ideas pass from one participant to another, triggering new ideas which are received by other minds, triggering yet more ideas until the limited objective is achieved. The think tanks can then be disbanded or given new objectives.

These small idea reactors or think tanks work quite well but the endeavour is to see what enables a large society-wide reactor to be set up and kept running. The main difference between small idea reactors and a large society-wide idea reactor is that a large reactor is non-linear in its operation. It is not set up with a specific goal in mind. It is random and unpredictable in its results. It works with a multitude of simultaneous ideas. Only a few of the ideas going on at any given time will, even if we understood them, have any practical meaning for any one of us individually but will almost certainly have meaning for other individuals.

It is impossible to predict what new thoughts any random idea will trigger as it ricochets from mind to mind gaining new twists and insights along the way. At the same time, if the number of fissile minds participating in the process is sufficiently large, ideas will lead to yet more ideas. Under conducive conditions, this will lead to experimentation and if the conditions are also conducive to enterprise, new ventures will arise. This will lead to further ideas and so on and so forth. Unless of course, the initial ideas are stopped dead in their tracks by control rods made up of unreceptive, closed minds.

Most of us are not in universities or research laboratories, on the cutting edge of science, nor are we in think tanks developing policies and products, where we have the good fortune to be surrounded by enquiring minds, where we understand and appreciate each other's ideas as we work towards a defined objective. We live in societies interspersed with both receptive and unreceptive minds. Our ideas too are very often just that—ideas. Random ideas. Not ideas that are directed towards finding solutions to a given problem. Our ideas could be about anything from how to build a slightly better mouse trap to inventing a more useful vegetable slicer. About finding a better way to deal with nosy neighbours or how to do your own thing without upsetting the padre or how to sidestep traditional homilies if they don't make sense in a changed world. The range of our ideas is endless but most of our ideas are not world changing and we don't rush to publish them in trade journals. More often than not we simply try to get some feedback for our ideas by sharing them with the nearest or most convenient listener, a friend perhaps or a spouse. If that person is conservative in his or her outlook, believing that the traditional way of doing things is always the best way, he or she will be disparaging of new ideas and almost always shoot them down. Ideas that might have led to worthwhile ends will instead hit a dead end.

Some originators of new ideas do not give up so easily and try to bounce their idea off a few more people. The chances of finding a responsive mind depends on the ratio of open minds and control rods in any society. Depending on that probability a potentially good idea will either progress or come to a dead end.

One of the reasons why some societies are more progressive than others is because these societies have a greater percentage of open minds. The total number of open minds in a population is not as important as the ratio of open and enquiring minds to closed and unreceptive minds in that population. It is not enough for a society to have a few brilliant scientists and thinkers. Society as a whole must be open to new ideas. Hence my emphasis on the need for a universal primary education including what is now considered secondary education and the changes required in the existing syllabi. We need to be able to consider new ideas, rationally evaluate them and then act upon them. We need to increase the awareness of the entire community. In this context, we must look at the role of women closely.

Women comprise half the population and are as dispersed in society as any subgroup can be, perhaps not always in the workplace but certainly in everyday social interaction. In many countries women are still at a disadvantage when it comes to education and liberty of action. Worse, in many societies they are not only denied a secular education but schooled instead in the traditions of that society, and taught that these traditions are inviolable. The teaching of tradition may in itself not be harmful for the generation of new ideas, but in the absence of other education, tradition becomes the only prism through which they view the world. They acquire a vested interest in upholding it and are more likely to shoot down any new idea, and diminish their value in general, thereby becoming the handmaidens of orthodoxy. While the minds of women are as astute as those of men, the fact is that most ideas formed are dependent upon the knowledge and experience already held in the mind. Limiting the exposure of women will result in limiting the ideas they form as well as the ideas they approve. Naturally, women, or men, for that matter, who are schooled in such a manner will be resistant to change and to any idea advocating it, which is what ideas are all about. Instead of being given an education, they are in effect being de-educated, suppressing even the native intelligence we are all born with.

An open mind can belong either to a man or a woman, and so can an unresponsive mind. Women, however, have for centuries been treated differently and denied the opportunity to make their minds more responsive. In the most primitive of tribes today there is little difference between men and women apart from that dictated by their physiological differences, in that child-bearing and rearing is done by women while activities that require more brawn, such as hunting and warfare, are handled by men. Women in primitive societies today are not regarded as possessions. From this I conjecture that this must have been the case in all primitive societies everywhere.

With slow growth in population leading to larger tribes, especially in areas with more game and edible fruit, the tribes must have come into regular contact and conflict with each other. The desire to increase the numbers of their own tribes could have led to warfare with the twin objectives of diminishing the numbers of the other tribe and abducting their women in order to increase their own birth rates. Thus the status of women might have changed from being roughly equal to men to becoming possessions, whom it suited the men to keep subjugated. This is not intended to be a study of how women came to be in subjugation to men but is merely a passing thought. What matters here is that when education became more widespread and universities began to establish their roots, women were largely excluded. This is not to say that men did not often suffer the same treatment, only it was more common in the case of women. Again, in most societies where the freedom of action for women was severely circumscribed, it was less so in the case of even disadvantaged or poorer men. In many societies this is still true.

In most such societies, where meaningful education given

to women is limited, there is often a small number of elite women who do get a decent education and are often showcased as achievers. Their example is unrealistically pointed out to other women so that they too can change their situation. This is the same as having a few brilliant people in a society—it does not in any significant way alter the ratio of open minds to unresponsive minds or increase the chances of ideas fructifying. What is applicable to women is applicable to everyone. If there are large swathes of the population who have not been given meaningful education, as is still unfortunately true of many countries, these people, whether men or women, act as agents for smothering ideas. Many countries regularly put out data regarding literacy rates but these figures include those who have only a rudimentary ability to read and write. That is not the education required. It is only the very start of an education.

The reason for looking at women separately is that they are so well interspersed in the population that they are often, perhaps from within the security of their homes, the first to have a new idea bounced off them and if they have been brought up to frown upon new ideas, very few ideas will meet their approval. The educational and economic suppression of women, along with their grooming into the Panglossian belief that the existing way of life and scheme of things is the best it can possibly be, impedes the progression of ideas. By depriving women of a meaningful education, those who would like to perpetuate the existing order have knowingly or unknowingly created a strong bulwark against change.

To enable the influential to achieve this, men in traditional societies, including the common man, are often compensated by de facto property rights over the women in their lives, whether it is their daughters, sisters or wives, thereby giving them an illusion of power in a system that has effectively locked them into the powerless state they are in.

The question that arises is this: in a society where women are denied education and their rights as individuals are severely curtailed, if everyone is happy, both the elite and men and women at large, since they know no other way of life, who or what is it that suffers? The progression of ideas suffers along with all the progress and growth it promises and the potential happiness it could have delivered. It is for each society to consider whether the trade-off is acceptable. When the rough equality between men and women in primitive tribal days (assuming this was indeed the case) changed to the subjugation of women and women being turned into possessions (which we know to have been the case), it stayed this way for a long period of time and in some societies continues even today.

Slowly things began to change for women. The change began almost imperceptibly and was first seen in Western Europe. Faltering starts in this direction were made elsewhere too, but petered out before they could make more progress. It is difficult to trace how exactly such a dramatic change in the attitudes of both men and women took place. There must have been a million conflicts and adjustments over generations as the relationship between men and women evolved to where it now is in Western civilization. Those battles of adjustment must not have been of much significance except for the individuals involved but the overall effect they had is of truly epic importance with consequences of greater significance than any revolution or any rise and fall of empire. We will never know the details of all those conflicts but we can identify the prominent trends and landmarks along the way to women's emancipation.

The first step in this journey of change may well have been taken by the troubadours, who sang of chivalry and courtly love. The movement started in the region of Al-Andalus (what is now Spain) and was probably inspired by Arabic traditions. The word troubadour possibly originates from the Arabic word 'tarab'—to sing.[3,4] From Spain it spread to Italy and Greece and related movements sprang up across Europe: Minnesang in Germany, Trovadorismo in Galacia and Portugal and the Trouveres in northern France. The earliest troubadour whose work survives is Duke William IX of Aquitaine (1071–1126). Troubadours sang until the middle of the fourteenth century and gave rise to the European practice of courtly love, wherein the woman of one's affections had to be wooed. Amour Courtois (Court Love)[5] was idolization of the woman and an ennobling discipline. The lover (idolizer) accepts the independence of his mistress and tries to make himself worthy of her by acting bravely and honourably (nobly) and by performing whatever deeds she might desire, subjecting himself to a series of tests (ordeals) to prove to her his ardour and commitment.

In the songs of the troubadours and the practitioners of courtly love, we see the beginnings of the change of women's status. Women now needed to be wooed to be won. It was no longer enough to possess a woman through brute force or financial or positional advantage. She had to come of her own accord, of her own will. Her mind began to matter and needed to be addressed. She needed to be listened to and her ideas were to be considered. From an idea-smothering entity she became an active participant in the realm of ideas. This may have started among the elite but their practices and attitudes tend to be emulated and can become common in society.

Perhaps the wooing of women led to subtle changes in societies where the practice was prevalent. Prior to this, in most parts of the world and even today in large parts of it, women had no say in the choice of their husbands. They were routinely bartered by their families for money or family positioning or family obligations or to curry favour with the powerful. As customs changed from acquiring women to wooing them, women gained the power to either accept or reject, among a suitor's other assets, his ideas and values. I believe this led to a somewhat gentler and more congenial environment for the exchange of ideas. This belief stems from the presumption that wooing a woman involves talking and not the use of power, whether physical or monetary. The practice of wooing was bound to make men more receptive to the idea of discussion and negotiation. Sociable people can better exchange ideas.

The next step to women becoming equal participants was education. Here too it appears that the first steps taken were in the Islamic culture. The tradition of women's literary circles in the Arab world dates back to the pre-Islamic period when the eminent literary figure Al-Khansa would stand in the Ukaz market in Mecca, reciting her poetry and airing her views on the scholarship of others.[6] This led to a culture of literary criticism among Arab women and continued under the Umayyed dynasty, (644–750 CE), in Damascus, thereafter in Baghdad and later on an offshoot in Al-Andalus until 1031 CE.[7] The University of Al-Karaouine in Morocco traces its origins back to 859 CE, when it was founded by Fatima-al-Fihri, herself a well-educated woman.[8] The Al-Karaouine Institution is regarded by the Guinness Book of World Records to be the oldest continuously operating academic degree-granting university in the world.

In Europe women's education began much later. In medieval Europe, the education of girls and women was at best patchy and was controversial in the light of pronouncements by some religious authorities.[9] St Thomas of Aquinas (1225–74 CE), who was perhaps one of the greatest teachers of his time, declared what was clearly a widely supported notion regarding women: 'The woman is subject to man on account of the weakness of her nature ... Man is the beginning of woman and her end, just as God is the beginning and end of every creature. Children ought to love their father more than they love their mother.'

Around 1405 CE Leonardo Bruni wrote to Baptista di

Montefeltro, the daughter of Antonio II da Montefeltro, the Duke of Urbino, commending the study of Latin but adding that 'subtleties of Arithmetic and Geometry are not worthy to absorb a cultivated mind, and the same must be said of Astrology. You will be surprised to find me suggesting that the great and complex art of Rhetoric should be placed in the same category. My chief reason is the obvious one, that I have in view the cultivation most fitting to a woman. To her neither the intricacies of debate nor the oratorical artifices of action and delivery are of the least practical use, if indeed they are not positively unbecoming. Rhetoric in all its forms—public discussion, forensic argument, logical fence and the like—lies absolutely outside the province of a woman.'[10]

Both examples give us a fair idea of the social and educational status of women in Europe in the Medieval and Early Modern period.

Actual progress in institutional terms, for secular education of women, began in the West much later, in the middle of the nineteenth century, with the founding of colleges offering education to young women. Women's education was still a controversial subject in 1848, when Queens College for women first opened in London.[11] Once women began to graduate from institutions of higher education, there steadily developed a stronger academic stream of schooling, and teacher's training of women in larger numbers, principally to provide primary education. Women's access to traditionally all-male institutions of higher learning took several generations to be completed.

It is critical to note that while the troubadours of Europe got their inspiration from the Islamic Caliphate of Cardoba and the education of women had a head start in Islamic culture, the emancipation of women did not progress in the Islamic world as it did in Western Europe.

Along with the emancipation of women came a flow of ideas

from Europe, in sharp contrast to the lack of emancipation of women in Islamic culture and a lessening of the flow of ideas after the demise of the Cordoba Caliphate. It is interesting to note that the end of Muslim rule in the Iberian peninsula was in 1492, when Emir Muhammad XII surrendered the Emirate of Granada to Queen Isabella I of Castile and King Ferdinand II of Aragon. It was these Catholic monarchs who, that same year, financed the voyage of Christopher Columbus, who went on to discover America for the Europeans.

Nothing in the foregoing, in any formal sense, proves that the growth of societies, nations and entire cultures is dependent on the way they treat their women but the logic, I think, is compelling and the correlation between the emancipation of women and the progress of societies is glaringly evident. Many studies have been carried out that show the benefits of women's education. These studies range from the benefits of having a larger educated workforce, to better management of family finances and the health benefits to families that have educated mothers. I know of no study that shows anything detrimental to society arising from the education of women, although there are studies that show a negative effect on families by way of increased divorce rates and the neglect of children by women working outside the home. However, as far as I am aware, there are no studies showing that the emancipation of women leads to greater creation and flow of ideas. Yet when a large percentage of the population changes its orientation from being negative towards new ideas to becoming generators and conduits for new ideas, from being control rods to becoming fissile minds, it is a great change. It is a force multiplier. Traditionalists will always try and resist this but the stakes are too high to allow them to succeed. New ideas are always about change and are only adopted by those who find merit in them, no matter how comforting the old ways are to others.

Having considered the role of tradition-bound minds and

uneducated minds as control rods in the idea reactor, let us look at other types of control rods that may affect the emission and flow of ideas.

There are areas of enquiry where our minds don't venture. People do not have the same taboo areas but most of us have certain areas in our minds that have a 'Do Not Enter' sign on them. These areas are not of our volitional choosing but have been deeply programmed into us from a very young age, before we developed our ability to sift through information. This vulnerability to early programming certainly has evolutionary benefits. It is easy to visualize how a fear of falling, or fire, or loud noises, or wild animals, or strangers increases our chances of survival. The same mechanism in our psyche can also instil in us unwarranted beliefs, fears or abhorrences. The fears could pertain to an individual or to an entire culture, from a fear of spiders to fear of the wrath of a god. Our beliefs too can be wide-ranging, from veneration of the elderly to the extent that new ideas are stymied just because it is feared that the elders may disapprove, to a firm belief that certain rituals can alter the laws of nature. The objects of our abhorrence are widespread too, starting from a dislike of anything different—whether people of different races, religious beliefs or sexual orientations to an abhorrence of reptiles, even harmless ones.

Some of our beliefs may be acquired later in life but are reinforced in us so often that they are as deeply ingrained in us as our earliest programmed beliefs. The inviolability of the nation state along with its notions of patriotism and the sacrifice required for its perpetuation is one such area, in line with earlier held notions of the divine right of kings and the sanctity of a geocentric universe.

I must emphasize here that I am not making a statement for or against the desirability of any particular belief; I am making a statement for the desirability of being able, without prejudice, to look at and examine deeply held beliefs and fears and evaluate them to the best of our abilities. I have no answer as to how we may remove our own blinkers of prejudice, other than expressing the hope that a good education may tell us that we all have some blinkers that only we can remove, and that once we understand this we may pass on fewer blinkers to the next generation.

There is no denying that the more 'Do Not Enter' areas there are in our minds, the less ideas will be generated. We must always keep in mind that in the dynamic setting of the idea reactor it is impossible to tell what trains of thought can be set off by a random idea.

So far we have considered factors that prevent or diminish the generation of ideas. Let us now examine circumstances where after an idea has been generated, it is not released.

In the normal course of things, for an idea to be worth its name it must have the potential to be of benefit to someone. If I were struck by an idea of a sure way to lose money on the stock market, it would not be of much use to me, nor would I have great success if I tried to sell the idea to someone else. I would not call it much of an idea and in the course of time, forget all about it. If, on the other hand, I were struck by an idea for a sure-fire way of making money on the stock market, I would perceive value in the idea and take steps to benefit from it. I could proceed to invest in the stock market and profit directly from the idea. If I lacked sufficient capital, I could consider taking a partner or enter into a contract with a person with sufficient amounts of money so that we could both benefit from my idea. For this, I would have to be sure that the contract would be honoured and if it were not, that I would have recourse to an effective and speedy justice delivery system. Lacking the backdrop of such a system, I would probably not enter into such a contract and would prefer to keep my idea to myself. Or else I could consider writing down my potentially lucrative idea and publishing it as a book, thereby benefiting from its sales. But if I lived in a society where the pirated printing of books was the norm, I would hesitate to publish my book, unless I cared only to earn a reputation from it. But if the society where I found myself to be turned a blind eye to plagiarism, I might be daunted yet again. And so it goes.

The same applies to young people, who statistically come up with the lion's share of great ideas. If they are working or studying in universities or research institutes where their ideas are routinely appropriated by their seniors or professors, giving the originator of the idea, at best, a passing mention as perhaps an associate member of the research team, these young people will tend to sit on their ideas and not release them. As we all have a sense of the worth of our ideas, it is paradoxically the best ideas that are sat upon and stifled. This may well be the main reason why in some institutes with a large number of graduates and researchers only a few worthwhile original research papers are published. It may not have much to do with either the calibre of the students and researchers or the institutes but rather with the lack of security for their ideas.

The first immediate output of an idea reactor is intellectual property, which is what ideas are. It is difficult to imagine a situation where the creation and release of intellectual property can take place without the creator of the intellectual property being rewarded for the idea created by him or her. The lack of an effective legal framework which protects intellectual property acts as another control rod. It is of no use if the requirements for the creation of ideas are in place but the ideas are not released. The ideas, for all purposes, may not have formed at all. An effective legal system protecting intellectual property, including patent laws, copyright laws, trademark protection laws and contract laws must be in place if we are to reap the benefits of an idea reactor.

It is pertinent to note here that in modern Europe laws encouraging the flow of ideas evolved in tandem with increased economic activity and prosperity over a period of time. The history of patents and patent laws is generally considered to have started in Italy with the Venetian Statute of 1474, a decree by which new and inventive devices, once they had been put into practice, had to be communicated to the Republic of Venice in order to obtain legal protection against potential infringers. The period of protection was ten years. Patents, however, had existed before the Statute of 1474. In England, grants in the form of 'letters patent' were issued by the sovereign to inventors who petitioned and were approved. A grant to John Kempe and his Company in 1331 for woollen weaving is the earliest authenticated instance of a royal grant made with the avowed purpose of instructing the English in a new industry. The practice of granting full industrial patents and monopolies became common in Italian states by the 1420s.[12]

Interestingly, the European Renaissance began at the same time as the awareness of intellectual property and the need for property protection. The two dovetail nicely. As the scope and practice of intellectual property laws increased, Europe moved from the Renaissance to the Industrial Revolution (eighteenth to ninteenth centuries).

In 1624, the parliament of England passed the statute of Monopolies. This act arose from the misuse of the 'letters patent' as a means of earning money instead of protecting patents. This is evidenced by the fact that patents were given out for even salt and starch. These 'letters patent' began to be granted for long terms instead of limited periods and created monopolies with exorbitant prices which stifled competition.

The Statute of Anne Copyright Act, 1709, named after the then Queen of Great Britain, came into force in 1710, at the beginning of the Industrial Revolution. The statute was concerned with the reading public, the continued production of useful literature and the spread of education. The central plank of the statute is a social quid pro quo: to encourage 'learned men to compose and write useful books' the statute guaranteed the finite right to print and reprint those words. It established a pragmatic bargain involving authors, booksellers and the public. The Statute of Anne ended the old system whereby only literature that met the censorship standards administered by the booksellers could appear in print. Furthermore, the statute created a public domain for literature, for prior to this all literature belonged to the booksellers forever. Copyright, rather than being perpetual, was limited to a term of fourteen years with a renewal term being available to the author (and only if the author was living at the end of the first term).[13]

Trademarks are the oldest form of intellectual property protection. The earliest use of trademarks probably served the twin purposes of a mark of ownership and an indication of the source of origin of the goods that bore them. Egyptian structures erected as early as 4000 BCE show quarry marks and stone cutters' signs. Potters' marks appear in relics left from the Greek and Roman periods.

The Industrial Revolution sparked the advent of modern capitalism. The guild systems gradually disintegrated and free business was established. Trademarks rather than obligatory guild membership began to identify the source of goods. Around this time special criminal laws protecting trademarks were developed through early anti-forgery, anti-counterfeiting and fraud laws. Civil protection was gradually and systematically established against those who would use another's mark without permission.

Since early commerce was limited to the immediate locality, few merchants needed marks on their products. As manufactured goods began to be marketed and sold over greater geographical areas and as trade and commerce grew apace and competition proliferated, the need for legally protected trademarks became imperative. Today there are a large number of goods with a truly global outreach. The products and the companies that make them are often household names worldwide. These products and companies would never have achieved this without legally protected brands and trademarks.

The whole set of laws that protect intellectual property enhance the creation of ideas and their release. Most of these laws began to be enacted in Europe and were carried over to America from the start of the Renaissance. It is not a coincidence that the creation and flow of ideas spurted significantly with the enactment and enforcement of these laws. The absence of such laws acts as a powerful control rod preventing the creation and release of ideas. A lack of these laws, properly codified and enacted, may be the foremost reason why the ancient civilizations of Egypt, India and China and later the Muslim Caliphates did not progress rapidly from the high points they all achieved when they were at their zenith.

To those who fret over the high cost of goods under patent protection, especially medicinal drugs and vaccines, I would like to point out that the choice is not between getting these products at a high price for a limited number of years while under patent protection, with lower prices thereafter, or getting them at low prices from the start. The choice really is between getting the goods at a high price for a limited period of time or not getting the goods at all. There is no moral judgement in this stance. It is simply an acknowledgement of the way an idea reactor works. If a country feels that the price of a certain drug, deemed essential, is too high for its citizens, it can subsidize the price directly or persuade the patent-holding drug company to let the country manufacture a generic version of the drug for its own use. In either case the idea generator will get its due share. That is the way ideas are generated and released.

Contrary to what many, especially in the developing world, might implicitly believe—that intellectual property rights are niceties not really applicable to them but indulgences affordable to the rich world—the reality is that it is the protection of intellectual property that creates wealth in the first place. If a society is to reap the wealth inherent in ideas, it must spare no effort to protect and reward these ideas. Even the ancient Greeks were aware of the power of intellectual property rights in spurring new inventions. As early as 500 BCE, in the Greek city of Sybaris located in what is now southern Italy, there were annual culinary competitions. The victor was given the exclusive right to prepare his dish for one year. Encouragement was also given to all who discovered refinements in luxury. The profits arising from these discoveries were secured to the inventor by law, although it was not then recognized as patent law, for the space of a year. The ancient Sybarians were percipient in limiting the period of protection. Without a time limit, patents become monopolies. Efforts must be made to prevent the evergreening of patents.

The justice delivery systems of all countries are faced with many tasks other than intellectual property protection and the implementation of contracts. Maintaining law and order and ensuring the safety of life and property are among the more important functions of a justice delivery system. These are also necessary for economic growth. The lack of law and order is a major deterrent to the release and implementation of ideas. People do not release ideas or start ventures if there is a high risk that the fruits of their labour will be appropriated by brigands or their lives put in danger. In such a background, it is a much better survival tactic to lie low and not attract attention.

When an idea interacts with a mind that is aware and receptive, a new idea may be formed but not necessarily released. The generation of an idea is an involuntary act but the release of an idea is not involuntary. A mind will release its new idea to the world only if it wants to. That often depends on whether or not it sees any advantage in releasing it. It is very difficult to force an idea out of someone. Conditions must exist for the originator of an idea to release it and benefit from doing so. The analogy that appears very apt for this is Aesop's fable about the North Wind and the Sun, where they both decide to see which of them can get a cloak off a traveller. The North Wind blows with all its fury, only to make the traveller grasp his cloak tighter. The Sun on its part shines warmly, making the traveller want to take off his cloak. The difference in the two approaches is trying to force an idea out of someone or creating conditions so that he or she wants to release the idea. Sometimes the originator of an idea, far from seeing any advantage in releasing an idea, can perceive a threat to his or her well-being if a particular idea is released.

The control rod, which prevents the release and implementation of ideas for the fear of brigands, does not differentiate between the colour of the brigands. They could be of any kind—lawful or unlawful. I refer here to confiscatory rates of taxation, which are lawful as per the law of the land but completely dysfunctional as far as the economy is concerned. If you were living in India in 1974, the highest tax rate applicable to you as an individual could have gone up to 97.5 per cent. Most brigands would probably have been more generous to their victims, leaving them with a little more, not out of the goodness of their hearts but because it made little sense to kill the goose that laid the golden eggs. Not surprisingly, very little economic activity took place in India at that time. The little that took place was on a very small scale designed to stay below the taxman's radar. From 1950 to 1980 the GDP growth rate in India averaged 3.5 per cent while the per capita income growth averaged 1.3 per cent. Thereafter tax rates were brought down gradually and by 1998 the highest tax slab was down to 30 per cent. The GDP growth rate responded by going up to almost 10 per cent within a decade. There is not much reason to strive for growth and profits if the profits are nearly all going to be taken away by exorbitant taxes. Without the security of property and profits, the incentive to take risks vanishes.

If you had an idea for manufacturing a perfect widget and needed a hundred clearances, licences and permissions from different authorities to set up a plant to manufacture the widgets, you would need to be either a very patient person with a smattering of Methuselah genes or a large corporation with departments to tackle and 'manage' the various permissions before you entered the quagmire. Add to that the likelihood that you would regularly be visited by friendly inspectors to check that you were diligently following every requirement of every obscure rulebook of every department, and the chances are that you would hesitate to venture forth.

Red tape is a control rod that has little to do with the formation of ideas but much to do with their release and transformation into ventures. It works particularly well against small businesses and new entrepreneurs, who do not have the manpower and other resources needed to manage the red tape, which large corporations are more easily able to navigate. So why don't individual entrepreneurs join hands with large corporations? In purely economic terms, it should not matter if the idea of a prospective entrepreneur is coupled with the resources of a corporation; in other words, if the idea is sold to a large corporation, growth would still ensue. In practice, however, this does not quite work this way. Many ideas of potential entrepreneurs are about fairly small business enterprises which, while sufficient for the needs of the entrepreneur, are too small in scale, at least initially, to interest corporations. Red tape prevents these ideas from ever reaching the marketplace. If an idea does interest a large corporation, it will, knowing that it is negotiating from a position of strength, tend to offer terms not always advantageous to the originator of the idea. This, of course, can only come about if an intending entrepreneur takes his idea for sale to a corporation. In the absence of effective intellectual property rights the entrepreneur would know that even by talking about his or her idea, he or she would be giving away for free what was intended to be negotiated.

If an entrepreneur decides, in the face of all the hurdles, to take the plunge, and manages to get the venture off to a good start, it is not the end of his or her problems. Red tape affects not only the starting of a business but also its continued running. Often the stress of navigating it is so great that even successful ventures are persuaded to sell out. Again, in economic terms, there is nothing wrong with an entrepreneur cashing out other than that it encourages the formation of conglomerates and monopolies, distorting the marketplace and giving a competitive edge not to a better product or service but to those with the ability to manage the red tape. Red tape favours large corporations.

Amongst other things, it impedes the transition of ideas into businesses, encourages monopolies, is a major source of corruption, eats into time and other resources and makes a country less competitive in the international marketplace since it varies considerably from country to country. To illustrate the wide variation amongst countries, consider the time needed to set up a business and to close a business. One day is needed to start a business in New Zealand and 694 days in Suriname. To close a business less than five months are needed in Ireland as opposed to seven years in India and eight years in Mauritania.

While researching this book, one country, India, stood out in some surprising ways. On the one hand India has become the fastest growing major economy since 2014. On the other hand it is ranked as one of the most difficult places in which to do business. In 2015, the World Bank Group ranked India in the 130th position overall,[14] for doing business. In the ten different aspects of doing business, India's rankings are anything but encouraging. All the rankings are out of 189 countries:

For starting a business, the number of procedures needed to be completed in India and the time required for them is more than double that of the average of OECD (mostly developed countries

Topic Rankings	2015 Rank
Starting a business	155
Dealing with construction permits	183
Getting electricity	70
Registering property	138
Getting credit	42
Protecting investors	8
Paying taxes	157
Trading across borders	133
Enforcing contracts	178
Resolving insolvency	136

that are signatories to the Convention on the Organization for Economic Cooperation and Development) countries. The minimum paid in capital requirement as a percentage of per capita income is 188.8 per cent as against 15.3 per cent for OECD countries but, more pertinently, the average requirement for other South Asian countries, with which India can best be compared, is 24.1 per cent. How do we reconcile the sustained high GDP growth with the abysmal rankings, not to mention the woefully inadequate state of infrastructure in India? If the rankings are accurate, I can only conclude that the entrepreneurial instinct in India is strong enough to counter the impediments it is faced with. Somewhere in the lumbering elephant of the Indian economy lies a hidden crouching tiger. If that tiger were to be unleashed, I suspect we would get to see an economic performance the likes of which has seldom been seen. I do not know how and if the tiger will ever be unleashed and I do not believe the unleashing can be done by merely pruning the ends of the red tape tree. The answer lies in fractal geometry. Instead of pruning the ends of the red tape tree, (which will grow back its cut twigs over time), it is better to cut whole main branches. Entire departments and even ministries being cut may be the best way to unleash the tiger. Admittedly, the task is daunting but the rewards may well be unbelievably great.

With a good education system, a good communication system and a good justice delivery system in place, ideas will arise and be released. If the ideas cannot be implemented because of a maze of red tape, it will give rise to despondency, cynicism and anger among citizens.

There is one control rod that I have not yet mentioned: labour. It is difficult to view labour as a control rod. The availability of labour is a great enabler for getting ideas to work. Without the availability of labour our best ideas would remain just that— ideas, concepts in our heads, squiggles on paper or sequences of binary digits in the ethereal world of computer memories. In the Classical Economics of Adam Smith, labour is one of the triad of the factors of production, the other two being land and capital (originally referring to capital stock such as buildings, tools and machinery). In today's industry, relatively little land is needed in ventures other than those involving agriculture. Land as a factor of production may now be subsumed under capital. The factors of production today are capital (including land cost for buying or renting a factory and other business premises), labour and knowledge or intellectual property or, to use a common word, ideas.

Labour is as important today as it ever was. I do not differentiate here between management and labour, or between physical and mental labour, but refer in general to 'the labours of men'. The entrepreneur or CEO who initiates a venture may be said to represent the idea. All other efforts, including the devising of marketing strategies, management and what is traditionally regarded as physical labour, come together to take the idea to the marketplace and are parts of labour. The availability of different types of labour is clearly a must for the implementation of an idea. The availability of this labour can only be viewed as an asset. It takes a rare and special kind of genius to turn a vital asset into a liability or a control rod to hamper the implementation of ventures.

Exit policies in some countries have managed to do just that. In these countries it is impossible to lay off people, not only during a business downturn cycle but even when the venture has become unviable. Perhaps what is best for the venture is to shut it down and pay off the manpower and make the capital, including land and manpower, available for other ventures, which may be more successful. Exit policies prevent that.

There is the bizarre case of a fertilizer plant set up at Haldia near Calcutta. The project was started in 1971 by Hindustan Fertilizer Corporation Ltd,[15,16] a government-owned venture. A township was built to house the employees along with a captive power plant. Everything went well except that no fertilizer was ever produced. Until at least 2002, the 1400-odd employees were still attending office. I have no idea what they did there. Their website shows the annual capacity of various finished products as 843,250 tons and the latest approved cost as ₹2820 million (in 1979 nine Indian rupees equalled one US dollar). Under Expected Commercial Production it says: 'No firm date as the commissioning activities has been suspended since October 1986'. Not surprisingly, under Financial Performance the losses for just the three years 1996–97, 1997–98 and 1998–99 were estimated to be ₹18,210 million, many times the initial cost of the project.[17,18]

Restrictive exit policies for labour, where they exist, are made with the avowed purpose of protecting the interests of labour, but they end up doing the opposite in two ways. First, having seen what happens to other companies when they try to lay off people, many ventures, especially those with a large labour component,

will be deterred from entering the market. Second, if a company does enter and has sufficient capital, it will try and automate as many of its processes as it can, trying to minimize the labour employed. If there is a pickup of demand during a business cycle a company will hesitate to add to its payroll numbers, knowing that when the demand returns to the normal trend, it will be difficult to lay off the extra employees. They prefer instead to lose market share or outsource some of the processes to what is euphemistically called the unorganized sector.

The unorganized sector does not typically yield data of any kind and is below the radar of both labour inspectors and tax collectors. Without any means to effectively protect any rights they may have under the law, it can only be assumed that workers in the unorganized sector get a worse deal than their peers in the organized sector.

Let us return again to the problem in India, where it is difficult to lay off people in even moribund plants. I quote from the Government of India, Ministry of Labour, website: 'The National Sample Survey Organisation carried out a sample survey in 2009–2010 and its results showed that out of a total work force of 465 million, only 28 million workers (6 per cent) are employed in the organized sector and the remaining in the unorganized sector.'[19, 20]

There are more interesting statistics available. As per the Planning Commission of India, on 31st March 1999 the total employment in the organized sector was estimated to be 28.113 million while in 2010, it was 28.708 million. This means that there has been an increase of 595,000 organized jobs over a 12-year period. This translates to an annual increase in employment of 0.17 per cent in employment.'[21] An increase in employment of 0.17 per cent during a period when the Indian economy was growing at an incredible rate of 7.3 per cent is difficult to reconcile with.

There is certainly a need to protect the interests of workers as much as there is to protect all our interests, for at the end of the day we all work in one capacity or another. But keeping workers employed in failed ventures is clearly not the way to do so. Such artificial employment, wastes capital and perhaps most importantly, destroys the self-esteem of the workers whose jobs have been thus protected.

In concluding this chapter on factors that inhibit the generation and release of ideas, it may be interesting to note that the neutron absorbers of which control rods are made are also called neutron poisons. It is an apt name as the control rods effectively absorb and kill all emitted neutrons, bringing to a halt any sustained nuclear reaction. Similarly, the control rods mentioned above, along with others that may have eluded me, all act as idea poisons, bringing to a halt the sustained progression of ideas and the hope of a better tomorrow.

REFERENCES:

1. http://en.wikipedia.org/wiki/List_of_early_modern_universities_in_Europe. Accessed on 26 April 2016
2. J.D. Bernal, 'Dialectical Materialism and Modern Science', *Science and Society*, No. 2, 1937, pp. 58–66
3. http://en.wikipedia.org/wiki/Troubadour. Accessed on 26 April 2016
4. Said I. Abdelwahed, *Troubadour Poetry: An Intercultural Experience* (Al-Azhar University-Gaza) 2004
5. http://en.wikipedia.org/wiki/Courtly_love. Accessed on 26 April 2016
6. *The Arab Human Development Report 2005: Towards the Rise of Women in the Arab World* (New York: UNDP, Regional Bureau for Arab States, 2006), pp. 212–1
7. http://en.wikipedia.org/wiki/Women's_literary_salons_and_

societies_in_the_Arab_World. Accessed on 26 April 2016
8. https://theurbanmuslimwomen.Wordpress.com/2008/08/04/fatima-al-fihri-founder-of-the-oldest-university-in-the-world/. Accessed on 26 April 2016
9. Gail Ukockis. *Women's Issues for a New Generation* (Oxford University Press, 2016)
10. http://history.hanover.edu/texts/bruni.html. Accessed on 26 April 2016
11. http://en.wikipedia.org/wiki/Female_education. Accessed on 26 April 2016
12. http://en.wikipedia.org/wiki/History_of_patent_law. Accessed on 26 April 2016
13. http://en.wikipedia.org/wiki/History_of_copyright_law. Accessed on 26 April 2016
14. http://www.doingbusiness.org/rankings. Accessed on 26 April 2016
15. http://www.rediff.com/news/2000/jul/13flip.htm. Accessed on 26 April 2016
16. http://indiatoday.intoday.in/story/hindustan-fertilizer-corporation-getting-ready-to-wind-up/1/245106.html. Accessed on 26 April 2016
17. http://www.fert.gov.in/hindustan0001.asp. Accessed on 26 April 2016
18. http://www.fert.gov.in/hindustan9899asp. Accessed on 26 April 2016
19. http://vikaspedia.in/social-welfare/unorganised-sector-1/categories-of-unorganised-labour-force. Accessed on 26 April 2016
20. http://en.wikipedia.org/wiki/Labour_in_India. Accessed on 26 April 2016
21. httpp://planningcommission.nic.in/data/datatable/data_2312/DatabookDec2014%20114.pdf. Accessed on 26 April 2016

4

THE COOLANT AND THE PIPELINE—
TAPPING THE IDEA REACTOR

In a nuclear power plant, a coolant carries the energy created in the reactor to a heat exchanger, where it is used to generate electricity. The coolant also prevents the reactor from overheating or having a meltdown. The coolant is carried to the heat exchanger through a pipeline without constrictions and leakages.

Money is the coolant of the economic engine. It is by means of money that ideas are taken to the marketplace. By converting ideas into hopefully profitable ventures, money prevents the build-up of frustration which often results in deviant social behaviour.

The pipeline that carries ideas to the marketplace is a set of business-enabling laws strengthened by an effective justice delivery system. Like any good pipeline it must be free of constrictions caused by red tape and free of leakages caused by corruption or taxes levied before profits have been earned.

♦

In this chapter we will look at what is required of a good coolant and how money measures up in this capacity. Along the way we will also look at the pipeline which enables the transfer of innovation from the idea reactor to the marketplace.

But first I would like to share a few thoughts on what a build-up of energy in the idea reactor can lead to. In almost all countries in the world, there are impediments to putting ideas to work. Perhaps it will never be possible to remove them all but the degree to which these impediments exist makes a great difference. A few impediments may even be a good thing in that they force the emergence of better ideas that can circumvent or overcome impediments. However, beyond a certain tipping point, when very little of the energy of the idea reactor can be led to the marketplace because of impediments, the first signs of the impending meltdown begin to appear in the form of deviant social behaviour.

The impediments can be many and differ from country to country and from time to time. They can vary from outright rejection of private enterprise as was the case under most communist regimes until recently, to excessive government-imposed regulations and licensing requirements as is the case in many overly bureaucratic countries. They are also found in misgoverned countries where heavy, continuous bribes have to be paid to permit even the smallest economic ventures, and in countries that tend to levy heavy taxes before profits are earned. Then there are countries where there is ineffectual legal recourse for lenders faced with wilfully defaulting borrowers, making potential lenders unwilling to lend money in the first place. Or else the legal system is unable to rein in monopolistic market behaviour, whereby established and entrenched players deny space to more efficient ideas.

The impediments to ideas being converted to ventures also include those elements of societies that are extremely conservative and so entrenched in their way of life that they frown upon even the slightest change from what already exists. And that is what ideas bring to the table: change, hopefully for the better. If a society feels it does not need new ideas, it could well spare itself the trouble and expense of educating its people and trying to set up an idea reactor. I suspect certain dictators would wholeheartedly endorse this view.

As the frustration caused by the inability to pursue ideas builds up, the first signs of a meltdown begin to appear. The signs vary depending upon circumstances, the culture of the society and the perceived power and ruthlessness of the regime in power. Cultural values such as tolerance or the virtue of accepting one's lot and deference to authority may delay the signs of the impending meltdown as will a society living in fear of a harsh regime. But the meltdown will come anyway. If the build-up of ideas that cannot be implemented and the frustration this generates is great, the trigger that causes the meltdown could come from anywhere, as unpredictably as it did in Tunisia in 2010, where the suicide of a fruit vendor unable to meet bribery demands unleashed the Arab Spring, causing the overthrow of not one but many governments in the region. Even as I write, the movement has not yet played itself out.

To be sure there will always be signs that all is not well and anyone with an ear to the ground should be able to discern hints of deviant behaviour born out of frustration. In the erstwhile USSR, the predominant sign was rampant alcoholism. In Islamic countries, with a few exceptions, power and wealth are perpetually ensconced in the hands of a few and escape into alcohol is not possible, so violence aimed at different sectarian groups, random bombing and suicide bombing is how the malaise shows itself. In some Latin American countries where wealth and businesses are largely controlled by a few families, the only avenues open for economic well-being are the drug and kidnapping industries. In India, the malaise may be showing itself in the practice of female foeticide, even among the well-to-do, and the abuse of women.

In all countries nearing a meltdown, there is a departure from civic norms and a disdain for the ruling regime, whatever its dispensation may be. When the death of a member of the ruling dispensation is met with relief rather than sorrow and when derogatory jokes about politicians and corruption begin to outnumber others, it indicates that things are not well. But I overreach myself, psychologists and social scientists will surely be able to throw sharper light upon this. I, for my part, believe the meltdown starts with a sense of despondency over what might have been.

Getting back to coolants, textbooks list their main properties as:

1. Having a high thermal capacity or the ability to carry heat from the source of heat to the intended point of use.
2. Having low viscosity or the ability to flow easily as it carries heat from the heat source to the intended point of use.
3. Being non-toxic and chemically inert, neither causing nor promoting corrosion of the cooling system.

There are two other characteristics of coolants that are not mentioned in engineering textbooks because they are taken as a given and not worth listing. They are:

4. Having a constant thermal capacity. This is omitted by textbooks as materials available in nature do not change their thermal capacity in their natural form.
5. Being available in the required quantity to meet the needs of the reactor.

Let us now consider these characteristics with the analogy of money as a coolant for the economic power plant.

MONEY MUST HAVE VALUE

High thermal capacity: In terms of money, thermal capacity is the ability of money to buy goods and services. The word 'high' implies a comparison with other coolants. One way of making a comparison between the currencies of different countries is to consider the number of days or years required to earn the money on a per capita GDP basis to buy a specific basket of goods and services. The less time required to earn that money, the higher its thermal capacity and the greater the ability of money to take the ideas generated in human minds to the marketplace.

MONEY TRANSACTIONS MUST BE EASY

Low viscosity: This was once a problem with money but now with internet-based transactions the flow of money is instantaneous. It has very low viscosity. Earlier, before the invention of money, transfer of assets was slow and cumbersome, when large quantities of grain or animals had to be exchanged to effect a transaction. When coins were in use they still needed to be transferred physically. With current banking practices the speed has increased and is only limited to the speed of transfer of information which is practically instantaneous.

MONEY TRANSACTIONS MUST BE TRACEABLE

Being non-toxic and chemically inert, neither causing nor promoting corrosion of the cooling system: The advent of money, while it speeded up transactions, also encouraged and promoted the corrosion of the cooling system primarily by way of corruption and theft. It was far easier to spirit away a bag of gold or a fistful of dollars than to walk away with a herd of cattle or bushels of grain. For much of its history, money, despite its many advantages, has been corrosive and the economic engines of most of the world have been operating with a leaky pipeline.

However, with online transfer of funds, which has made the movement of money almost instantaneous, the process has become far more transparent. Information about most transfers can be retrieved and scrutinized. This is a development that needs to be encouraged and enhanced. Further, with banks refusing to accept deposits of significant amounts of cash, the corrosion causing aspects of money are beginning to recede. This process needs to be strengthened. Pressure must be brought to bear upon the Swiss and other tax havens to become more transparent.

MONEY MUST RETAIN ITS BUYING POWER

Having a constant thermal capacity: As pointed out, this is not mentioned in engineering textbooks because materials in nature do not change their thermal capacities. This is fortunate as it would be practically impossible to design a cooling system where the coolant kept changing its thermal capacity. Money losing its value is like a coolant losing its thermal capacity. In a situation where money loses value and accumulated savings get reduced, the money may be insufficient to take the energy of ideas and to convert those ideas into workable ventures.

The degradation of money or the loss of buying power has been a problem ever since money was conceived. This is also known as inflation. When the prices of a few goods rise it may simply reflect greater demand than supply. When there is a general rise in the prices of all goods and services it is always caused by the oversupply or degradation of money, normally through the innocuous-sounding term 'deficit financing'. While governments and central banks can print money at will, they can never mandate through a fiat that it retain its value. Printing money excessively always leads to the loss of its purchasing power. During the period when metallic coins were the chief medium of exchange, rulers often tried to reduce the quantity of the most precious metal, which was usually gold, and increase the quantity of other metals, but this sleight of hand did not work for long. While rulers or governments may have been able to dictate prices within their borders, the medium of exchange lost purchasing power dramatically once it went outside their borders.

To examine the role of money and inflation, let us start with the history of money, its evolution and what is expected of it. Before money was invented, all goods exchanged hands by way of barter mostly between strangers or through giving gifts among better-acquainted people, who expected that the gifts would one day be reciprocated. However, barter trade has its drawbacks, the chief among them being what is known as the coincidence of wants. Coincidences are required both in terms of the goods being offered for exchange being wanted and also being wanted at the same time. This is often not the case. A farmer might need, for example, milk for his children on a daily basis, but his crops, which he exchanges in order to get milk are only available in their seasons. Further, neither fruits and vegetables nor milk can be stored for very long as all are perishable commodities.

There is also the question of exchange rates. How much is a measure of milk worth in apples and how much is it worth in cabbages? Barterers would always need to have a sense of the exchange rates of different commodities against each other. If there were only ten commodities being considered for exchange, each against any other, it would require the barterers to consider forty-five different exchange rates. If, however, a common medium of exchange, such as a shekel of barley or a specific number of cowrie shells, was accepted by all, only ten possible exchange rates or prices would need to be kept in mind. Trading therefore becomes much simpler if a good is commonly accepted as a medium of exchange. This medium of exchange becomes money. There is another advantage to using money—it permits the buying and selling of goods even when there is no immediate need for them. Shekels of barley can be kept for a few years and cowrie shells for even longer. Money becomes a store of value.

I mention shekels of barley and cowrie shells because these were amongst the earliest of commodities to be used as mediums of exchange. The shekel was an ancient unit of both weight and currency. It was first used in Mesopotamia about 5000 years ago to define a specific weight of barley and equivalent amounts of materials such as silver, bronze and copper. The use of a single unit to define both mass and currency was later employed to define the British pound, which was originally valued as one pound mass of silver.[1]

Cowrie shells were used as money in large parts of Asia and Africa for a long time, starting about 4000 years ago.[2] It is easy to see why. Money needs to be portable, long-lasting, available in sufficient quantities to enable the growth of trade and yet in limited supply in order to retain its value as a medium of exchange. Further, it must be difficult to counterfeit. In this last aspect, cowrie shells performed better than gold or silver or other metals.

Cowries could not be debased by filing away the edges, as people often did with gold or silver coins, nor could they be mixed with other materials as was common with metal coins. Electrum is a naturally occurring alloy of gold and silver, with trace amounts of copper and other metals. The gold content of naturally occurring electrum in modern western Anatolia ranges between 70 per cent and 90 per cent, in contrast to the 45–55 per cent of gold content used in ancient Lydian coinage from the same geographic region, where the first coins in the world were minted some 2700 years ago.[3] We can see the wilful debasement of money at work here. We can also see that this tendency to debase money has been around for a long while. This is not surprising, for debasing money and circulating more than was originally there is the easiest way for a ruler to garner wealth, power and popularity. Either it did not occur or it did not matter to those early Lydian rulers that the extra debased money they circulated created no extra wealth, but instead took wealth away from those who had saved and accumulated money. Not much seems to have changed in this regard in the last 2700 years.

Gold, silver and cowrie shells owed their appeal as mediums of exchange and stores of value to their limited supply. They have no intrinsic value. Even their use as articles of personal adornment arises from their limited supply and scarcity and perceived high value. When supply increased, for whatever reason, it led to inflation and in extreme cases even the demise of the commodity as money, like in the case of cowries. When supply decreased, it no longer oiled the wheels of trade and growth, leading to stagnation and the running down of the economic engine followed by rampant debasement of money in an attempt to get the economic engine going again, further exacerbating an already bad situation.

An ideal situation would be a gradual increase in the supply of the commodity being used as money in tandem with economic activity. Such an ideal situation is unlikely to prevail for a length of time. We cannot really expect the supply of any commodity to keep magically in step with economic activity. This is, however, possible with fiat money (which I will soon come to), provided we can eschew unchecked money printing and deficit financing by our governments. As wealth is created in the marketplace, money will grow automatically. The solution to our ills is not a return to the gold standard but the prudent spending of money by governments.

The cowrie, after being accepted as money for thousands of years and being impervious to debasement and counterfeit, finally met its nemesis in an unexpected manner. It was counterfeited by nature. The cowries that had been used as money for thousands of years were Cypraea Moneta. Almost all of them came from the Maldive Islands and were transported to the littoral countries of the Indian Ocean by Arab sailing ships and from the early sixteenth century by European ships too. Then large quantities of a very similar cowrie, Cypraea Annulus, were discovered off the coast of Zanzibar and were accepted to be of the same value as C. Moneta. This caused a great oversupply of cowries and consequent inflation. The inflation was such that the very counting of the shells, even for everyday purchases, became a near impossibility and spelt the end of cowrie shells as a unit of money.[4]

The same thing once happened with gold and silver. The European Price Revolution refers to a series of economic events from the second half of the fifteenth century to the first half of the seventeenth century. The Price Revolution refers most specifically to the relatively high rate of inflation across Western Europe, with prices on average rising about sixfold over 150 years.[5] That works out to an annual inflation rate of barely 1.2 per cent. In recent years most developed economies have had an inflation rate in the region of 3 per cent and emerging markets have inflation rates that are higher still.[6] A 3 per cent inflation rate over the 150 years of the Price Revolution would have seen not a sixfold rise in prices but an 84-fold increase in prices.

The only term that can be used to even come close to describing the current prevailing situation is 'price explosion'. It is surprising that we are so sanguine about the high rate of inflation today. It is pertinent to remember that a 1.2 per cent rate of inflation seemed high and unusual enough to earn the sobriquet Price Revolution. It must tell us that inflation, unlike death and taxes, is not inevitable.

The Price Revolution was caused by an unusually increased supply of both silver and gold. The increased supply of silver, which gave the first thrust inflationary pressure, came from increased production of silver and copper in south German mines. This occurred due to two technological advances. The first, and perhaps more important, was the Saigerhiitten prozess, a chemical process that utilized lead in smelting to separate silver from copper ores. The other was mechanical pumps to drain water from flooding mines, enabling deeper shafts to be constructed. This increased output was shortly followed by huge imports of silver from Spain's new American possessions.

Similarly, the supply of gold increased, starting first in 1470 CE in the Portuguese African Gold Coast fortress of Sao Jorge, from where 'Sudanese' gold, which the West Africans were extracting from the Senegal, Niger and Volta river basins, was sent to Europe. This was followed some years later by large shipments of Spanish Inca gold.[7]

When the supply of a commodity used as money increases it always leads to inflation. When the supply reduces it is worse. One of the reasons for the decline of the Roman Empire was the shortage of silver, with the mines past their peak production. Output from the silver mine at Rio Tinto in southern Hispania, a major source of Roman silver, peaked in 79 CE. This shortage of silver prompted the debasement of the silver coin, the Denarius coin, which started out as a coin of almost pure silver, became the Antonymous coin of the second half of the third century which had a silver content of only 2 per cent.[8] As the content of silver in Roman silver coinage reduced, prices rose. To meet expenses more coins with even less silver were minted, leading to further inflation. It was a vicious cycle.

The single largest expense of the Roman Empire was the payment and upkeep of its armies. The legions spread out within and along the borders of the Empire saw their purchasing power dwindling and unrest rose. Emperors began to be deposed and were replaced by their generals. It would be simplistic and untrue to say that the shortage of silver was the only cause of the fall of the Roman Empire but it was certainly an important factor.

The need to debase the currency arose when the government began spending more than it earned, whether by way of taxes or other receipts, and in the case of Rome by way of tributes from newly conquered territories. Could Rome have done otherwise? It is a moot point. The hard reality is that when governments spend more than they have, it always leads to debasement of currency and inflation. Inflation may take time to show itself, but it will, eventually.

Gold, silver and cowries are examples of commodity money. These had value due to their scarcity and as happened with cowries, they lost value drastically, thanks to oversupply. Other commodities of direct use which have been used as money may also have an intrinsic value of their own, which will always be retained. Regardless of inflation, grain, cattle and other livestock in agrarian communities, animal pelts in cold regions, rum, peppercorns and cannabis where they are difficult to come by and surely many other commodities will always retain the value derived from their usage. The relative value of these commodities certainly varied with season and circumstance, but the intrinsic value of directly used commodities does not change.

In the case of grain, in a good harvest people ate better and stored away more grain. In a poor harvest the opposite happened. A shekel of barley or any other grain stayed a shekel of grain and gave as much nourishment in times of plenty as in times of little. The more commonly used of these commodities as mediums of exchange were grain, cattle and other livestock. Grain because it was of universal usage and readily tradable and had a shelf life of a couple of years. Cattle and other livestock because it was largely an agrarian world where the wealth of a person was measured by the number of livestock owned. Indeed many words referring to money or wealth have their origins in cattle. The word 'fee', for instance, derives from *feoh* in Old English, where its meanings included livestock, cattle, money and property.[9] In the familiar phrase 'goods and chattels', 'chattels' is derived from cattle. In classical Latin, the value of one's animal herds was one's 'pecunia' which led to the word 'pecuniary'.[10]

Livestock and grain were among the earliest mediums of exchange, probably dating back to the first agricultural settlements around 10,000 years ago, long before metals appeared on the scene. I imagine the first metal objects were paid for in grain and livestock.

The different commodities used as mediums of exchange and stores of value had different attributes. Some kept for a long time and were better stores of value, some were more readily acceptable and were better mediums of exchange, some were easier to transport and encouraged trade over longer distances, and some were more abundantly available so there was something to trade with in the first place. Whatever the merits or demerits of a particular commodity to be used as money, all commodity money was honest money. You got what you saw.

Of course, you had to keep your wits about you. It would not be to your advantage if you got saddled with a sick cow or insect-infested grain or a short weight of silver, but there was never any doubt that left you wondering if it was indeed a cow or simply a piece of parchment promising you a cow. In direct commodity trade, the cow you saw was the one you got. In the case of the parchment promising a cow, the health and other qualities of the cow were open to doubt; or whether the grain promised was actually edible, or what if the silver that had been promised to you had also been promised to others.

The next step in the evolution of money was representative money. Representative money introduced convenience and personal safety as merchants no longer needed to carry valuable commodities to pay for their purchases. However, it also introduced a degree of dishonesty to the value of money. Historically, the use of representative money pre-dates the invention of coinage. In the ancient empires of Egypt, Babylon, India and China, temples and palaces often had commodity warehouses which issued certificates of deposit as evidence of debt, a form of representative money.[11] This can also be called commodity-backed representative money. Essentially, representative money is a receipt or certificate that can be exchanged for a fixed quantity of the commodity warehoused. The acceptability of the certificate as a medium of exchange depended on the credibility of the issuer of the certificate. It could be the crown, the temple or church, a bank or a goldsmith. Over time this role has been taken over by central banks.

It did not take long for the issuers of these receipts to realize it was unlikely that all the holders would simultaneously wish to claim the commodities warehoused with them. They began to issue these certificates totalling well in excess of the commodity held by them. In the case of banks the certificates or money was issued as interest-bearing loans, generating far more profit for the bank than would otherwise have been possible. In the case of kings and governments, this ability to create money out of nothing helped to increase their wealth and power and generate a feeling of well-being by partly sharing the money in the form of subsidized bread and circuses. This has been done frequently by all hues of ruling dispensations since early Roman times. The wealth acquired in this manner by governments helped them to show their largesse, retain popularity, enrich themselves individually and wage war. The act of printing and spending more money than a government has is politely referred to as deficit financing. It debases money, which ceases to be a good store of value and is unable to act as a good coolant for the economic engine.

Wealth, unlike money, cannot be printed and created out of nothing. Deficit financing only shifts wealth disproportionately from the savers and the less well-off to the issuer of money, normally the government. The government may then show its munificence by partly sharing the wealth appropriated with those it wishes to influence, as subsidies and other giveaways, and partly retaining the wealth for its factotums.

The individuals who issue money often partake of it by voting themselves greater salaries, perks and pensions and by receiving kickbacks from inflated spending. The irony is that the less well-off, towards whom the subsidies and giveaways are ostensibly directed, end up paying for these.

Deficit financing causes inflation, resulting in higher prices of goods and services. Higher prices only affect a person to the extent of money spent. Any money that is saved and invested in an instrument yielding a return that is at least equal to the rate of inflation is not affected by inflation. The poor, who spend most of their money on everyday necessities and can save little, are the worst affected. The rich, who spend a very small portion of their money on life's necessities, are the least affected. In the same way the poor are more affected by taxes other than income tax such as sales tax, excise and service taxes. The rich, almost by definition, own many assets other than cash that will appreciate in value with inflation. They are also able to pay for the best financial advice and probably end up gaining from the inflation. The poor end up financing not only the budget deficit and ensuing government profligacy but also the profits made by the rich from the effects of inflation. Easy money to the government through deficit financing also tends to increase the size of governments. This, more often than not, increases bureaucratic control and red tape, further impeding the growth generated by the flow of ideas to the market.

There is nothing strange about a society that is willing, even keen, to extend a helping hand to the distressed among them, but inflation causing deficit financing is not the way to do so. Any spending done by a government to ameliorate the condition of its disadvantaged must be done with the money that the government has.

Once representative money became the norm, the world muddled through, oscillating between periods of price stability and rampant inflation. Underlying the rise and fall of the value of money was the widespread belief that there must be a basis, to some extent, on which to peg its value. Many rulers and governments, while debasing their money, probably regarded their act as a temporary measure, hoping to rectify the situation in the future. Whenever the gap between the value of the commodity held and the value of the money in circulation became excessive, money lost value. Governments would then suspend their obligation to exchange currency for the underlying commodity. Within their borders rulers could proclaim by fiat the value of their currency and enforce it. Fiat money was most commonly resorted to when money had lost most of its value and had little value outside the borders of the issuing country. During the days of the USSR, in the 1960s and early 1970s, three roubles could buy a bottle of champagne at a fine restaurant within the USSR, but outside the borders of the USSR, when those three roubles were exchanged for local currency at the rate offered by money changers, it was barely enough to buy a shot of vodka in a local bar. Value less fiat money was looked down upon by other countries, which refused to accept such money as means for payments due. International payments had to be made in gold and silver. This led to the gold standard.

The gold standard was not designed deliberately but evolved with the major trading nations of the time, that put their credence in gold rather than in the banknotes of other nations. This led to the gold bullion standard, where instead of coins, banknotes were used for trade, with the central banks agreeing to sell gold bullion on demand at a fixed rate of exchange for their currencies. With increasing international trade and not enough gold to back it, other steps needed to be taken.

In 1944, delegates from all 44 Allied nations gathered at the Mount Washington Hotel in Bretton Woods, New Hampshire, USA, for the United Nations Monetary and Financial Conference. They set up the Bretton Woods system of monetary management and established the rules for commercial and financial relations among the world's major industrial states. The Bretton Woods system is the first example of a fully negotiated monetary order intended to govern monetary relations among independent nation states. The delegates also established the International Monetary Fund (IMF) and the International Bank for Reconstruction and Development (IBRD), which today is part of the World Bank Group.

The chief feature of the Bretton Woods system was an obligation for each country to adopt a monetary policy that maintained the exchange rate by tying its currency to the US dollar with the IMF bridging temporary imbalances of payments. The US dollar was chosen because it was the only currency strong enough to meet the rising demands for international currency transactions. The strength of the US economy, the fixed relationship of the dollar to gold (at $35 an ounce), and the commitment of the US government to convert dollars into gold at that price made the dollar as good as gold. In fact the dollar was even better than gold: it earned interest and was more flexible than gold.[12]

It was too good to last. The dollars held by other countries soon exceeded the gold reserves held by the US government. It became impossible for the US government to redeem them and pay out gold. On 15 August 1971, the United States unilaterally terminated convertibility of the US dollar to gold. With no commodity backing it up, the US dollar ceased to be representative money or commodity-backed money and became fiat money. As the US dollar was the world's reserve currency and since almost all the world's currencies were pegged to the US dollar, all other currencies effectively became fiat currencies. Whereas earlier the few currencies that were fiat money were looked upon in askance, after 15 August 1971, all the world's currencies, for the first time in history, became fiat money. The world's central banks continued to hoard gold but it was more out of force of habit than because gold had anything to do with backing up their currencies; habit, and the realization that when push came to shove it was gold that would save them and not paper currencies.

Gold has sometimes been used to good effect to bail out a country in dire straits, as in 1991 when India airlifted 67 tons, about 15 per cent of India's gold reserves, out of India, to secure a loan from the IMF. The gold was used as collateral for the IMF loan and had no role to play in shoring up the Indian rupee. Any other commodity, had it been acceptable to the IMF, could have been used as collateral, whether barrels of oil or shekels of barley. The advantage of keeping reserves in gold is that it tends, in these inflationary times, to retain some value over a period of time and is also easy to handle. These are the same reasons that caused money to be created in the first place. The IMF did not accept rupees at the then current value of gold as it probably feared that India would simply inflate its debt away.

Once the world's currencies had all become de facto fiat money, it did not take long for the world's governments to think they had been freed of the tyranny of circumstance. They probably imagined, if one is to judge by their actions, they could simply print their way to prosperity. They were like the proverbial kid in the candy store, buying whatever took his fancy without actually paying for it. But it was all adding up on the tab and would eventually, willy-nilly, have to be paid. This not being a fair world, the burden would fall on the less well-off in each country.

Once a country steps on the slippery slope of using deficit financing for subsidies and other giveaways, it finds it hard to stop itself. Apart from the difficult task of weaning its citizenry away from the perks to which they have become accustomed, servicing the debt incurred, with interest and repayment obligations, is a difficult exercise. The servicing of debt consumes a progressively larger percentage of the GDP and of government revenues. This leaves less money for all other government spending, including money to eventually repay and retire the debt. If increasing debt continues for a long time it leaves governments with three alternatives, either singly or in combination.

First, a government can renege on its foreign debt, either partly or fully (I rather like the term of letting the creditors take a hair cut, a term that recently came into usage when the Greek and Cyprian banks simply forfeited a percentage of bank deposits, which almost makes it sound like the creditors were being done a favour), making it difficult to secure foreign funding in the future.

Second, it can inflate away its internal debt or foreign debt in its own currency by printing more of it, thereby diminishing the real value of both the money and the debt. This cost is borne by the individuals or countries holding the debt. This works to the great benefit of the USA as the dollar is the currency in which almost all international transactions are denominated. To a smaller extent it also works to the advantage of the Euro-zone.

The third option is for the government to tighten its belt and ensure that it spends less than it collects in order to eventually pay off the debt it has incurred on behalf of its citizens. It is the citizens who must pay for the past profligacy of the government in the form of higher taxes. The interests of a government and those of its citizens are not, it seems, always identical. This tightening of the belt can be extremely painful. The economy slows down, people lose jobs, inflation which is still high decimates savings that had been made for such an eventuality. Living standards decline. The worst affected are the less well-off in any country and the irony is that most of the subsidies and other freebies that led to deficit financing were given out in the name of the poor.

The value of money in any country is best measured by comparing the value of the country's currency against the currencies of other countries. At the present time, when countries are trying to outdo each other in printing money, the comparative values of currencies do not vary a great deal. However, when measured against a standard basket of goods and services, almost all currencies are losing value. In 2011 the world inflation rate was estimated to be 5 per cent, with developed countries averaging at 3 per cent and developing countries at 6.3 per cent inflation.[13] The world average was four times the inflation rate experienced during the 150 years of the Price Revolution. At these inflation rates, money is no longer a store of value and disposable incomes flow to assets that are seen as better stores of value, such as gold, real estate and other commodities. These assets are then exchanged for other needs by converting them into money and holding the money for the shortest time possible before purchasing those needs. While money stays a medium of exchange it is no longer a store of value, which is its most vital role.

Within a country, citizens have no alternative to using the money decreed by fiat as the medium of exchange. In international trade, only the more stable and comparatively value-retaining currencies are used as mediums of exchange.

The nature of money, as summed up in an old ditty used as a mnemonic by students of economics, is, 'Money is a matter of functions four, a medium, a measure, a standard, a store.'[14] Modern textbooks list only three functions of money: as a medium of exchange, a unit of account and a store of value, not considering a standard of deferred payment a distinguished function but rather, subsuming it in the others.

These three functions of money are not equally important in the role money plays in our lives. The use of money as a unit of account is certainly convenient and makes accounting simpler but the need to account has less to do with the nature of money and more to do with the nature of human beings and our need to tally our lives. Surely, before money came into use, accounts and tallies were kept with the medium of exchange in use at the time, whether it was the number of sheep or shekels of barley or strings of cowries.

The same logic applies to the use of money as a medium of exchange. It depends on the ability of money to act as a store of value. If money loses this ability it ceases to be used as a medium of exchange as we have seen in the case of cowrie shells. In a scenario where money is constantly losing value it can continue to be used as a medium of exchange because there are few alternatives, but the aim of parties who make a transaction will be to try and hold money in its liquid form for the shortest time possible, preferring to exchange it for desired goods or services. Holding money becomes a liability.

This is not what money is meant to be. The chief function of money is to act as a store of value. The other functions of accounting and as a medium of exchange will follow more or less automatically.

Is there any way we can ensure that our money retains its value? Since the advent of money, it has been subject to debasement by those in a position to do so, be it kings, governments or banks. During the era of precious metal coins this was done by diminishing the quantity of the precious metal in the coins. During the period of representative money, more money was circulated than held in the reserves. Currently, when all money is fiat money, it is debased by governments that spend more money than they have earned by way of taxes and other receipts but exclude the debt they take on to bridge the gap between their revenue and spending. This debt has to be serviced by paying out interest, making subsequent budgets that much more difficult to balance. When it is time to repay the debt, fresh debts are taken on, probably of a higher amount, resembling a giant Ponzi scheme where the youngest generation struggles to pay for the largesse enjoyed by previous generations. No Ponzi scheme can continue indefinitely and this one run by the governments of most nations shows signs of unravelling. Innovative schemes are being floated to hide the severity of the situation and being considered by some as sensible steps. The US Fed has started an operation whereby it exchanges short-term debt for lower-yield long-term debt, congratulating itself that it has not increased its balance sheet. This would be true only if the factor of time were ignored. If the same debt is taken on for a long period of time the aggregate debt has in reality increased. Fittingly, governments have borrowed the name of a convoluted dance form and lent it to a convoluted financial operation—Operation Twist.

Inflation has many consequences, most of them harmful. Many economists believe that by printing greater amounts of money a stalled economy can be got going again, but this is open to debate. Even if the economy began to function, it would be weighed down by the debt-servicing burden caused by the printing of money. To manage this, governments would have little choice but to keep interest rates unrealistically low, further disincentivizing savers. Continuing inflation is pernicious. It is psychologically debilitating and socially divisive. It impacts human behaviour. Further, inflation devalues money. Even if there is no profit to be earned from buying something, it makes sense to buy it anyway, as the money available today will buy less tomorrow.

Purchases that once seemed frivolous and unaffordable begin to appear wise decisions. Luxury goods that used to be the preserve of the well-heeled become common aspirations, making the well-heeled in turn seek yet more expensive brands. Money becomes a hot potato that everyone tries to get rid of because it is losing value. A paradoxical situation arises where people need to earn more money to maintain their standards and then realize they need to earn yet more the following year and then try to quickly spend what they have earned instead of postponing the spends for the future. It is like running on a treadmill to stay where you are but falling back a little every year. Human behaviour changes and some of these changes can be seen during periods of hyperinflation.

There are poignant memoirs of quite ordinary people that emerged from the period of hyperinflation in the German Weimar Republic (1921–23), easily accessible on the net, that show some of these changes.[15]

In an article posted by Aschwin de Wolf,[16] he quotes Theodore Dalrymple on the culture of inflation: 'asset inflation—ultimately, the debasement of the currency as the principal source of wealth—corrodes the character of people. It not only undermines the traditional bourgeois virtues but makes them ridiculous and even reverses them. Prudence becomes imprudence, thrift becomes improvidence, sobriety becomes mean-spiritedness, modesty becomes lack of ambition, self-control becomes betrayal of the inner-self, patience becomes lack of foresight and steadiness becomes inflexibility; all that was wisdom becomes foolishness.' He further goes on to quote Jorg Guido Hulsmann, senior fellow at the Ludwig von Mises Institute: 'The spiritual dimensions of these inflation-induced habits seem to be obvious. Money and financial questions come to play an exaggerated role in the life of man. Inflation makes society materialistic. More and more people strive for money income at the expense of personal happiness. Inflation-induced geographical mobility artificially weakens family bonds and patriotic loyalty. Many of those who tend to be greedy, envious and niggardly anyway fall prey to sin. Even those who are not so inclined by their natures will be exposed to temptations they would not otherwise have felt. And because the vagaries of the financial markets also provide a ready excuse for an excessively parsimonious use of one's money, donations for charitable institutions will decline.'

Although hyperinflation is a traumatic experience for any country, long-term inflation ranging from 5 to 15 per cent per annum is far more pernicious. Hyperinflation is an event of limited duration. When a country enters a state of hyperinflation, it soon leads to a breakdown of the existing system, to be replaced by a new order which hopefully manages to bring inflation under check. Recent hyperinflationary periods have normally lasted between one and three years. High inflation rates, on the other hand, can last for years, even decades. A period of one to three years is probably too short a time to completely change the structure of society and put an end to long-held values such as common decent behaviour, pride in one's profession and a sense of empathy towards fellow beings. Indeed it is possible that members of the same class in society, especially the middle class of professionals and wage-earners who are most affected by hyperinflation, may band together, their anger focused upon a villainous government or inimical foreign powers or rapacious businessmen or a combination of all three. A greater camaraderie and kinship within society may also be fostered by the traumatic experience, as in times of war and natural calamities.

It is quite different with consistently high inflation. In this scenario, a person sees the constant diminishing of the buying power of one's savings and salary and stares at an increasingly bleak future. The experience is that of an inexorable diminishing of the self. Along with this comes a diminishing of the moral fibre and good ethics that bind people together at other times. Any means that are employed to ameliorate one's personal economic situation begin to appear fair and acceptable. Corruption increases, as borne out by statistical analysis of inflation and corruption.[17] Promises and contracts are dishonoured, civil services deteriorate as bureaucrats cannot readily command bribes. The environment is degraded for monetary gain or out of sheer lazy convenience. Only the small isolated areas which are the domains of the powerful and influential are spared the ignominy of trash at their doorstep. Thus the notion of the common good of society vanishes, to be replaced by an overwhelming desire to stay ahead of the debilitating inflation by any and all means. Behaviour that would once have been regarded as abhorrent and irrational now becomes the norm.

Even governments do not remain unaffected. In an attempt to meet ever-increasing expenses, they introduce taxes which would in normal times have seemed strange. Two examples spring to mind, although there must be many more around the world. The first is the German city of Bonn putting up expensive parking meters for prostitutes who stand on the roadside hoping to catch the eye of a customer. It is difficult to think of a better way to further dehumanize an already dehumanized existence. The second is the capital of India, New Delhi, one of the more expensive cities in the world, imposing a luxury tax on all hotel rooms that cost over eight dollars a night. A luxury tax on what could be little more than a hovel or shanty? It would seem that inflation makes people brazen too.

Some economists and central banks are apprehensive about a zero or very low inflation rate. They are even more apprehensive about a very low negative inflation or deflation rate. They worry that in a scenario of prevailing deflation, buying decisions will be postponed with buyers expecting lower prices in the future, and business will slow down. They also fear that business profits and consequently government revenue will drop, largely because businesses cannot reduce certain costs such as wages or rent. Deflation, they maintain, can be even more disruptive for the economy than inflation. However, their apprehension is only valid in the case of long-term deflation. Human behaviour is not impacted by short-term and small inflationary or deflationary movement of prices. Human behaviour is impacted by inflationary or deflationary expectations. It is only the long-term prevalence of either inflation or deflation or the expectation of long-term inflation or deflation that impacts human economic behaviour. If one expects long-term price stability, with only a minor movement of prices likely in both directions, a dip in prices will spur buying in order to take advantage of a temporarily lower price, thereby helping to move prices back up again. This is an opportunity all purchase managers are constantly on the lookout for.

The anxiousness with which the central banks of America, Europe and Japan are hoping to see a rise in inflation has another explanation altogether. The only reason for this is so they can reassure themselves that their unprecedented printing of money is having the desired result of getting economic activity going again. If money is sloshing around in the system, prices must go up. If prices are not going up, it can only mean that the money is sitting in banks and other financial institutions, propping up their balance sheets. It is not being put to use either by businesses in making capital investments or by consumers borrowing to spend. I fear that central banks and governments are trying to address malfunctioning economies at the easiest point and not addressing the root cause of the problem, which is low economic activity. That could also be for reasons other than money supply.

THE SUPPLY OF MONEY MUST BE ADEQUATE

As economic activity increases, more money will be needed to cater for increased trade and to stimulate enterprise. Can the supply of money keep pace with economic growth? It is possible and it does not depend on either a gold standard or the running of the money printing presses. It depends on the velocity of money, as we will examine in the next chapter which is about markets. Efficiently functioning markets have the ability to increase non-inflationary money supply.

The next thing to consider is the pipeline that carries the ideas married with investments to the market, where the value inherent in ideas is realized. It would at first glance seem almost trivial to try and analyse the functioning of a simple structure like a pipeline but it is a very important part of the economic power plant and deficiencies in the pipeline can have severe consequences.

It is easy to imagine what the design parameters for such a pipeline, or indeed any pipeline, need to be. It would need to:

1. Be as short as possible so that no energy is dissipated unnecessarily.
2. Be without constrictions or narrowing of the pipeline, where pressure can build up and cause leakage of resources.
3. Be without any other unrequired pipelines leading away from the main pipeline, which can bleed away the viability of funded ideas before they reach the market.
4. Be of sufficiently sturdy material so as to prevent leakages.

Let us now consider how these requirements apply to the pipeline carrying ideas to the market. The pipeline is the sum total of a set of laws, policies and practices that enable business ventures to function.

1. The pipeline should be as short as possible: The length of the pipeline can be measured in many ways. It can be measured by the number of days required to start a business, the number of days to get a building licence, the number of days to get the myriad clearances and permits before a business can start and the number of days to close a business if it does not work out, thereby releasing the assets of the business which may be put to better use elsewhere. The UNO releases data for countries in an ease of doing business index, and it is not just for comparative purposes and ranking pride that the government of any country needs to study this data. It can

help a government pinpoint the areas it needs to focus on to improve the performance of its economy. Without speeding up the process and shortening the pipeline, many ideas will be stillborn and many ventures that could have been fruitful may never bear fruit.

2. The pipeline should be without constrictions: Constrictions are caused when numerous clearances, permits or licences are required before a business is set up and for its continuing operation. When ventures are faced with bribery demands they tend to pay up for fear that the venture may not start at all. Almost always, it is not just one clearance or permission that is required but a series of them. In ill-administered countries, the entrepreneur will not be surprised, even after he has started the business, to find the representative of some obscure department of the government come by and inform him that he requires permission from them too.

In such a situation, the pipeline carrying the venture to the marketplace starts to resemble a string of sausages with regular constrictions along the way, with each point of constriction a point of leakage from the pipeline. Inevitably these leakages will push up the price of goods offered on sale, if and when they do reach the market, resulting in fewer buyers. I sometimes wonder if we would have had airplanes today had the Wright brothers lived in a country with pipelines resembling sausage strings.

3. The pipeline should have no other pipelines bleeding money away before profits are made in the marketplace: While the first two points refer to the bleeding away of resources by way of corruption, the third and by far the largest component of continuous depletion of money is quite legal. These are the taxes that are levied before any income is earned. These are referred to as indirect taxes and comprise excise tax, value added tax (VAT) or sales tax, service tax, or any tax other

than income tax. There are two main reasons why these taxes are levied instead of relying on income tax. The first is that they are easier to collect than income tax and the second is that these taxes accrue to different bodies like the central government, the state government or local municipalities, all of which are then independently funded.

It is certainly easier to collect taxes from businesses, at the factory gate, city entrances and shop tills than to collect taxes from millions of reluctant taxpayers. But what if taxpayers were not reluctant taxpayers and were instead eager taxpayers? Could we then dispense with taxes before profits were generated and wages earned? I think it is possible to turn taxpayers into eager taxpayers. It all depends on the interplay between the nature of money, our human condition and our longevity, interest rates and income tax rates. To achieve this we do not have to bribe the taxpayer or promise him or her the earth. We simply have to ensure that at least part of the taxpayer's money is what money is supposed to be—a store of value, but more on this later.

4. The pipeline should be built of sufficiently sturdy material to prevent leakage: The material of which the pipeline is built are the sound laws and policies which can be legislated and promulgated to prevent the leakages described above. The mesh of wise and enabling laws needs to be reinforced by an effective justice delivery system to ensure that once the pipeline is opened up by legislative action, it remains open. Indeed some of these laws are probably already in place in most countries in the form of anti-corruption laws and need to be fully implemented by the justice delivery system.

While it is easy to imagine that the leakage of money from the pipeline before it reaches the marketplace can increase the cost of goods and services, thereby depressing demand, it is at times difficult to comprehend the extent to which this demand can be reduced. It does not matter if the leakage is caused by illegal means such as corruption and bribes, or by legal means including all taxes other than income tax. If the energy generated in the idea reactor, coupled with the money generated by savings from past endeavours, is bled away, it results in increased prices for goods in the marketplace that find fewer takers. To show just how disastrous the consequences of this may be, I give two examples.

The first example I would like to hold up for scrutiny is the Indian food processing industry, its potential and what it has actually achieved. There are two reasons for the underperformance of this industry. The first is the bleeding away of the coolant before it reaches the marketplace through both taxes and leakages caused by constrictions in the design of the pipeline. While it is possible to quantify the leakages caused by taxes, the leakages caused at the points of constriction are difficult to quantify and are best left to the imagination of people who have some experience in doing or attempting to do business in India. The second reason is an Act of Parliament specifically aimed at distorting a level playing field and actively discouraging competition.

I chose to look at the Indian food processing industry because of a few startling facts. India is the second largest producer of fruits and vegetables in the world. In the year 2010–11, fruit and vegetable production in India was 213 million tons. The secretary to the Ministry of Agriculture says that wastage is over 72 per cent. To quote him, 'The real challenge starts after the production. More than 72 per cent of the vegetable and fruits are wasted in the absence of proper retailing.'[18] The amount of fruits and vegetables wasted in India is more than that produced by most other countries, and enough to provide every man, woman and child of India's 1.2 billion people with 350 grams of fruits and vegetables every single day of the year. What do these figures mean in the context of India? Is India a land of such abundance that it can afford the monumental wastage it experiences? Sadly, such is not the case.

In its newsletter of March–April 2009, the World Bank, citing estimates by World Health Organization (WHO), said that 49 per cent of the world's underweight children, 34 per cent of the world's stunted children and 46 per cent of the world's wasted children live in India. According to United Nations Children's Fund (UNICEF), 42.5 per cent of India's children are underweight (moderate and severe), 48 per cent are stunted and 19.8 per cent are wasted.[19] If you are, as I was, unsure of the difference between stunted children and wasted children, WHO clarifies the matter.[20] Stunting or low height for age is caused by long-term insufficient nutrient intake and frequent infections. It generally occurs before the age of two and its effects are largely irreversible. Wasting, or low weight for height, is a strong prediction of mortality among children under five. It is usually the result of acute significant food shortage and/or disease. There are twenty-four developing countries with wasting rates of 10 per cent or higher, indicating a serious problem. The same web page of UNICEF goes on to give the prevalence of wasting in children under five in India as 20 per cent, one step below Sudan which has a wasting figure of 16 per cent.

If the wastage of fruits and vegetables in India could be eliminated or greatly reduced, it would go a long way towards improving the nourishment levels of its people, including its children. I have focused only on the wastage of fruits and vegetables, but the wastage of all of India's fresh produce including pulses, milk (both of which India is the largest producer of), grains and meats is far higher than world standards. Why has the food processing industry in India not been able to process and preserve more of its produce?

Food processing, like any other economic activity, has its technical aspects but we can safely say that it is not rocket science. The capital required to start a food processing enterprise is modest.

India does not lack technical expertise, entrepreneurial enterprise nor sufficient capital to have a thriving food processing industry. Further, Indian farming is of relatively low cost, resulting in Indian vegetable prices being 53 per cent of world prices and fruit prices 63 per cent. India produces an estimated 11 per cent of the world's vegetables and 15 per cent of the world's fruit. With all this going for it, India's share of the global export market is 1.7 per cent for vegetables and 0.5 per cent for fruits.[21, 22]

There are two main reasons for the dismal performance of India's food processing industry. One is a piece of market distorting legislation called the Agricultural Produce Market Committee Act (APMC Act). This Act forces farmers to sell perishable items like fruits and vegetables to only a limited number of licenced traders at APMC 'mandis' (markets), thereby encouraging cartelization in agriculture marketing. The APMC Act was instituted in the mid-1960s to ensure farmers got the right price for their produce with immediate cash payment. Meanwhile, traders who continue to hold licences by default for generations have become a strong cartel. The Act discourages competition by limiting the number of players and naturally lends to collusion.[23] It is a stringent Act providing for up to six months' imprisonment for any buyer or seller trading outside the APMC mandis. The Act also prevents food processors or retailers from buying directly from farmers. The result is that fruit and vegetable prices for the consumer are 350 per cent of the farm gate prices.

The second reason for the dismal performance of the industry is to do with money being bled away by means of taxes before its products reach the marketplace. This has the same effect on trade as having a portion of the merchandise pilfered in transit. The following table, which lists food processing levels and taxation rates of a few countries, shows taxes before profits on food products in India to be in excess of 30 per cent. This is not like pilferage during transit but a highway heist that has severe consequences on prices and profits. When the effects of these taxation levels are compounded by the effects of the APMC Act which drives up prices from the farm gate level to the wholesale level by 175 per cent, meaning that if a certain fruit cost ₹100 at the farm gate, it would be sold at ₹275 at the wholesale level, where most fruit and vegetables are bought by food processors. It is hardly surprising that India's level of food processing is only 2.2 per cent, resulting in massive wastage of its agricultural produce and consequent malnutrition of its population.

In perhaps the only nod to free trade the APMC Act explicitly exempts head loads, or goods carried to and fro from the markets in baskets on human heads, thereby ensuring the availability of at least some agricultural produce at reduced rates. This ensures the continuation of loading produce on human heads is the preferred means of transport to the marketplace for many farmers and small traders. I do not know if this carrying of head loads impacts the average height of Indians but the enduring deficiency of nutrition certainly does have a long-term effect. India has the third shortest people in the world, with the average height of a man being 5 feet 3½ inches (1.61 metres) and that of a woman 5 feet (1.52 metres). The two places where people are shorter than Indians is Bolivia–Aymara and Indonesia.[24]

Table 5.1 shows tax rates on processed foods and the extent to which fruits and vegetables are processed in a few diversely located and economically well-off countries. The taxes are those that are levied before the marketplace and do not have anything to do with income tax which is levied on earnings and therefore taken from the wealth created in the marketplace. In terms of our analogy to the nuclear power plant, this is a heated coolant that is bled away from the pipeline before it reaches the heat exchanger and not from the useful energy released in the heat exchanger.

The table (Table 5.1) shows taxes on processed foods and the level of fruit and vegetable processing in selected countries.

In the table 5.1, I have included restaurant taxes because they are very much a part of the food processing industry. The food processing industry is a big force multiplier. Apart from having the potential to save large quantities of food from being wasted, it is a very powerful tool in the progression of women's emancipation. The more evolved the food processing industry, the more its products move up the value chain, and the more time it saves for the housewife or any other consumer.

Our human condition dictates that we eat every day, usually two to three times a day. Our human condition also requires us to process what we eat. We have moved far away from our days as hunter gatherers when we could eat food completely unprocessed. We do not even regard some basic foods as processed, such as a bag of flour. If we were to process all our food from its natural state in our homes there would be little time for at least one adult in every family, normally the housewife, for anything else. It is the food processing industry, more than any other, that frees up her time for other endeavours, resulting in an enhanced quality of life and greater prosperity, both for herself and her family and the community as a whole.

The affordability of eating out is a step in the same direction. Apart from the time it saves, there is pleasure derived from eating out and choosing from a much wider fare than an individual home can provide. I believe the ability to eat out occasionally also affects the culture of a community. The very act of eating in the presence and company of others imparts a sense of conviviality and lubricates the interactions of the members of the community.

While I have no research to back this last point a great deal of work has been done on the high transaction costs between strangers. This trust deficit hampers the exchange of ideas. Even if social interaction is at a minimum while eating out, the very act of eating in the company of others who are also partaking of similar fare makes them seem less as strangers and enhances a

TABLE 5.1
Taxes on processed food and percentage of fruit and vegetable processing

Country	Excise (%)	Sales Tax (%)	Octroi (%)	Cumulative Taxes (%)	Fruits and Vegetables Processed (%)*	Taxes on Restaurants (%)
USA	Nil	No VAT. Most states have no sales tax on food items but 14 of 50 states have sales tax of about 5 per cent	Nil	0–5	80	Different states have different taxes averaging about 7 per cent
Malaysia	Nil	5 per cent at time of import or manufacture of grocery items	Nil	5	80	Nil
Philippines	Nil	12	Nil	12	78	12
France	Nil	5.5	Nil	5.5	70	5.5**
Thailand	Nil	7	Nil	7	30	7
India	12 per cent	12.5	4.75 (Mumbai)***	32	2.2	Sales tax on food 12.5 per cent. Sales tax on beverages whether alcoholic or not—20 per cent + Service tax—3.09 per cent +carryover from excise on any processed ingredients

*The percentage of fruits and vegetables that are processed has been taken from, *Value Addition of Horticultural Crops*, published by Springer, 2015, edited by Amit Barua Sharangi and Suchanand Data

**From 1st July 2009, France reduced the sales tax levied on restaurant sales from 19.6 per cent to 5.5 per cent. 19.6 per cent was the agreed upon rate for restaurant taxes by the European Union. France cited the importance of eating out to its economy as the reason for the reduction.[25]

***Octroi rates in India vary from municipality to municipality. The rate mentioned here is for Mumbai, one of India's largest municipalities and markets.[26]

sense of community. Interestingly the word 'convivial' which today means sociable and lively has roots in the Latin word 'convivium' meaning feast, dining party, entertainment and banquet, while the word 'conviver' defines 'an eating or drinking companion' comes from the Spanish 'convivir' which means to live together, to coexist, to live side by side. The opposite of a convivial society would be a privatized and polarized society where transaction costs are high and the exchange of ideas difficult. Little things like eating in the company of others finds no place in economic models but they help define us and our human condition.

Our human condition in all its many facets is important to consider when thinking of an economic engine that will deliver what we expect of it. It is important to remember that an economic system is designed for us and we are not to try and redesign ourselves for any arbitrary system or economic model. Our apparent strengths, weaknesses, idiosyncrasies and foibles do not even need to be labelled as such. They are a given. That is what we are. Of course, we are not all alike and go through life focused on different things. That is our strength as a species and not a weakness. If we were all a big herd doing the same thing we would have few ideas to exchange with each other. A good economic system should enable us all to live our lives differently. This paragraph about our human condition has little to do with the running of a nuclear power plant and the analogy seems to be breaking down. However, I visualize it not as a breakdown of the analogy but as our human condition being superimposed on the analogy of the nuclear power plant and the economic engine. Perhaps if we are able to keep in mind our human condition, the dismal science of economics will not remain so dismal.

While the effects of drawing away money, coupled with ideas and other business inputs before demand is generated and profits made, may have startlingly ruinous effects as in the case of the food processing industry, taxation and corruption taking away money before the idea reaches the marketplace has ill effects on every industry. Taxes, other than those on profit and income, increase costs and prices and depress demand.

The consequences of bleeding money away from the pipeline and of stymieing market forces in even one segment of the economy can be severe. In addition to the millions of stunted and wasted children, India also has a very low life expectancy figure. Thirty-two countries/administered areas of the world have life expectancy figures of over 80 years. Ninety-two countries have a life expectancy in excess of 75 years. In 2015 India was ranked 163rd with a life expectancy of 68.13 years.[27]

Fruits and vegetables, which are wasted so abundantly in India, are a major source of micronutrients, both minerals and vitamins. Numerous studies have shown the importance of micronutrients in countering stunting and wastage among children and in better resisting infections and increasing the life expectancy of the entire population.[28,29,30] Further, these micronutrients play a vital role in warding off or limiting the effects of many diseases and ensuring the optimal development of the body.

The economist Amartya Sen has observed that malnutrition and famine have more to do with problems of food distribution and purchasing power than lack of food production. He states that in recent decades there has been sufficient food to feed the entire world population. That is the reality of India too. With a wastage rate of 72 per cent, it is not food production but affordability that is the problem.

It matters not a whit whether the increase in prices and the ensuing reduced affordability is caused by corruption or government policy that encourages cartelization or by taxes increasing the cost of goods before they reach the marketplace. The deprived will be equally deprived irrespective of what has pushed these essential goods out of their reach.

It seems to me that the price to be paid in terms of a

malnourished population, stunted and wasted children, widespread blindness and other rampant diseases, leading to people with poor health and reduced longevity, is far too high a price to be paid for one piece of market-distorting legislation and a propensity for taking away money before goods reach the marketplace and needs can be met.

Staying with India and its penchant for taxing goods and services and prevailing corruption a little longer, let us consider the tourism industry. India is a large and diverse country, almost continental in size. It is blessed with a widely varied geography, from the Himalayan mountains with their glaciers and ski slopes to the sandy dunes of the Rajasthan deserts, to its rain forests and mangrove swamps of the Ganges delta. India also has 7517 kilometres of tropical coastline, including about 1400 kilometres of tropical island coastline and reef atolls and lagoons.

In addition to its geography, India can showcase 7000 years of its history, starting with one of the earliest human civilizations, the Harappan civilization, which was contemporaneous with the civilizations of Mesopotamia and ancient Egypt but far more widespread. Archaeological sites show houses of baked bricks, public baths, advanced sanitation systems, docks and granaries, at the dawn of human urban civilization. There are numerous Harappan sites in India and they are so well guarded by the authorities that there is hardly any awareness of their existence by even the local population, let alone any effort made to bring them to the notice of tourists. There is a site just 20 kilometres from Delhi at Hindon but hardly any of the 20 million residents of Delhi are aware of it.[31]

India is a treasure trove of history, from the grandeur of the Mauryan Empire, the Mughal Empire to the British Empire, to mention just the most well known of India's historic periods. The founder of the Mauryan Empire was contemporaneous with Alexander the Great and is said to have met him.[32] At the peak of his empire, Ashoka issued many edicts carved into rocks and stupas. Some of these edicts and many of the stupas or religious buildings he built 2300 years ago are still there to be seen.

Also a part of Indian history is a long line of kings and dynasties, with nearly all of them leaving their mark on the landscape by way of forts and palaces and temples. The temples, ranging from the ascetic to the wildly erotic temples at Khajuraho and Konarak, give an insight into the way of life and thinking prevalent in different periods of Indian history. India was ruled by Islamic rulers for nearly 700 years and dozens of their architectural achievements, including the iconic Qutub Minar, the Taj Mahal and the Jama Masjid, are on display. Four hundred and fifty years of India's interaction with European powers followed, starting with the landing in Goa of Vasco da Gama in 1498, just six years after Columbus reached America and culminating in 200 years of British rule. Most of the grand churches, forts, Gothic and Edwardian buildings they built, including the elegant Victoria Memorial in Kolkata and the magnificent Viceroy's Palace, now the official residence of the Indian President are still in use.

With the advantages conferred upon it by its geography and history along with its many art, music and dance forms and varied cuisines, India ought to be one of the world's leading tourist destinations. Such, unfortunately, is not the case.

The Table 5.2 lists countries with international tourist arrivals, the total earnings from tourism and the average amount that a tourist spends in each of these countries. Since tourism generates a great deal of employment, the last column mentions the per capita GDP of each country to give an indication of manpower costs.

The bottom half of the table comprises countries, the tourist arrivals of which might conceivably be compared with the tourist arrivals in India.

The table illustrates three points: first, the high earning potential from tourism; second, the subnormal performance of the Indian tourism industry; and third, the very high cost of visiting

India. India seems to be one of the most expensive countries in the world to visit and it is certainly not a value-for-money destination. A tourist spends just a little more when visiting the United States than India. The country that is next to India in per tourist spend is Singapore, now ranked as the most expensive country in the world.

TABLE 5.2

Country	Tourist Arrivals (2012) (million)[33]	Earnings from Tourism USD (2012) (billion)[34]	Earning per Tourist USD	Per Capita GDP (2012) USD (United Nations) (nomin)[35]
France	83.01	63.530	765	39,617
USA	66.97	299.092	2,988	51,163
China	57.73	54.937	952	6,070
Spain	57.70	63.198	1,095	28,278
Italy	46.36	43.036	928	33,069
Turkey	35.70	32.249	903	19,653
UK	29.28	45.966	1,570	39,367
Malaysia	25.03	20.251	809	10,422
Ukraine	23.01	5.988	260	3,872
Thailand	22.35	37.740	1,689	5,775
Canada	16.34	20.696	1,267	52,283
Poland	14.84	11.835	798	12,820
Singapore	11.10	19.261	1,735	42,141
Morocco	9.38	8.491	905	2,952
Indonesia	8.04	9.463	1,177	3,557
India	6.58	18.340	2,787	1,516
Tunisia	5.95	2.931	493	4,150
Brazil	5.68	6.830	1,213	11,347

Manpower is a major input in the cost of tourism, and India, which has the lowest per capita GDP among the countries listed in Table 5.2, has a comparatively lower manpower cost input. It is difficult to understand how in an industry that is relatively labour intensive, a tourist needs to spend the same amounts when visiting America and India, when the per capita GDP of America is $51,163 and that of India is $1,516.

But cost is not the only consideration in determining the popularity of a tourist destination, although it is a major factor. What is important is the overall quality of the experience, and whether it brings the tourist back for a second visit and inspires her to recommend the destination to her friends. Few people visit countries solely to marvel at ancient architecture. Vacationing in other lands is all about being convivial in the modern usage of the word—sociable, lively and festive. Certainly heritage sites have their attractions but only if they are backdrops to a convivial experience, and not the only attraction. A tourist might, after seeing the sights, wish to sit in a bistro for a bite to eat along with coffee or a glass of wine. This is not readily available in India. New Delhi, India's capital city, has a permanent population of 14 million in addition to a floating population of 2 million. For these 16 million people, Delhi in 2012 had 484 restaurants that had been granted the licence to serve a glass of wine.[36] This number has diminished since as 44 or almost 10 per cent of these restaurants refused to get their licences renewed, leaving only 442 such places for 16 million Delhi residents and the odd tourist.

Why is the density of restaurants which can serve a drink so low in Delhi? It is certainly not due to paucity of capital nor is there a dearth of entrepreneurship in India. The answer lies in the near impossibility of obtaining the permits which would enable an entrepreneur to open such a bistro.

To get an idea of how difficult it is to obtain such a licence, I urge a visit to the restaurantindia.in website which enumerates these licences.[37] They include a food licence from the Food Safety and Standards of India,[38] a trade licence from the local authorities,[39] an eating house licence from the police,[40] a licence to serve any alcoholic drink,[41] a pollution certificate,[42] a music licence to be able to play recorded music,[43] and a certificate of environmental clearance.[44] Other licences include one from the fire department, a licence from the electricity department in case a lift is installed, as well as one from the Labour Commissioner. A licence is also needed under the Shops and Establishment Act to open a place of business. None of these licences are easy to get and all of them require numerous other certificates, details, plans and proofs. If the gauntlet is run, all the licences obtained and the small restaurant that can also serve a glass of wine is ready to open, it will finally need a signage licence to enable it to put up its name on the door.

If the restaurant owner decides to give his patrons a more convivial atmosphere by providing music, perhaps by having a singer strumming his guitar or a crooner belting out her songs or a tabla player working magic through his fingers, he would come under the purview of entertainment tax. If he plays recorded music but leaves clear a small area where patrons may dance if they wish to, he would still be liable to pay entertainment tax. The Delhi High Court has judged in just such a case that 'considering the facts of the case, we find no distinction between a case where performance is by a person other than the person who has made the payment and the case where the facilities are provided by the assessee i.e. the petitioner in the present case and the entertainment is in pursuance of the facilities provided.'[45] In other words even if his patrons entertain themselves because he has left them a space to do so he is liable to pay entertainment tax. If he has the space and decides to put up a pool or billiard table he would then have to pay the luxury tax.[46]

And obtaining these licences is not a one-time exercise. They have to be renewed, forms filled at regular periods and various inspectors kept satisfied.

Simply contemplating the route to starting and then running a restaurant that is congenial to creating a convivial ambience would deter an aspiring restaurateur from starting out, to the loss of tourists coming into India, local Indian residents, the restaurant business, the job prospects of the many who would be employed by expanding restaurant numbers, the entire Indian tourism industry and indeed to the growth of the Indian economy as a whole.

This tendency to tax whatever is possible before profits are made is effectively killing the goose that lays the golden eggs, well before the eggs have been laid. The luxury tax is a case in point. I quote from the rather self-congratulatory opening paragraph of a Delhi government website:[47] 'As an attempt to mobilise a new source of revenue the Govt. of Delhi decided to explore a hitherto untapped source of revenue namely the Hospitality Industry. The Luxury Tax was introduced w.e.f. from 1.11.1996 on various hotels, lodging houses, clubs etc.' 'Luxury provided in hotel' refers to accommodation and other services provided in a hotel, including air conditioning, telephone, radio, music, extra beds and the like, which cost ₹500. At the current exchange rate ₹500 is less than 8 US dollars. Affordable luxury indeed!

What this means is that the only tourists who avoid paying luxury tax, which is currently 12.5 per cent, are backpackers, mostly young people who do not mind roughing it out and are prepared to live in rudimentary lodgings that are below the radar of tax inspectors. They congregate in large numbers in places like Goa and Manali and because of their numbers are able to create their own convivial communities. The other set of tourists who come to India are the well-to-do, mostly older people who do not mind paying to be pampered. India largely misses out on middle- income, middle-aged people who travel with their families and form the bulk of tourists in other places.

Entrepreneurs desist from opening up convivial places of gathering, fearing that their ventures will lead to more unhappiness than money. Tourists other than backpackers desist from revisiting India or recommending it to friends fearing that even their high spending will not bring them much joy. Ventures into the hospitality industry are thus begun only by those with an ability to manage the bureaucracy or corporates with deep pockets and the ability to hire people to manage the bureacracy. They are aware that with the existing restrictive regimen they have little to fear by way of competition and can charge whatever the small market can bear. The small friendly family-run restaurant which serves conviviality along with its fare is completely missing.

Happiness and joy or the lack of these are nebulous, difficult to quantify and not normally associated with economics but they can be powerful incentives or deterrents to the way people act. Again, much like the traveller in Aesop's fable, if the environment is conducive, people will doff their cloaks and set up ventures and even create some of the infrastructure without the government needing to spend much. Entrepreneurs will do what needs to be done to attract tourists. Tourists, like they do elsewhere, will come in large numbers if they are assured of a joyful experience at a reasonable price.

With increasing tourist arrivals and an increased number of stakeholders in the local communities, much of the unkempt look and litter on the streets are likely to disappear. The role of the government would be limited to ensuring law and order and perhaps goading the local community towards higher hygienic standards. There is also likely to be a subtle change in the demeanour of local residents once tourists start coming in. Whether dealing with them directly or indirectly, their self-confidence will increase. They will be welcoming and interact more with the tourists. That in itself is an education and a fertile interface for more ideas to be generated, further strengthening the output of new ideas and new ventures.

Neither this book nor indeed this chapter is about India or specifically about its food processing and tourism industries. There are many other countries which to a greater or lesser extent follow similar policies and have similar results. These two examples have been picked up solely to try and illustrate how taxes before profit, needless red tape and corruption with its delays and costs can stall and defeat industries even in areas of very high potential. Food processing and tourism are certainly not the only industries that suffer. While the impact on other industries may not be as glaringly self-evident, it certainly has a major impact on the food processing and tourism industries. Fewer business ventures will start and there will be less demand for goods as the taxes and costs imposed by corruption will put many products and services out of reach of potential customers.

Needless to say, the costs imposed by any country upon its industries can be of great benefit to competing industries in other countries, as evidenced by the tourist arrival figures of countries much smaller than India in the same region and which lack the historical and geographical advantages of India. It is interesting to note that the other large country of Asia, China, has tourist arrival figures almost ten times those of India.

I have been going on about the harmful effects of all taxes before income is generated and the folly of bleeding away money before goods reach the marketplace. I hasten at this point to reassure the reader that I am not trying to conjure up some sort of tax-free Utopia. Taxes are necessary for a government to do what we cannot do for ourselves at an individual level. These include external defence, a justice delivery mechanism including both the police and the courts, ensuring the delivery of compulsory primary education of good quality, primary and preventive health care, and building infrastructure. We need taxes for a lean administration to do what we cannot do for ourselves and to facilitate us in the things we can do for ourselves.

The question that I am trying to address is not the necessity or desirability of taxes. They are both desirable and necessary. The question is the point in the economic engine cycle at which it is best to garner taxes. Every service and goods provider, whether it is a manufacturer, trader or wage earner, expects to make a profit from providing goods or services. Every punter on the stock market, or for that matter on the race track, expects to make a profit. These are the profits, if realized, that need to be taxed. Any tax that tends to reduce the number of potentially profit-making transactions or the number of people participating in these transactions is counterproductive. As a society it makes no difference where we get the money for our collective needs, provided we get the amount needed. It makes eminent sense to get our taxes in the way least harmful to the running of our economic engines.

Perhaps the earliest chieftains, roving brigands, lords and kings, who provided the citizenry little other than an implied promise of protecting them from other roving brigands, understood this for they took only from the harvested grain and seldom touched the ploughs, the draught animals or the seed stored for the next planting. It would not have made much sense to them to harm future production and consequently harm their own future tax revenue.

Governments tend to rely on indirect taxes, like excise, sales tax, VAT, local business taxes, service tax, etc. This reduces the number of transactions that take place by increasing the cost of the goods or services offered.

There are two reasons for governments relying on indirect taxes. The first and less intractable reason is the multiplicity of administrative levels, such as national governments, state governments and municipalities. Different taxes accrue to each level of government. It is necessary for each level of government to collect its own taxes, by way of income taxes normally retained at the national or federal level, sales taxes at the state level and property and octroi taxes which were usually earmarked for the municipal level. Today, with instant transfer of funds, the different levels of government could be funded as soon as taxes are received provided a formula is agreed upon as to the ratio of the funds to be given to the different levels of government. There would be no need for state and local bodies to go, cap in hand, to the next level of government.

It should be simple to work out a formula for sharing the money collected as income tax, based upon the actual money collected at the different levels over the past few years. We could also seize this opportunity to change the manner in which our taxes are used without being bound by how much money is collected at each taxation point. We could use our taxes to incentivize certain behaviour patterns and disincentivize others. If this idea is ever taken seriously and debated upon, I am certain that many more suggestions will come up for consideration, and what any particular country or society chooses will, I suppose, depend upon the maturity of that society and the sagacity of its leaders.

I now ask the reader to allow me to share my personal idea of how taxes may be levied and shared.

First, the major taxes would be income taxes levied on both individual earnings irrespective of source and on profits made by businesses. Excise taxes are justifiable only on those items that we need to actively discourage the usage of. On health grounds alone, excise duties could be levied on tobacco products, strong liquor, sugary drinks and similar items. On environmental and conservation grounds, excise taxes could be levied on fossil fuel power plants and motor vehicles giving off greenhouse gasses and other particulate emissions above specified levels. Electrical appliances below defined efficiency levels could be taxed.

It is important to remember that excise duties levied on a limited number of products should not be viewed as a source of income for the government but as a financial prod to move things in desired directions. The efficiency and emission limits set must be achievable within a reasonable period of time. New targets may be set as and when there are advancements in technology that make achieving these possible. If along the way the government earns revenue from these taxes, it should be regarded as a bonus.

Now for the devolution of tax money. Let the money from personal income taxes and residual excise taxes be put in one pot and the money from corporate taxes be put in a second pot. Let the central government retain a certain percentage from both pots, as money for doing the things that only a central government can do—ensure the security of the country, the safety of its citizens and the protection of their lives, liberty and property. The central government must also ensure the sanctity of the country's money and create conditions for growth and prosperity. If any central government can enable the efficient running of the economic power plant and all the parts that make it run, it will have done all that can be asked of it. This is no mean task.

A central government should not encumber itself with tasks best administered at subsequent levels of administration, closer to where the money is spent, both to encourage transparency and to enhance employment opportunities. Besides, the officials who actually sanction and spend the money will be better able to see why the money needs to be spent and the results of the spending. This applies to any welfare spending, which must be initiated and executed at smaller regional levels depending on local conditions. It is possible, even likely, that different states, prefectures, or counties will spend the money allocated to them in different ways. This is not a negative outcome. It is like running many experiments simultaneously and learning from the results.

In any attempt to list the areas essential to the working of the economic engine and on which a central government must focus, it is impossible to list them in any order of importance. The engine comprises many parts like links in a chain, and like any chain its strength is only as much as that of the weakest link. The engine will not work satisfactorily until all the parts are up and running.

1. External defence in all its complexities, including intelligence gathering and preparedness to tackle terrorism. This will provide a secure environment for the running of the economic engine.
2. A good education system, especially universal and free primary education, an extensive and cheap system of communication, the nurturing of an environment where all ideas may be freely expressed, and safeguarding all property rights including intellectual property.
3. An effective and speedy justice delivery system with sufficient courts and judges.
4. Maintenance of the sanctity and purchasing power of our money. Money is above all else a store of value. No country can hope to prosper in the long run if the value of its money and the savings of its citizens are constantly degraded. The most effective means for safeguarding the value of money is for governments to spend within the taxes they have collected. The inflation target to aim for is a narrow band oscillating around a zero inflation rate.

The inflation figure to focus on is the consumer price inflation rate. Core inflation figures are often put out that ignore food and energy costs as these are considered too volatile to give an accurate picture. While this is true, the problem can be obviated by putting out five- and ten-year inflation figures along with monthly and annual figures. This will stabilize the volatility. Inflation figures that exclude these two major heads of expenditure for the average person are not very relevant.

5. A free and fair marketplace across the country.

If this seems like a return to the laissez-faire practised in parts of Europe and North America from the late eighteenth to the early twentieth centuries, with some safeguards thrown in, it is. I am not advocating a complete abdication of the government but simply reiterating the role of the government in maintaining a free and fair marketplace.

Apart from passing laws and implementing policies that ensure transparency and fairness while resisting the temptation to overregulate and stifle the market, the government may need to intercede, especially in periods of turmoil. It may, for example, need to ban the export of staple foods during a famine. Or at times of war proscribe certain economic activities to direct more resources to the war effort. However, governmental intercession in the marketplace should be a rare event, other than modifying fair play norms as market players find loopholes in the existing rules.

Laissez-faire has, over the years, acquired an unsavoury image with robber barons riding roughshod over the rights of workers and their communities with a total disregard for the environment. All this may well have transpired in the past but it was a different world then. Society was largely feudal and slavery not yet fully abolished. Workers had few rights, whether they worked on a farm or in a factory. In today's world, a policy of laissez-faire could not lead to such excesses.

According to legend, the word laissez-faire originated at a meeting between the French finance minister Jean Baptiste Colbert and a group of French businessmen led by a certain M. Le Gendre in 1680. When the minister asked how the French state could be of service to the merchants and help promote their commerce, Le Gendre replied simply: 'Laissez-nous faire' ('Leave us be', literally,

'Let us do'). This anecdote was related by the French minister and champion of free trade, Rene' de Voyer, Marquis d' Argenson, who himself is accredited for a similar but less celebrated motto: 'Pas trop gouverne' ('Govern not too much'),[48] which I think is a more apt description of what is needed. The historical record is unambiguous. Free markets have always performed better than planned or controlled ones and have always delivered a better standard of living.

After the central government has retained the funds it needs for its functions, it must automatically transfer the balance to the next administrative level. We had put the money from personal income taxes along with the residual excise taxes into one pot and corporate income taxes into another pot. From each of these pots the central government had taken an equal percentage for itself. The money left in the personal income tax pot should be divided among the states as per their population. Of the money remaining in the corporate income taxes pot, perhaps 25 per cent should be returned to the states in the ratio of the corporate taxes deposited by each state and the remaining balance should be added to the first pot and again divided among states as per their population. This ought to have the salutary effect of making states compete for businesses to be located in them.

The states can, in turn and in a pre-agreed manner, divide the taxes that come to them as soon as they are received, with the cities and municipalities located within them. Countries of different sizes will have different internal administrative set-ups and must devise formulas that best suit them.

In the existing scheme of things, income taxes, excise taxes and service taxes are often collected by the central government, sales taxes by state governments and octroi and other entry taxes, when levied, at city gates. This may have once been the best possible solution to the fact that all governments at all levels need money to function. They did not have the luxury of debating the best point from which to collect taxes without harming the economic engine. For one level of government to extract tax money collected by another level of government it would always have been an uphill task, fraught with delays and excuses. That is no longer the case. With the possibility of rapid money transfers, it is no longer a question of whether this can be done but whether we want to do it.

The problem of dividing tax money between different administrative levels is not the main reason why so many different taxes are levied. The main reason is that governments are fearful that if they rely solely on income tax they may not garner enough taxes for their needs. Their fears are not completely unjustified. It is certainly easier to collect taxes at the factory gate than trying to pry out a little money from each of millions of tightly clutched fists. The task of an individual tax collector or tax department has always been difficult and is never pleasant. The skills required are an almost equal mix of detective work and psychological terrorism backed by fairly draconian laws, with the power to confiscate assets. In most countries even disputed tax claims, claimed by the tax department, need to be first paid and then disputed.

The history of taxes and tax collection makes interesting reading right from early Egyptian times.[49] The methods employed to collect taxes have been quite coercive and intrusive while protests against taxes have been emotional and even dramatic. During the various reigns of the Egyptian pharaohs tax collectors were known as scribes. At one point scribes imposed a tax on cooking oil. To ensure that citizens were not avoiding the cooking oil tax, scribes would audit households to ensure that appropriate amounts of cooking oil were consumed and that citizens were not using leavings generated by other cooking processes as a substitute for the taxed oil.

Other famous protests against taxation include Lady Godiva's naked ride through the city to persuade her husband, Leofric,

Earl of Mercia, to bring down taxes and the Boston Tea Party which led to the American Revolutionary War.

With this historical background, it is understandable why governments would have serious reservations about relying solely on income taxes. Is it possible that a system could be devised whereby citizens come forward as willing, even eager, taxpayers? Perhaps. The possibility hinges upon the interplay between the nature of money, our human condition, interest rates and the rates of taxation. Let us look closely at each of these four elements before we try and formulate such a system.

We have seen that of its three functions, namely, as a medium of exchange, a unit of account and a store of value, it is as a store of value that money plays the most important role. The other two functions are a consequence of this. We have also seen that it is mainly because of governments spending more money than they have that inflation occurs and money loses value. We cannot deride deficit financing by governments without a passing reference to Keynesian economics. John Maynard Keynes (1883–1946) was a British economist who propounded a theory based on the circular flow of money, which argued that when spending increases so do earnings which leads to more spending and earning. In a normally functioning economy this forms a cycle of earning and spending. When the Great Depression started in 1929 and people began losing jobs, their natural reaction was to hoard money and cut back on spending. Under Keynes' theory, this stopped the circular flow of money, bringing the economy to a standstill. Keynes' solution to this poor economic state was to 'prime the pump'. He argued that the government should step in and increase spending, either by increasing the money supply or by actually buying things itself.

Before Keynes, classic economic theory did not perceive the need for government intervention in the market. The stand of classic economics is well summarized by Say's Law which says that products are paid for with products. A modern way of expressing Say's Law is that there cannot be a general glut or surplus of goods in general; there may be excess supply of one or more goods but only when balanced by excess demand or shortage of other goods. Thus there may be a glut of labour but this is balanced by excess demand for produced goods. Modern advocates of Say's Law see market forces working quickly via price adjustment to abolish both gluts and surpluses. Keynesians feel that price adjustment, especially of labour wages, cannot be quick enough as it is difficult to persuade people to take a cut in nominal wages, even if it may not amount to a cut in real wages in a deflationary situation. Keynes himself famously remarked, 'In the long run we are all dead.'

Say's Law was the result of a debate. The major figure on one side of the debate was Thomas Malthus, better known for his theory of population. He argued that crises (recessions) were the result of a 'general glut' of goods. The production of goods could outrun the ability or desire of people to purchase these goods, and it was this oversupply or underconsumption that led to an economic crisis. On the other side of the debate were David Ricardo (known for his theory of comparative advantage in trade), Scottish philosophers and economists James Stuart Mill (1773–1836) and John Stuart Mill (1806–73) father and son, and Jean Baptiste Say, a French economist (1767–1832). Their arguments were based on barter trade. In a barter world, buying cannot be done unless one sells at the same time, and selling cannot be done unless one buys at the same time. In a world of barter the only way one can finance purchases is by selling and there is no reason to sell except to finance purchases.[50] In a barter world savings are impossible. Once money is introduced into the argument, it is possible to save, as money is a store of value. The central notion that Say had concerning money is that if one has money, it is irrational to hoard it. The assumption that hoarding is irrational was later attacked by underconsumptionist economists, such as John M. Robertson, in his 1892 book *The Fallacy of Saving*, where he called Say's Law 'a tenacious fallacy, consequent on the inveterate evasion of the plain fact that men want for their goods, not merely some other goods to consume, but further, some credit or abstract claim to future wealth, goods, or services. This all want as a surplus or bonus, and this surplus cannot be represented for all in present goods.' Robertson refutes Say and maintains that people wish to accumulate a 'claim to future wealth', not simply present goods, and thus hoarding of wealth may be rational.[51]

When there is a shortage of money in the economy for whatever reason, classical economists say that market forces will see transactions taking place with prices being lowered. Keynesians believe this process is too slow and would prefer it if governments pumped money into the system by lowering taxes and increasing spending. While classical economists say that savings are undesirable because any money saved will stop driving demand and slow transactions in the market, in reality savings do not vanish from the market. Most savings are kept in banks or other financial institutions which, to pay the interest incumbent upon the savings kept with them, loan out the money to businesses and individual consumers at a higher rate of interest, ensuring that almost all savings remain active within the overall economy.

Keynes was primarily concerned with boosting demand by putting more liquidity in the market. He argued that the solution to the Great Depression was to stimulate the economy through a combination of two approaches:

1. A reduction in interest rates (monetary policy)
2. Government investment in infrastructure (fiscal policy).

Keynes did not advocate subsidies or other government giveaways as a method to spur demand. However, there is an allusion to a form of redistribution of wealth in the development of the 'Keynesian multiplier', developed by Richard F. Kahn in 1931. Exogenous (from outside the working economic model) increases in spending, such as an increase in government outlays, increases total spending by a multiple of that increase. A government could stimulate a great deal of new production with a modest outlay if:

1. The people who receive this money spend most of it on consumption goods and save the rest.
2. This extra spending allows businesses to hire more people and pay them, which in turn allows a further increase in consumer spending.[52]

The idea that the people who receive the money spend most of it on consumption goods implies that the money goes to the less wealthy rather than the rich who would save most of it. Perhaps the best way to do this is for the government to forgo the taxes on goods and services and make up for the loss of revenue by income tax. The consequent effective lowering of the prices of goods and services would certainly spur demand and encourage capital spending by businesses to enhance capacity. Businesses would also need to hire more people, further increasing employment and demand for more goods and services. The rich who might end up saving some money (freed from purchases) are too few in number to make any significant difference to demand.

After the crash of the stock market in 1929, the trigger for the Great Depression, business confidence was at an all-time low. Between 1929 and 1933, prices fell by 20 per cent and unemployment rose from 4 per cent to 25 per cent. In the same period 40 per cent of American banks failed and went bankrupt due to bank runs. Much of the economic damage of the Great Depression and shortage of money was caused directly by bank runs. Yet, despite the shortage of money, there were few takers for fresh debt, with businesses unwilling to make new investments.

Interest rates fell and continued to fall. By 1940 commercial banks in New York and Chicago were giving loans at a little over 3 per cent after factoring in their spreads of 1½ to 2 per cent.[53] There was little room for further reduction of interest rates as Keynes had advocated. America was for all practical purposes in a liquidity trap, although Keynes himself denied it.

Keynesian economic policy is credited for having pulled America out of the Great Depression and also for the post-war economic expansion from 1945–1970. But this is only partly true. During the years of the Great Depression American deficit financing by the government was only about 5 per cent of GDP. This is a high number but not nearly as frightening as the 13 per cent GDP (amounting to $1.4 trillion) in 2009[54] and a similarly high figure for 2012. The annual deficit came down to $435 billion in 2015 but the gross federal debt rose to 103 per cent of GDP. During the post-war expansion, the US government budget was actually in surplus in 1947, 1948 and 1949 and the deficit stayed mostly below 1 per cent until 1970.[55] The deficit, as a percentage of GDP, crossed into the double-digit territory in 2009, where it has stayed since. If a relatively small amount of government spending was sufficient to pick the economy up after the greatest economic cataclysm of the twentieth century, and no deficit financing was required for post-war economic expansion, then Keynes's advocacy of government deficit spending is clearly not the complete solution for picking up an ailing economy. Indeed neo-classical economists of the Austrian school believe that the post-war boom was largely the result of free market reforms and deregulation.[56] In the light of this it should not be too surprising that seven years of unprecedented monetary stimulus have barely dented the economic crisis since 2008.

I do not believe that diminishing the value of money through deficit financing, except as a very temporary step in the most excruciating of situations, can ever be a good strategy. Keynesian economics has over the years acquired the status of a 'received truth' and most of us regard it as self-evident. At the first sign of an economic slowdown, governments tend to move the printing presses into higher gear. They should perhaps be studying the situation more closely and trying to see just where in the economic engine the problem lies.

Governments report their fiscal deficits as percentages of their GDP. I do not think this figure imparts material information and is in fact misleading in that it tends to allay apprehensions of government overspending. If anyone, say, a housewife or an advertising executive, has a budget within which to work and the budget is overshot, the overshot amount would be calculated as a percentage of the original budget. In the case of the housewife the amount overshot would not be calculated as a percentage of the earnings of her extended clan and in the case of the advertising executive it would not be calculated as a percentage of the entire corporation's turnover. However, this is the way governments report their deficits, as a percentage of the value added by the labours of the entire country, or the GDP of the entire country, a figure that has no bearing upon government budgets, their revenues or their spending.

Table 5.3 lists the top 8 deficit running countries, showing their deficits both as percentages of their GDP as well as percentages of their revenues.

It is apparent from this table that the fiscal deficit numbers reported as a percentage of GDP and the fiscal deficit numbers as a percentage of government revenues are quite different from each other. I think the fiscal deficit as a percentage of government revenues is a ready number for measuring a government's profligacy and its regard or disregard for economic prudence. It also serves as a pointer for countries that are prone to inflation.

When a government gives out subsidies and other handouts without having the money to do so and resorts to deficit financing, it is ostensibly with the purpose of helping the poor, as we have already discussed. Ironically, it is the poor who are most affected by inflation as they are by all taxes that are not income taxes but those levied on goods and services. If a poor man spends nearly all his income on goods and services then nearly all his income is depleted by the sum of inflation and the cumulative taxes on goods and services. If a rich man spends, let us say, only 10–20 per cent of his income on goods and services then only 10–20 per cent of his income is affected by inflation and taxes on goods and services and the balance is unaffected and available for investment. The rich are almost always able to invest their surplus in a manner that yields them returns greater than inflation. This makes them richer. If the rich invest their surplus in assets such as precious metals and real estate, thereby driving up the prices of those goods, no productive activity has taken place. The poor have in effect financed both the excessive spending of the government and the increasing wealth of the rich. They pay for it by either paying more or depriving themselves of a dwelling and forgoing the little security that a few bits of precious metals have traditionally afforded even the poor in most parts of the world. The gap between rich and poor thus increases. An avowed concern of all governments is at least a degree of egalitarianism and of diminishing the gap between rich and poor. It is surprising, then, that they continue to espouse policies that exacerbate the gap.

This discrepancy of wealth is measured by the Gini coefficient, named after Corrado Gini, an Italian statistician. It sums up the gaps between people's incomes into a single number. If everyone in a group has the same income, the Gini coefficient is 0; if all income goes to one person, it is 1. Another way of looking at inequality is to look at the number of US dollar billionaires and see the amount of wealth they have as a percentage of the GDP of their countries. According to a special report on the world economy by *The Economist* in 2012, America has the largest

TABLE 5.3
Top eight deficit running countries*

Country	GDP[57]	Government Revenue[58]	Government Expenditure	Absolute Deficit	Deficit as % of GDP	Deficit as % of Government Revenue
		($ billion)				
India	1,670.00	181.30	281.60	100.30	6.00	50.74
Venezuela	367.00	103.40	139.40	36.00	9.81	34.81
Japan	5,007.00	1,739.00	2,149.00	410.00	8.18	26.58
USA	16,720.00	2,849.00	3,517.00	668.00	4.00	23.45
Spain	1,356.00	505.10	597.30	92.20	6.80	23.28
Ireland	220.90	75.30	91.30	16.00	7.20	21.24
Malaysia	312.40	65.72	79.40	13.68	4.38	20.81
Greece	243.30	106.20	116.00	9.80	4.02	9.23

* 2013 figures

number of billionaires at 421, their total wealth equalling 10.5 per cent of GDP, while the total wealth of India's 48 billionaires equals 10.9 per cent of GDP. Russia and China have almost the same number of billionaires at 96 and 95 respectively, but while Russia's billionaires account for 18.6 per cent of GDP, China's billionaires account for only 2.6 per cent of GDP.[59]

Wealth per billionaire measured as a percentage of GDP is highest in India. When 48 individuals out of a population of 1.2 billion can have wealth amounting to 10.9 per cent of GDP, it is clearly not a very equal society. The higher the Gini coefficient, the higher the inequality in a society, and the higher the inequality in a society the more fractured its functioning. This is especially true when the inequality widens as we see happening now in almost all countries. The Gini coefficient has been steadily increasing in most countries since the 1980s. It has become more difficult for all sections of society to agree on economic issues, as we see in the hardening of positions across the world on whether to cut government spending or increase taxes in an attempt to improve government finances. Without doing at least one of the two there is no hope for future governments being able to avoid deficit financing.

There will always be rich people and poor people. But if we are to have a more equitable system where the poor are not continually impoverished through no fault of their own and the rich not continually enriched through no genius of their own, our first step is to eliminate inflation and restore to money its prime function as a store of value.

Having considered the nature of money, let us consider our human condition. Our human condition is a multifaceted edifice which is contemplated upon by poets and philosophers. I merely endeavour to address a fairly mundane aspect of our condition. We are born helpless, need many years to grow up, the larger part of our life is spent in earning and providing for ourselves and our families, and as we grow old, our capacity to earn diminishes until we are forced to depend either on our savings or on handouts from others. Within this universal human condition there are large variations among individuals. Some will study more and start earning later whereas others will start earning sooner. Some will earn more than others. Some will earn steadily during their working lives, while others will have spikes and troughs of income over the years. Some will go through life meeting the usual expenses whereas others will have the misfortune of incurring large unexpected expenses.

To smoothen life's uneven bumps and vagaries, we resort to saving for the proverbial rainy day, apart from saving for our old age. Taking a loan to meet expenses is an option but loans are not always readily available and to be eligible for a loan one usually needs to demonstrate an ability to repay the loan or an evidence of assets, for which savings are helpful. While we all need savings, the indigent need them more, for their lives are more uneven and they usually do not depend upon a regular source of income. It is generally assumed that the poor have no savings in the first place and to talk of their savings is meaningless. This is not true. The poor save too, even if they earn a negative rate of interest.

Stuart Rutherford has done some pioneering work in studying the money management and saving methods of the very poor in slums and villages across the world. I quote from the book he co-authored, *Portfolios of the Poor*,[60] where he writes: 'no matter where we looked, we found that most of the households, even those living on less than one dollar a day per person, rarely consume every penny of income as soon as it is earned. They seek instead, to "manage" their money by saving when they can and borrowing when they need to ... Second, we saw that at almost every turn poor households are frustrated by the poor quality—above all the low reliability—of the instruments that they use to manage their meagre incomes.' To my mind the most important instrument for them is one with which the poor can reliably save and where their savings retain their original value.

In *The Economics of Poverty*, Stuart Rutherford quotes the example of a woman, Jyothi, an informal savings collector, in Vijayawada, an Indian town, who visits 50–60 houses a day for 220 days, collecting 5 or 10 rupees a day from each house. At the end of 220 days she gives back money equal to 200 days' collection in one lump sum, retaining the balance 20 days' collection as her fees. Expressed as an annual percentage rate Jyothi's fee works out to about 30 per cent of the money collected. Her clients, however, calculate it as a mere 9 per cent and feel it is a cheap rate for a highly valued service.

Our human condition dictates that we save. How we save, how much we save and under what terms and conditions we save depend to a large extent upon the options available to us. Sometimes we are prepared to save even if at a negative rate of interest. We must consider better instruments of saving. Before we do that, let us consider interest rates.

Interest rates are a contentious issue. If you are a net borrower, you would like interest rates to be as close to zero as possible and if you are a net lender, you would want interest rates to be as high as possible. Is there an interest rate upon which we can all agree, that we can define as an almost natural rate of interest? I believe there is. It stems from our human condition and it is around 2 per cent annually for savers.

Two per cent net of inflation. As observed, our human condition dictates that we save. Let us put some numbers on our human condition. Let us imagine a person, who I hope is close to the average. He finishes his studies, gets a job, settles down, and at the age of 25 starts putting some money away as savings and continues working until the age of 65. Let us further assume he earns 100 units of currency per year (we can multiply this number by any other to arrive at figures in any currency that are plausible for the different currencies and economic levels of each country). Let us further assume that his earnings are constant through his working life. This last is unlikely to be true as earnings normally rise until they reach a peak before trending down. But if his earnings rise over the years, his situation will only improve. Out of his 100 units of earnings, he is required to pay 20 units as income tax—the maximum rate. Under the scheme I am suggesting, this would entitle him to put 20 units—the same as the amount of tax he has paid—into a special long-term savings account which would give him an interest of 2 per cent per annum. Let us take a glance at his finances. He has earned 100 units, given 20 units as tax and put 20 units in a long-term savings account. He is left with 60 units which should suffice for his expenses. The great thing about this long-term savings account is that it would be linked to inflation. At quarterly intervals, the balance amount in the account would be enhanced by the consumer price inflation index and the interest on his savings earned would be inflation plus 2 per cent. If he started to save at age 25 and if he kept deposited 20 units in the savings account (after paying an income tax of 20 units) every year until the age of 65, he could withdraw from that account 75 units every year after he turned 65, on which he would pay 15 units tax (at the same 20 per cent tax rate) and be left again with 60 units, evening out his earnings throughout his life. At the end of his life, he would be left with nothing. This plan has been modelled on a life expectancy of 83 years, that of the life expectancy in Japan which is the highest in the world for any major country. It would take actuaries no time at all to come up with an insurance policy guaranteeing the income for the full life term, provided they got their cut from the balance if the beneficiary died earlier.

Two per cent per annum for savers is not a sacrosanct number. It can be changed, but carefully. With an increase of 0.5 per cent in the interest rate a person who started saving at the age of 25 could now be sure of getting the same constant income if he worked and saved until the age of 60 and not 65. Perhaps many societies would prefer this. However, the more interest an economic system gives its savers, the more interest it will need to charge its borrowers.

Banks have an interest rate spread, also known as the bank spread. This is the interest rate charged by banks on loans to private sector customers minus the interest rate they give to their depositors. Bank spreads vary from country to country. Japan has amongst the lowest bank spreads in the world. In 2012 Japan had a bank spread of 0.9 per cent followed by Bangladesh at 1.3 per cent, and South Korea and New Zealand at 1.7 per cent.[61] Some countries have bank spreads of over 5 per cent. A few even have spreads of over 10 per cent. Netherlands is shown to have a negative bank spread of 1.1 per cent, which must imply that banks are losing money by lending it out. Equally surprising is Madagascar with a bank spread of 49.5 per cent, Malawi 21.3 per cent, Tajikistan 17.5 per cent and Peru 16.8 per cent. I suspect not many loans are being taken out in these countries.

By and large, the higher the spread the more profitable the bank. On the other hand, the cost of borrowed money is higher, which affects every other industry and leads to higher prices, tending to slow down the economic engine. There are four main reasons why banks have high spreads:

1. There are too few banks in the country and not enough competition amongst banks.
2. Over-regulated banking with the government owning and controlling many banks.
3. Banks have a large exposure to bad debts, caused either by poor judgement by bankers or influence from parties that don't share the same interests as the bank, or by banks not exercising due diligence while giving out loans.

4. An ineffective legal system, leading to inordinate delays for banks to get redressal for loan defaults and not being able to seize assets pledged to them as collateral.

The reason I look at bank spreads at all is out of a sense of bewilderment. If we recognize that simply by raising the rate of interest to savers by 0.5 per cent we can lower the retirement age from 65 years to 60 years, how can we be sanguine about bank spreads in excess of 5 per cent? If savers get 2.5 per cent, how can banks that only act as intermediaries between savers and borrowers get twice as much? We certainly need to look into bank spreads and try and bring them down to reasonable levels. Perhaps we can even mandate a maximum spread.

Classic economic theory tells us that the rate of interest on money is a function of supply and demand. If there are too many savers and too few borrowers, interest rates will drop. If, on the other hand, there are fewer savers than borrowers, interest rates will rise. In practice, though, interest rates are greatly influenced by central banks. The current almost worldwide flood of easy money at low interest rates is as a result of actions taken by central banks.

Since 1996, Japan's benchmark interest rate has been close to zero.[62] This means that savers get practically no interest on their savings. We also know that Japan's bank spread is just under 1 per cent. This means that the Japanese banks' best borrowers are able to borrow money at a little over 1 per cent interest per annum. This is advantageous to Japanese businesses as they are able to invest and grow on the back of easy borrowing. This is good for the supply side of the economy. We also know that Japan has the highest life expectancy in the world, at 83 years. This low interest regimen has not been so good for the elderly. Going back to the case of the hypothetical saver who started saving at the age of 25 and was able to save 20 units out of his 100 unit earnings after paying tax, at an interest rate of 2.5 per cent, on his savings he could retire at the age of 60, ensuring a lifelong income of 60 units, after paying 20 per cent taxes on drawings. If the money saved earns no interest, after retirement at 60 the person would earn an income of 30.4 units, which after the same taxes, would amount to only 24.3 units.

As a consequence, the Japanese majority cannot hope to retire at 60 years and would have to continue working much longer. Aware that they will soon face a dearth of money, the elderly spend frugally and save as much as they can. This cannot be pleasant for them. It is also bad for the demand side of the economy. The situation was acceptable for the economy of Japan when a large part of the demand that drove its economy came from overseas markets, where Japanese goods were prized. This is no longer the case. With increasing competition from China and other countries in Asia and stifled internal demand caused by a need to save, the Japanese economy is showing signs of weakness.

Japanese who have been dismissed by their companies and are unable to find further employment find themselves in dire straits. Japanese culture is perhaps more focused on honour and pride than many others. The code of Bushido was born from Neo-Confucianism and was influenced by Shinto and Zen Buddhism and stresses on, among other things, frugality, loyalty and honour unto death.[63] For a culture steeped in such notions, it must be unsettling to see senior citizens resorting to petty crime with the purpose of landing in prison where they are guaranteed food, shelter and medication. Japan's population over the age of 60 grew by 17 per cent between 2000 and 2006. The number of prisoners in the same age bracket in the same period grew by 87 per cent.[64] The trend is increasing and Japan has been forced to set up prisons for the elderly.

Having made my case that there is a narrow band of interest rates that can be considered natural and desirable, let us look at rates of taxation. Higher tax rates do not always lead to higher government revenues.

The Laffer curve represents the relationship between possible rates of taxation and the resulting levels of government revenue. It illustrates the concept of taxable income elasticity, that is, taxable income will change in response to changes in the rate of taxation. It postulates that no tax revenue will be raised at the extreme tax rates of 0 per cent and 100 per cent and there must be at least one rate where tax revenue would be a non-zero maximum. The Laffer curve is typically represented as a graph which starts at 0 per cent tax with zero revenue, rises to a maximum rate of revenue at an intermediate rate of taxation and then falls again to zero revenue at a 100 per cent tax rate.[65]

The curve is attributed to Arthur Laffer in 1974. Laffer himself does not claim to have invented the concept, attributing it to fourteenth-century Muslim scholar Ibn Khaldun. The logic behind the Laffer curve has also been apparent to others. In 1924, preceding the Laffer curve by 50 years, US Secretary of Treasury Andrew Mellon wrote: 'It seems difficult for some to understand that high rates of taxation do not necessarily mean large revenue for the Government and that more revenue may often be obtained from lower rates.'

The exact contours of the Laffer curve are not known and are often disputed. Different studies have suggested widely varying rates of maximum taxation.

Many countries have successfully increased revenue collection by lowering maximum rates of taxation. During the Reagan presidency, the top marginal rate of tax in the United States fell from 70 per cent to 31 per cent, while revenue continued to increase every year from $885 billion in 1980 to $1930 billion in 1990. During this period, government revenue as a percentage of GDP increased from 31.8 per cent to 32.2 per cent.

The Laffer curve is likely to be different for different economies and countries. In America, for example, 55 per cent households pay federal income tax. In India only 3 per cent of the population, which roughly translates to 12 per cent of households, pay income tax. Lower tax rates, coupled with the incentive of being able to save an amount equal to the tax paid at a reasonable rate of interest without the fear of inflation eating into the savings, should induce many more taxpayers to come forward and pay taxes. The increased income tax collections could easily surpass the revenue collected by indirect taxes levied on goods and services. This would eliminate a major leak from the pipeline, lower the price of goods and services and encourage growth.

An important criticism of the Reagan years is that while there was growth it was uneven and the bottom quintile had an actual decrease of income. I do not think this was due to the lowering of the maximum income tax rate. We must look for the reason elsewhere. The Reagan years saw a significant rise in automation and computer-enabled operations, requiring a newer degree of competence from the workforce. It is probable that the bottom quintile lacked these attributes and was driven to lower-paying jobs or even unemployment. The fault may have lain in an uneven educational system which failed to deliver on the requirements of the day, rather than on a lower rate of maximum taxation.

The system of taxation and savings proposed in this book precludes any dropping of income in the lower quintiles. In fact, it starts by immediately increasing the money in the hands of the lower quintiles by eliminating taxes on goods and services on which the less wealthy spend the greatest portion of their income.

To summarize, the salient features of the scheme of taxation proposed in this chapter are:

The elimination of taxes on goods and services, like sales tax, or VAT, excise, service tax, octroi and any other similar tax levied before profits are made or wages earned. This would effectively lower prices of goods and services, spurring demand and growth.

It is an equitable step and would benefit the less wealthy, who would see the greatest per cent increase in the money in their hands.

The revenue lost to the government from the above taxes is intended to be more than made up by increased income tax collections from both individuals and companies. Individuals will be encouraged to pay more taxes by lowering the maximum tax rate and by giving them the opportunity to save an amount equal to taxes paid in inflation-protected savings, earning a real rate of interest between 2 per cent and 2.5 per cent per annum. While the right to save in this scheme is generally to be earned by paying taxes, an exemption from this requirement must be made for those whose earnings are below the minimum tax rate bracket. They must be allowed to save enough in this scheme to ensure a secure albeit frugal old age.

All income, regardless of source, including regular income, income from stock market profits, income from capital gains and even drawings from this savings scheme, must be liable to taxation. There must be no exemptions or loopholes. Capital gains must be allowed the benefit of indexation for prices increased by inflation, but in a low inflation regimen, this will not amount to much. There is another component built in, making this scheme more equitable. While calculating the returns these savings would give in old age, taxation at a proposed 20 per cent maximum tax rate is allowed for. In reality, those with earnings or drawings below the maximum tax slab would be paying the tax at a lower rate and their money in hand would increase.

While proposing a maximum tax rate of 20 per cent it might be said that I am presuming to know where the Laffer curve lies. This is not true. This is at best an educated guess for which I am relying on the power of lower taxes and secure savings to induce better tax compliance. Every country will discover its own Laffer curve once this has been tried out. The final validation of this proposal will come if after a few years of implementing this scheme it is felt that taxes can be further lowered by a per cent or two. The world has often witnessed tax rates being reduced with government revenues rising. As mentioned earlier, examples include America and India. Reason tells us that there must be a low rate of taxation beyond which government revenues will fall. That low rate of taxation has seldom been tested.

Corporates do not need to save for their old age. Of course, they will be encouraged to disclose more profits by the lower rate of corporate taxes at 20 per cent, but perhaps we can help things along with a few steps that will be beneficial to us all in the long run. If we let them deduct up to, say, 5 per cent from their profits if they spend the money on socially responsible activities, we will benefit not only from their money but also from their insights and management capabilities. We should also perhaps let them deduct a similar 5 per cent if they spend the money on research and development. This would strengthen the capabilities and competitiveness of our companies.

The scheme for individuals could also have built-in flexibility allowing for limited premature withdrawals, leaving enough money in the scheme at all times to fund at least a minimum savings level for old age. This scheme would in effect serve the twin purposes of providing a social security net and a pension scheme. Governments would be spared the possibility of being faced with cascading pension account deficits. They would only need to ensure that this long-term savings account, linked to taxes paid, earned a real rate of interest of 2 per cent to 2.5 per cent.

This overall scheme, while ensuring a good rate of interest for savers, will also ensure the availability of funds for borrowers at reasonable rates of interest for fully secured loans.

With this in place, I believe we will have a well-functioning monetary system, efficiently transferring the energy of the idea reactor to the wealth-creating magic of the marketplace.

REFERENCES

1. www.etymonline.com/index.php?allowed_in_frame=0&search=feoh. Accessed on 26 April 2016
2. http://en.wikipedia.org/wiki/Shell_money. Accessed on 26 April 2016
3. http://en.wikipedia.org/wiki/Electrum. Accessed on 26 April 2016
4. http://www.conchsoc.org/interests/shell-money.php. Accessed on 26 April 2016
5. http://en.wikipedia.org/wiki/Price_revolution. Accessed on 26 April 2016
6. http://www.inflation.eu/inflation-rates/cpi-inflation-2011.aspx. Accessed on 26 April 2016
7. https://www.economics.utoronto.ca/public/workingPapers/UTECIPA-MUNRO-99-02.pdf. Accessed on 26 April 2016
8. http://en.wikipedia.org/wiki/Roman_currency. Accessed on 26 April 2016
9. http://wiki.mises.org/wiki/History_of_money_and_banking. Accessed on 26 April 2016
10. http://en.wikipedia.org/wiki/Feoh. Accessed on 26 April 2016
11. http://en.wikipedia.org/wiki/Representative_money. Accessed on 26 April 2016
12. http://en.wikipedia.org/wiki/Bretton_Woods_system. Accessed on 26 April 2016
13. http://www.indexmundi.com/world/inflation_rate_(consumer_prices).html. Accessed on 26 April 2016
14. http://en.wikipedia.org/wiki/Money. Accessed on 26 April 2016
15. http://www.historylearningsite.co.uk/hyperinflation_weimar_germany. Accessed on 26 April 2016
16. www.city-journal.org/html/inflation's-moral-hazard-13224.html. Accessed on 26 April 2016
17. http://www.econjournals.com/index.php/ijefi/article/viewFile/234/pdf. Accessed on 26 April 2016
18. http://www.spindian.com/newsportal/business/72-percent-of-

indias-fruit-vegetable-produce-goes-waste_10047895.html. Accessed on 26 April 2016
19. http://www.unicef.org/infobycountry/india_statistics.html. Accessed on 26 April 2016
20. http://www.who.int/nutgrowthdb/about/introduction/en/index2.html. Accessed on 26 April 2016
21. http://www.efymag.com/admin/issuepdf/Processed%20Vegetables.pdf. Accessed on 26 April 2016
22. http://timesofindia.indiatimes.com/city/mumbai/industry-seeks-APMC-Act-repeal-farmers-eye-overseas-sales/articleshow/7489831.cms. Accessed on 26 April 2016
23. Alok Jha, *Role of Dairy and Food Processing Industries for Promoting Economic Growth in Eastern India* (Banaras Hindu University). http://pdf.thepdfportal.net/?id=57141. Accessed on 26 April 2016
24. http://en.wikipedia.org/wiki/Human_height. Accessed on 26 April 2016
25. http://www.spiegel.de/international/business/au-revoir-la-tva-french-vat-cut-boosts-restaurant-trade-a-643420.html. Accessed on 26 April 2016
26. http://www.frizair.com/pdf/octroi_list.pdf. Accessed on 26 April 2016
27. https://www.cia.gov/library/publications/the-world-factbook/rankorder/2102rank.html. Accessed on 26 April 2016
28. http://jn.nutrition.org/content/133/11/4010S.full. Accessed on 26 April 2016
29. http://jn.nutrition.org/content/133/11/3879S.full. Accessed on 26 April 2016
30. http://lpi.oregonstate.edu/infocenter/foods/fruitveg/. Accessed on 26 April 2016
31. http://www.theindianhistory.org/what-were-locations-of-ancient-india-civilizations.html. Accessed on 26 April 2016
32. http://en.wikipedia.org/wiki/Maurya_Empire.Accessedon26April 2016
33. http://data.worldbank.org/indicator/ST.INT.ARVL. Accessed on 26 April 2016

34. http://data.worldbank.org/indicator/ST.INT.RCPT.CD.Accessed on 26 April 2016
35. http://en.wikipedia.org/wiki/List_of_countries_by_GDP_(nominal)_per_capita. Accessed on 26 April 2016
36. *Hindustan Times*, 19 June 2012. 'Rising Costs, Low Returns Force Resto Bars to Shut Shop'
37. http://www.franchiseindia.com/restaurant/Licences-for-Opening-New-Restaurant.6045. Accessed on 26 April 2016
38. http://foodlicensing.fssai.gov.in/userLogin/Login.aspx. Accessed on 26 April 2016
39. http://www.mastbusiness.com/bizguides/bg552. Accessed on 26 April 2016
40. http://www.delhipolicelicensing.gov.in/eating/eating-house.htm. Accessed on 26 April 2016
41. http://www.ccs.in/tipsy-liquor-policy. Accessed on 26 April 2016
42. http://www.dpcc.delhigovt.nic.in/indexdup.php. Accessed on 26 April 2016
43. http://www.pplindia.org/licctg.aspx. Accessed on 26 April 2016
44. http://www.hospitalitybizindia.com/detailNews.aspx?aid=17254&sid=23. Accessed on 26 April 2016
45. http://indiankanoon.org/doc/9679061. Accessed on 26 April 2016
46. http://delhi.gov.in/WPS/WCM/connect/doit_excise/Excise/Home/Functions/Entertainment+Department. Accessed on 26 April 2016
47. http://excise.delhigovt.nic.in/ex5.asp. Accessed on 26 April 2016
48. http://en.wikipedia.org/wiki/Laissez-faire. Accessed on 26 April 2016
49. http://www.taxworld.org/History/TaxHistory.htm. Accessed on 26 April 2016
50. http://ingrimayne.com/econ/Connections/Says.html. Accessed on 26 April 2016
51. http://en.wikipedia.org/wiki/Say's_law. Accessed on 26 April 2016
52. http://en.wikipedia.org/wiki/Keynesian_economics. Accessed on 26 April 2016

53. http://www.nber.org/papers/w16204.pdf?new_windows=1. Accessed on 26 April 2016
54. http://www.usgovernmentspending.com/debt_deficit_history. Accessed on 26 April 2016
55. http://en.wikipedia.org/wiki/Post-World_War_II_economic_expansion. Accessed on 26 April 2016
56. http://nationalpubliclibrary.info/articles/Post-World_War_II_economic_expansion. Accessed on 26 April 2016
57. http://en.wikipedia.org/wiki/List_of_countries_by_GDP_(nominal). Accessed on 26 April 2016
58. https://www.cia.gov/library/publications/the-world-factbook/fields/2056.html. Accessed on 26 April 2016
59. *The Economist*, Special Report on World Economy, 13 October 2012
60. Portfolios of the Poor by Daryl Collins, Jonathon Morduch, Stuart Rutherford, Orlanda Ruthven, Princeton University Press, 2009
61. http://data.worldbank.org/indicator/FR.INR.LNDP. Accessed on 26 April 2016
62. http://www.tradingeconomics.com/japan/interest-rate. Accessed on 26 April 2016
63. http://en.wikipedia.org/wiki/Bushido. Accessed on 26 April 2016
64. http://www.theguardian.com/world/2008/jun/19/japan. Accessed on 26 April 2016
65. http://en.wikipedia.org/wiki/Laffer_curve. Accessed on 26 April 2016

THE HEAT EXCHANGER—
THE RICHES OF THE MARKETPLACE

In a nuclear power plant, it is in the heat exchanger that the energy created in the reactor and carried by the coolant is tapped and put to whatever use we wish. Without the heat exchanger there would be no point in setting up a nuclear reactor and power plant. Deficiencies in the heat exchanger will diminish the output of the entire plant. If the exchanger is deficient in design and we are able to tap only very little of the heat generated in the reactor, we may even begin to question the potential of the reactor and the whole power plant.

It is the same with ideas, business ventures and the marketplace. It is in the marketplace that we harvest the fruits of our ideas and release the wealth inherent in them. It is the exchanger of the marketplace that releases a cornucopia of riches for our use. This is the last part of the economic engine. If we have been able to set up the other parts of the engine, which encourage the formation, release and implementation of ideas, sound money and business-friendly policies, we must be careful at this last stage where we harvest the fruits of the economic engine. This is also the place where our governments should tax us.

♦

Efficiency is the chief criterion when designing the layout of the marketplace and other considerations, such as the colour of the marketplace, are, as was the case of the colour of Deng Xiaoping's cat, which we referred to when discussing funding for education, quite peripheral to the issue. It does not matter whether the market is a free market or a controlled market or a mixture of the two. What matters is that the market efficiently values all products and services in a manner that does not depress either demand or supply and permits new products, services and ideas to be offered in the market. If the resultant market has more elements of a free market, so be it.

The market should approach Pareto optimality. Pareto optimality is a concept in economics, named after Vilfredo Pareto (1848–1923), an Italian economist. In a Pareto efficient economic allocation, no one can be better off without making at least one individual overall worse off. If a change permits a move that makes at least one individual better off without making any other individual worse off it is called a Pareto improvement. A Pareto improvement does not refer to a specific individual. For instance, if a change in economic policy eliminates a monopoly and that market subsequently becomes competitive, the monopolist will be made worse off. However, the loss to the monopolist will be more than offset by the increased efficiency in the market. This means the monopolist can be compensated for its loss while still leaving a net gain for others in the economy. When no further Pareto improvements are possible in any given system, it is said to be Pareto efficient or Pareto optimal.[1] In a further validation of my belief that a set of rules can apply to diverse phenomena, the economic theory of Pareto efficiency is also used by engineers when building a device.

In the real world a market will never attain Pareto optimal condition. It can only move towards it. This is because the market of a functioning economy is constantly exposed to new products and services, to new ideas and awarenesses. New offerings often command high premiums and face little competition. By the time the newness works itself into the system through a series of Pareto improvements, newer offerings have arrived in the market. A well-functioning economy is not a moribund edifice that can attain perfection in a state of stasis. It is a dynamic construct which not only allows for but welcomes new offerings which may be unsettling in the short term but in the long term are the way forward to growth and prosperity. When new ideas have played themselves out and no new ideas are forthcoming we may be entering a state of stasis. In a heat exchanger, this is called a state of thermal equilibrium, when no further energy can be transferred. If no new offerings in terms of goods or better prices are able to reach the marketplace, the economy becomes moribund. There is no impetus to growth.

The function of new offerings being brought to the marketplace does not depend on the marketplace. The onus is on new ideas being generated and on money being available to convert the ideas into goods that can be brought into the market through a business-friendly environment. The job of the market is to expose all supplies to every possible demand, thereby maximizing the chances of any offering in the market, whether it is a product, service or labour, meeting with a corresponding demand, and thereby delivering benefits to both buyer and seller.

The underlying logic behind the working of a heat exchanger and that of a marketplace is the same and is fairly straightforward. A heat exchanger is a piece of equipment built for efficient heat transfer from one medium to another, without needing the two mediums to be physically mixed. This is done by exchange of the kinetic energy of individual particles through the boundary between the two parts of the system.[2] It is much the same in a marketplace. A market needs to facilitate the exchange of goods, services and ideas without the necessity of moving people physically or requiring their physical intermingling. (Not that the physical intermingling of people is necessarily a bad thing in itself but this is not a function of the marketplace.)

In this chapter, I will look at the different parts of the marketplace and seek to understand what improvements can make it approach Pareto optimality. However, before I proceed to do so, I must point out that all countries have two different markets functioning, the internal market and the international market. The logic and objectives of the two markets are very different from each other and so are the strategies required to make them function optimally and to our benefit.

The consequences of whatever happens in the internal market, whether good or bad, remain within the market. Jobs are created or destroyed within the market, profits or losses remain within the market. Savings and investments are made within the market, thereby increasing productivity and lifting the living standards of those within the market. This is not the case with international trade. Jobs, profits and investments happen outside the market. Of course, no country can buy anything from another unless it is able to sell something else to it. All trade agreements are based on the assumption that if we all open up our markets to each other, the benefits of trade accruing to other countries will largely cancel out and we will all benefit from increased trades. This and David Ricardo's law of comparative advantage are the central tenets of liberal thinking and of bodies such as the World Trade Organization (WTO), the IMF and the World Bank. I will return to the subject of international trade later in this chapter and only wish to state at this point that the requirements of a country's internal marketplace and international marketplace are very different from each other.

The analogy of the marketplace to a heat exchanger applies more to the internal market than to foreign trade, where other considerations come into play.

The central logic of a heat exchanger is simplicity itself. A heat exchanger is essentially a membrane separating the heat-bearing fluid from the fluid to which the heat is to be transferred. Because of the temperature difference between the two fluids and the conducting nature of the membrane, kinetic energy is transferred from the hot fluid to the cooler one. The devil, as they say, is in the detail.

While devising better heat exchangers, engineers try to implement the following:

1. Ensure the largest surface area by various means including corrugation of the heat exchange membrane, thereby prolonging the period of exposure.
2. The flow of the fluid must be such that no cold spots develop along the membrane that is exposed to the hot energy-bearing flow. This is done by inducing a churn in the hot fluid, so that all molecules of the hot fluid come in contact with the membrane, and once they have given off their heat are replaced by new heat-bearing molecules.
3. The flow of the fluid must be such that no hot spots develop along the membrane in the colder fluid to which the heat is to be transferred. This again is done by inducing a churn in the cooler fluid. If the fluid becomes stagnant on either side of the membrane, the temperature difference is reduced, impeding the transfer of energy.
4. The membrane must be a good conductor of heat so that it does not itself absorb the heat to be transferred nor slow down the process of heat transfer.

The requirements of a marketplace are the same:

1. A larger surface area is equivalent to a larger set of possibilities for transactions to take place
2. A churn of the hot fluid is equivalent to the greater ease with which new products and ideas can reach the marketplace
3. A churn of the colder fluid to which the heat is to be transferred is equivalent to a greater diffusion of buying ability so that no monopsony (the opposite of a monopoly, when there is only one buyer for any good or service) is created, encouraging sellers to come out with Pareto improvements, raising the sophistication and competitiveness of the market as a whole.
4. The membrane separating the hot fluid from the colder fluid must be a good conductor of heat without itself absorbing much of the energy. This is equivalent to a marketplace with as low transaction costs as possible.

Let us look at each of these four areas and try and identify the practices that either promote or retard the efficient functioning of the marketplace.

1. When people first started trading, it must have been through chance occurrences. The market was very small and interactions so sporadic that neither seller nor buyer could predict them, much less plan for them. The next step, I assume once again because the details of early market evolution are lost in the past, was the practice of setting up a market at predictable times—for instance, during the time of harvest of different crops or with the change of season. The great advantage of a predictable market was that people could plan for it. They could prepare the goods they hoped to sell and a list of the things they hoped to buy. The increased activity of preparing goods for sale with a view to eventually buying

other goods increased the well-being of a community and increased its GDP, which of course was never measured as such in those days.

The increase in well-being in a predictable market must have been so pronounced that it soon led to more frequent markets, even weekly events, a practice still in vogue in many parts of the world in even the most developed markets in the form of flea markets. In less developed markets, the weekly bazaars still play an essential role in meeting purchasing and selling needs.

From a weekly market to a permanent market that would be open every day was but a small step. This small step, however, had a major impact. Not only did opportunities for the exchange of goods increase, but goods and services that might otherwise never have been exchanged came to be exchanged. Permanent markets where people regularly congregated became one of the major focal points of towns and cities. The gathering of people often coming from some distance on a regular basis gave an opening to establishments serving food and drink, barbers, tailors, shoemakers and many others. With each new business opening in the market, the number of people participating in the market grew, giving rise to yet more opportunities. The mere existence of a market can give rise to demands that can be readily met by willing suppliers. If a novel idea to meet a perceived need is born but there is no marketplace or the marketplace is difficult to access, the idea might never be put to practice.

Once permanent markets had been established, they evolved ways to further enhance their reach by conveying information about market offerings to potential buyers. Spreading information about products increases the possibility of transactions and sellers do this in several ways. They display their wares at shop windows to reach out to passers-by, they participate in exhibitions and trade shows, they advertise in the media, including trade journals. Purveyors of ideas and new findings present them at seminars and in specialized publications that target others with similar interests.

This exchange of information is non-adversarial in nature and to the benefit of both buyer and seller. Sellers hope to get as many customers as possible while attempting to get the highest price they can for their products while buyers seek the best products or services at the lowest prices. Thus the buyer seeks utility maximization while the seller seeks profit maximization. Utility maximization is not just about getting the lowest price for a product. A buyer may also be willing to buy an article at a higher price due to higher perceived brand value. The utility that is being satisfied here is a higher status in society as it demonstrates that the buyer is a person of great means.

This process leads to price discovery and in a competitive market ensures that the discovered price is as low as possible while permitting a reasonable profit to sellers.

In recent decades, the widespread use of the internet has given this process a major boost. It is now far easier than it has ever been for sellers and buyers to find each other. The internet with its search engines is so significantly superior to earlier means of putting out and accessing information about goods on both a local and international level that the once ubiquitous Yellow Pages have disappeared from many cities.

Except where impeded by governmental impediments, the evolution of the marketplace has been due to private initiative and technological breakthroughs. There is little that governments can do to further this process other than promote use of the internet at the cheapest possible rates. There is, however, much that they can do to delay the process by limiting free and unfettered access to information.

2. All new and innovative offerings should be able to reach the marketplace. An innovation that cannot reach the marketplace is a wasted innovation, a wasted idea and wasted energy. There are many ways in which a new offering is prevented from reaching the marketplace.

   The most direct way is by requiring new ventures to obtain licences and permits. The more permits needed, often from multiple authorities, the more the chances that a new initiative will not see the marketplace. Often the power to grant licences is parcelled out at the discretion of different departments of the government, making the process arduous and lengthy, taking months and even years. It does not take much imagination to see how such an arrangement can lead to corruption and crony capitalism. Crony capitalism is only possible with government inputs. One of the more blatant examples of crony capitalism is the story of Air India and the aviation industry of India.

   Indian aviation was started by Tata Sons Ltd (now Tata Group) in 1932. The venture was profitable from the start. In 1946 Tata Airlines changed its name to Air India. Over the years it expanded its network to many parts of the world and earned itself a sterling reputation for its service. In 1953 it was nationalized. In 1993 private companies were once again allowed to run airlines and a few companies quickly started business. In 1995 the Tata Group, the company with the most experience and best track record in the business, applied for a licence to open a new airline in partnership with Singapore Airlines, internationally one of the best-run airlines. The licence was granted but before the company could start operations the rules were changed to say that while foreigners and foreign companies could invest in Indian carriers, foreign airlines could not. In other words the people with experience in running an airline were barred from investing in an Indian airline while others were welcome to do so. The rationality, if any, for such a bizarre rule eludes me. The only plausible explanation is an insinuation attributed to the then chairman of the Tata Group, Ratan Tata, implying that the deal failed because the group did not bribe a Union minister a sum of 3.3 million US dollars.

It can be nobody's case that the venture would have been detrimental to anyone other than competitors who may have been offering an inferior product and politicians or bureaucrats who were unable to line their pockets. The failed Tata–Singapore Airlines venture attracted considerable media attention. Smaller ventures that go largely unreported often face the same problem in varying degrees. In some countries even a small venture like opening a grocery store requires multiple permits from multiple authorities. The result is always the same. The more the number of permits needed to enter the market and the more difficult they are to obtain, the more potentially better products and services cannot reach the market and the greater the corruption and crony capitalism in a country.

In many places and industries, state interference does not end after a business has obtained the required permits. In the Indian food processing industry if even a variant of an existing sauce is to be launched, permissions have to be taken, a process of many months and a considerable outlay of money. This is akin to a chef needing approval from a panel of government experts if he wishes to change an ingredient in one of his dishes. Many ideas are never tried out as the reward is simply not worth the effort.

Further, the fees for the permits and delays in obtaining the permits push up costs and increase the price of offerings, thereby reducing transactions in the marketplace and also reducing profits and tax revenue.

Countries should review their requirement for permits. Just how many permits do we really need to to open a corner grocery store or a small bistro or a large airline?

India is not the only country so mired in regulations. The eminent writer Niall Ferguson has said in his book, *The Great Degeneration*, perhaps tongue in cheek, that it would be impossible today for common salt to be approved for general consumption by the US FDA because of its hugely complex procedures. I sometimes wonder what the course of history would have been if the Wright brothers, for their 'improbable' heavier-than-air flying machine or Karl Benz for his 'ridiculous' horse-less carriage or the inventor of any major breakthrough, had the inventor been required to have his or her invention be first vetted by a team of government 'experts'.

Apart from the permits which are difficult to obtain, there are other circumstances that prevent goods from entering the market. Let us look at monopolies and cartelization. It is the natural tendency of all businesses to grow as much as they can and to try and monopolize the market. However, that is not what is best for the functioning of a marketplace. Monopolies or near monopolies and cartels can influence both suppliers and buyers to act in a manner so as to prevent the entry of new players with cheaper or better products. Indeed the possibility of creating monopolies and cartels is the strongest argument against the adoption of laissez-faire policies. Monopolies and cartels deny a level playing field to new entrants in the market and impede Pareto improvements in products and services.

There are some natural monopolies such as railroads, airports, seaports and power grids where it makes little economic sense to duplicate investments. If a railway company owns the railway tracks or an airline owns an airport or a shipping company owns a seaport, the company must be broken up so that the unduplicable asset is hived-off to become another entity which charges for the use of its assets to other users, in an open access system. The hived off parts of the business must be required to deal with each other at arm's length. There are other industries for which this approach can be advocated. Large supermarkets have over the years come to own large stores in city centres where new large stores are prohibitively expensive to establish. This gives them an unfair advantage when they introduce house labels which they sell at vastly cheaper prices than the competition, mainly by subsuming their profits from the manufacturing business and the store operating business into one head, trying to capture market share for their in house labels and denying entry to potentially better products. This is a classic example of predatory pricing.

Predatory pricing is a pricing strategy where a product or a service is set at a very low price, intending to drive competitors out of the market and create entry barriers for potential new competitors. If competitors cannot sustain equal or lower prices, they go out of business or choose not to enter the business. The predatory merchants then have fewer competitors and become de facto monopolies.[3] This practice prevents goods that are superior in price or quality from reaching the market, which is just what should not happen in an efficient marketplace.

There are many views as to what determines market dominance and gives firms the ability to abuse their dominant position. European Union anti-monopolies law can apply to dominant market players with 38 per cent market share, compared to the US where a market share of 60 per cent is usually required to trigger intervention.[4] That is when any company reaches a market share of 38 per cent or 60 per cent, respectively it is investigated if there is abuse of its dominant market position. In my opinion, to prevent cartelization and to provide a platform for new ideas, rules must permit a minimum of 5 to 10 competitors in each significant segment of business and a market share of 20 per cent and higher should trigger enquiries as to whether unfair trade practices are being employed to deter competition. I realize that my suggestion could ruffle the feathers of free trade advocates but it is my stand that it is the presence of many players that really supports free trade.

Trade unions can be monopolies too. When countrywide or industrywide trade unions negotiate high wages and other working conditions and get their governments to legislate those conditions into law, they prevent start-ups which do not have the wherewithal to meet those conditions from starting a venture and entering the market. Such a set-up can institutionalize both unemployment and a lack of churn, preventing the arrival of new offerings in the market. Before I am accused of being anti-labour, let me hasten to say that trade unions are good but they should be companywide and not countrywide or industrywide. The fortunes and rewards of the trade union must be linked to the fortunes of the company. I also feel that the trade union must be represented on the board of a company and have access to the company's financial information, so that when the fortunes of the company pick up, the trade union can rightly expect the fortunes of its members to pick up too. This can only augur well for the morale of any company and its chances of success.

Let us now look at subsidies, another market-distorting practice that hampers the flow of new solutions to an existing problem. I dare say most subsidies are started by governments with the good intention to alleviate perceived hardships in either the whole country or a section of its people. Let us, for the time being, ignore the niggling suspicion that subsidies can also be given for the purpose of gaining popularity in the constant battle for votes. However, the road to hell, as the saying goes, is paved with good intentions.

Subsidies distort economic behaviour. Subsidies alter the relative prices of goods and thereby tend to change decisions of production for businesses and decisions of consumption for all of us. To my mind, there are two main arguments against subsidies. The first is that they lock us into behaviour patterns that would otherwise not be sustainable. They bridge the gap between reality and wishful thinking. With subsidies no effort needs to be made to either adjust to the reality that started the subsidy or find other solutions to the problem, while consumption of those goods continues to rise due to the lower prices.. Subsidies in effect are addictive and tend to keep increasing until they can no longer be sustained and end with some sort of shock therapy and social unrest, which can lead to a regime change either through a democratic process or through street violence.

The second argument is that subsidies preclude the chance to find alternative solutions. If a good can be sold at one dollar and a subsidy lets it be sold at 75 cents, an alternative solution costing between 75 cents and a dollar will never see the light of day. Subsidies act in the same way as monopolies or a cumbersome permit regime in preventing the churn of new solutions or improvements from reaching the marketplace.

It is one thing to understand the ill-effects of subsidies but quite another to expect that subsidies will never be given out. Calamities, whether natural or man-made, will at times make subsidies unavoidable. When that happens, precautions can be taken to mitigate the disruptive effect of subsidies upon the functioning of the market. Subsidies are given to make a good more affordable. It could be given directly to consumers by way of cash transfer or it could be given to producers to enable them to sell the good at a cheaper rate. Of the two methods it is preferable that the subsidy is given by transferring money to the intended consumer without linking the subsidy to any proof of the good being actually purchased. In this way the consumer retains the ability to choose amongst any number of alternative means of satisfying his or her needs.

Through this approach the impediment to new solutions reaching the marketplace is removed. New solutions will not have to compete against an artificially cheapened product but will compete against the existing solution at the original price, increasing the possibility of improvement. The churn of new solutions is maintained. Competition is maintained in the market.

Another argument against subsidies is to do with consumption. When the price of any good rises, its consumption drops. This is true of almost all goods. The drop in consumption of a particular good due to price rise is quantified by a measure called PED (price elasticity of demand).[5] This gives the percentage change in the quantity demanded in response to 1 per cent change in price.

An exception to this behaviour of demand decreasing in response to price rise is seen in a class of goods known as Veblen goods.[6] Veblen goods comprise mainly luxury goods or positional goods that enhance the status of an individual in society. They include items like luxury cars, rare wines, designer dresses, bags and shoes. For these goods an increase in price increases their allure for aspirational buyers. An interesting thought comes to mind regarding Veblen goods. If Veblen goods were taxed heavily, it should make everyone happier. It would make the goods more expensive, making them more exclusive, increasing their snob value. That should make the manufacturers of the goods, the people who buy the goods for positional purposes and the government collecting the enhanced taxes—very happy. The taxes will not affect anyone not buying Veblen goods.

There is another class of goods known as Giffen goods,[7] which is really a set of circumstances that make demand grow because of a price increase. Imagine the food mix of a family that is not rich and has little money left over for discretionary spending. The mix consists of a cheaper staple food like grain or potatoes which is supplemented with a more expensive food like meat. If the price of the staple food rises, there will be no money left for the more expensive meat. The meat will need to be replaced with the cheaper staple food. In this case an increase in the price of the staple food causes an increase in its consumption. This set of circumstances is quite uncommon and is not applicable, for example, if the more expensive meat increases in price. The consumption of the meat will then drop in keeping with the law of demand, which states that, all else being equal, as the price of a product increases, the quantity demanded falls; likewise, as the price of a product decreases the quantity demanded increases. Veblen and Giffen goods are the only classes of goods which do not follow the law of demand. For all other goods, with lowered prices consumption increases.

If subsidies are given to producers so that their products, whether fuel, food, electricity or other goods, may be sold cheaper, there is no disincentive to continue consumption, even wasteful consumption, of the subsidised product. This ensures increased demand for subsidies. If, on the other hand, the money intended to ease the burden for citizens were transferred to them directly and the high prices of the goods intended to be subsidized were allowed to remain high, there would be an incentive to use the money wisely. Due to the prevailing high price of the goods for which the subsidy was received, attempts would be made to find a cheaper alternative to fulfil the basic need and the consumption of the goods would not be spurred by artificially low prices.

Another benefit of making a cash transfer or subsidizing the consumer rather than the producer is that the subsidies can be more precisely targeted, given to people below a certain income level or to people in a particular geographical area.

The process of changing from a system of subsidies being given to producers to a system which transfers the money intended for the subsidy directly to consumers may be administratively challenging at first but its benefits will make the effort worthwhile. It ensures that better goods and services enter the marketplace. It ensures that scarce goods are not wasted. It enables better targeting of subsidies, keeping the subsidy amount in check. If it also manages to reduce corruption by reducing the number of intermediaries and by eliminating any black market for underpriced goods, that would be the icing on the cake.

There are views held by some individuals, who would like to micro-manage the lives of the poor, that it is not a good idea for money to be given directly to recipients of subsidies as it might be used for other purposes, such as the purchase of liquor. This, I think, is a patronizing view implying that the less well-off who need to be subsidized are either incapable of handling money or so unmindful of their responsibilities that they need a nanny state to do it for them. To be sure, there may be some who buy liquor in lieu of food or fuel but it makes little sense to throw out the advantages of direct money transfers in favour of a few dysfunctional people. In their case, even if the goods intended to be subsidized are made cheaper by subsidizing the producers, there can be no guarantee that the intended goods will be bought.

There is another set of subsidies known as cross-subsidies, which are an attempt to equalize various conditions. These are often, but not always, to do with advantages or disadvantages of location and include things like freight equalization subsidies that attempt to equalize the price of various commodities across a country or subsidies given to backward regions. I think these subsidies are foolhardy. Every place has its advantages and disadvantages. How do you equalize the opportunities presented by pristine beaches and mountain views for tourism or a salubrious climate or a permissive culture to mineral deposits or potential dam sites for hydroelectric power or densely populated centres where businesses may thrive? Every place, every situation has a comparative advantage in doing what it does best. This is what David Ricardo, one of the most influential classical economists (1772–1823), stated in his theory of comparative advantage. The theory does not refer to one country having a comparative advantage over another in the manufacture of particular goods, but refers to a country having a comparative advantage in manufacturing one product over another.

The theory of comparative advantage is often used to further international free trade but is just as pertinent to internal trade. Every part of the country should concentrate on doing what it is most advantageously placed to do. Unlike in international trade, any money saved or extra profit made by following the logic of comparative advantage stays within the country and as there are no restrictions on internal capital flows or movement of people, the money is likely to be invested within the country, furthering economic growth. There is an irrefutable logic to Ricardo's theory of comparative advantage and governments should not try and subsidize away the inherent advantages of a particular region or situation. The theory is more commonly applied to international trade but there it operates within certain unstated limitations. I shall discuss them in further detail later in the chapter.

There is another aspect of subsidies I would like to draw the reader's attention to. Subsidies are given to benefit a segment of the population. Unless done with due care and consideration, they can separate society and build up powerful lobbies of interest groups that will make the removal or reduction of subsidies very difficult. Farmer lobbies the world over are an example of this.

Over the last few paragraphs we have been looking at the supply side of the market or the hot part of the heat exchanger and trying to identify the factors that prevent new offerings from reaching the marketplace. Let us now look at the demand side of the market or the cooler part of the heat exchanger and try to identify the factors that inhibit demand.

3. The most obvious factor that inhibits demand is lack of money. It goes without saying that the more money in an economy, the greater its buying power. However, I am not comparing the buying power of one economy with that of another but analysing the factors that will spur demand within the size constraints of any economy. It is not just the total aggregate of money available in the economy but also the dispersion of the money that generates demand. It is not just about the quantity but also about the quality of demand.

A well-functioning idea reactor throws up all sorts of ideas, which, if the conditions are right, lead to all sorts of products and services being offered in the marketplace. However, this is of no use if there is no demand and no buyers with the wherewithal to buy the products and services. Eventually the products will no longer be offered or even developed. Ultimately, the ideas themselves will not be taken seriously, seeming to be an exercise in futility and be then lost to history.

The range of ideas and the goods they lead to is endless. From slightly better mousetraps to geostationary satellites, from brain scans to miniskirts, from atom-smashing to bungee-jumping, the list is inexhaustible. The money needed to buy these products varies as widely, from what can be bought with loose change to big-ticket individual purchases like houses or cars to amounts that can only be put together by big businesses, financial institutions and even governments. Obviously, the things that can be bought with loose change need to sell many units for the businesses making them to be viable whereas more expensive items need to sell only a few units to be viable. The space shuttle, one of the most expensive projects ever, ended up building only six shuttles and I assume it was profitable for all the contractors involved in building them.

For the demand side of any economy to work to its full potential, the buying power must be so distributed as to generate demand across the full spectrum of goods reaching the marketplace, from what can be bought with pocket change to what requires a substantial amount of money. For goods that are not affordable to a single individual or even a single economic entity, there must exist a legal framework to permit collaboration among more than one economic entity towards a shared goal. This requirement for a varied dispersion of money is against a perfectly egalitarian society where everyone has the same buying power. While in a perfectly egalitarian society everyone can afford goods costing a modest amount of money, there will be no takers for goods that are more expensive. If, on the other hand, there is excessive concentration of money in a few hands, whether private or governmental, there will be too few buyers for goods requiring a modest amount of money. Concentration of buying power in a few hands occurs either when a government garners for itself a disproportionate buying power or when monopsonies are allowed to establish themselves.

The standard of living, the quality of life and, at lower income levels, the nutritional intake and longevity of people depend upon the buying power of individual citizens and is meaningless if correlated with the total buying power in an economy. In command or centrally planned economies as in all communist countries until recently, the living standards of the citizens could not be compared with those of the citizens of countries with comparable aggregate buying power but free markets. The citizens of command economies were condemned to strive for a distant utopia while their leaders planned and made investments in large projects aimed at that utopia. The problem was not one of aggregate buying power but of the dispersion of that buying power.

For this purpose a better measure for estimating the dispersion of buying power in a country is median income rather than average income. Median income is the income of a person who has as many people earning more than him as people earning less than him. Average income, on the other hand, can hide great extremes of both wealth and poverty.

An easy way to gauge the health of an economy is to look at the quality of goods offered on sale at the lower end of the market. If these goods are shoddy and of poor quality and their sales are dependent only on their low price it can only mean that buying power at the lower end of the market, where the bulk of the people reside, is low and the economy is doing poorly. If the quality of goods on sale at the lower end of the market begins to improve, it means the economy is doing better. In the erstwhile USSR, as indeed in most command economies, the government seemed to find enough money to spend on the things important to them, including military hardware and attention-grabbing monuments or projects. The government had in effect pre-empted the use of most of the money, leaving little in the hands of individual citizens to spur the demand for and hence the development of better products.

I do not believe there can be a set formula for how much money a government can pre-empt for itself and how much money should be in the hands of consumers. The amounts can vary with circumstance. However, there must be a constant awareness, both among the people who run the government and those who vote for the government, that too much money in government hands is bad for the economy and for the well-being of the citizenry.

When a government controls a significant portion of the money in the economy and becomes the sole buyer of many goods, it becomes in effect a monopsony and the consequences of this are detrimental to efficient market functioning. A monopsony drives down prices to often unsustainable levels. It increases corruption because the stakes for the seller are very high. The seller either has to get the business of the monopsonistic buyer or close down. Further, it discourages new entrants to the market even if the new product is better, due to the low prices and the existing crony capitalism between suppliers and the monopsonistic buyer.

Elements of monopsonistic behaviour can be seen in many situations. For instance, when a manufacturing plant opens in an isolated region where there are no other similar plants, it becomes a monopsonistic buyer of labour and is able to pay lower wages than it would have in the presence of competition. However, monopsonies are difficult to establish. When there is an overwhelmingly large buyer, for example the American supermarket chain Walmart, for a segment of goods, it can drive down prices, but only temporarily. If the segment is large and profitable, it will soon entice other competitors, thus ending the monopsonistic situation.

Effective monopsony cannot exist without a corresponding effective monopoly, whether government owned or private. Some examples of monopsonies are the armed forces of a country which are the sole buyers of military hardware, or a state-owned national railway, or in countries where the government is the largest supplier of education or health care. While most monopolies and their resultant monopsonies are government owned, they also exist where large infrastructure that is impossible to duplicate has been built and has not been broken up by antitrust action. Examples include railways, telecommunication networks, electrical grids and oil supply networks.

Monopolies and monopsonies can also be set up with government fiat. Perhaps the most outstanding example of this is the East India Company, which was incorporated by Royal Charter in 1600. The Charter granted a monopoly to all English trade in all lands washed by the Indian Ocean (from the southern tip of Africa, to Indonesia in the South Pacific). Unauthorized British interlopers were liable to forfeiture of ships and cargo.[8] Any monopsonies that the Company enjoyed was by virtue of the monopoly granted to it. The monopsonistic benefits were never spelt out.

Another outstanding example of a government granting a monopoly is the Agriculture Produce Marketing Committees (APMC) Act granted by the different state governments in India since the 1950s to cartels of traders. The scope of this Act goes beyond the Charter granted to the East India Company as it explicitly grants both a monopoly and a monopsony to the cartel of marketing committees. The Act makes it illegal for farmers to sell their produce to anyone other than the market committees, making the committees the sole buyers of all of India's agricultural produce. The Act also makes it illegal for retailers and food processors to buy from any source other than the committees. The measures in case of a breach of the law are stringent. Whereas the Charter of the East India Company provided for forfeiture of goods involved in breaching the Charter, the APMC Act provides for imprisonment of farmers who sell their produce outside the committees. It also provides for imprisonment for those who buy outside the committees. In view of the existence of the APMC Act, it is hardly surprising that there is such a great difference between farm gate prices and the prices at which produce is sold by the committees.

There is another peculiar monopsony in operation in India—the Minimum Support Price for foodgrains, a scheme in operation since 1966. In the 1960s, India was deficit in food-grains and needed to import grain to meet its needs. The Green Revolution led to more productive farm practices and the introduction of a minimum support price (MSP) scheme, guaranteeing that the government would buy any amount of grain at proclaimed minimum prices. This ensured that India's grain production went up. Today India exports grain. There is no denying that the MSP scheme went a long way in ensuring India's food security. Farmers could fearlessly grow as much grain as they were able to, without fear of market prices crashing. They were assured of getting a decent price for their produce. Somewhere along the way, the government started raising the MSPs of foodgrains. From defining the lower end of a viable price range, MSPs came to define the upper end of the range.

The price increase was probably a populist measure aimed at getting farmer votes, as about half of India's population earns its livelihood from agriculture. The government in effect became a monopsony as far as buying grain was concerned. But it was a monopsony with a difference, or rather two differences. First, monopsonies are able to push down prices, while this monopsony pushed up prices. Second, every entity including a monopsony buys only as much as is needed. This monopsony is committed to buying everything sellers bring to it. The upshot of this is that the silos and godowns of the Food Corporation of India—the government agency that handles MSP purchases—are overflowing with unimaginable quantities of rotting grain. The Global Food Waste Not Want Not report of 2013 says, 'considerably greater levels of tonnage loss exist in larger developing nations, such as India, for example where about 21 million tonnes of wheat annually perish due to inadequate storage and distribution—equivalent to the entire production of Australia.'[9] It is one thing to have a MSP as an insurance against a distressingly low price but quite another to use this as a means of increasing farmers' fortunes. India could, in theory, export its surplus grain to other countries. That, however, is a losing proposition for the government. According to a *Global Post* article of 2012, 'The Indian Government pays about $346 per tonne. To be competitive in the international market, a tonne would have to sell for about $260. That $86 difference constitutes a huge loss for a government already running a high fiscal deficit. The crops don't feed who they should and in the end, actually cost the government billions.'[10]

The absurdity of the situation is poignant. A low-income country like India ends up subsidizing foodgrains for richer countries while its own citizens have to pay a higher price as the base price has been set by high MSPs. Between the effects of the APMC Act and ever-escalating MSPs, food inflation in India has skyrocketed in the last few years and shows few signs of abating.

Excessive taxation resulting in concentration of buying power in the hands of the government or deficit financing which puts disproportionate buying power in the hands of the government tampers with the demand side of the market. Monopsonies have the same effect of concentrating buying power in a few hands. However, monopsonies are rarely set up by purely commercial organizations and almost always have a government input.

So far we have looked at ways of increasing the interaction area of the market to increase the chances of transactions taking place. We have looked at the supply side of the market and considered the factors that help or hinder new goods in reaching the marketplace and we have looked at the demand side of the market and seen how a good dispersion of buying power can give rise to a demand across the entire range of products put out by the supply side of the market. Let us now consider the final component of the market in terms of its analogy with the heat exchanger. It is the nature of the heat exchange membrane through which heat is conducted.

4. In the marketplace, the equivalent of the conductive membrane is the terms of trade. Terms of trade permit transactions to take place easily and at minimal cost. In a heat exchanger, the transfer of heat from the hotter side to the cooler side is made possible by a difference of temperature between the two sides of the conducting membrane. If there is no temperature difference, heat will not be transferred. In the marketplace the difference is between the price at which a product or a service can be provided and the price that buyers are willing or able to pay for the goods. The greater the difference, the greater the number of transactions that take place. If much of the difference between the price at which goods can be offered for sale and the price at which

they can be bought is siphoned away by the terms on which transactions are made, it will result in fewer transactions. This occurs by the following means:
a. High licence fees for operating a business
b. High interest rates
c. Taxes levied on sales transactions

Let us examine at each of these criteria in detail.

1. I differentiate between the difficulty in obtaining licences to do business and high licence fees. Whereas the difficulty of obtaining a licence prevents goods from reaching the market, a licence fee diminishes the number of transactions taking place. The higher the licence fees the less transactions take place. While it is rare for transactions to stop completely because licence fees are so high, it does happen on occasion. An example of this is the high licence fee charged to a restaurant for serving alcoholic drinks, including a glass of beer, in Delhi. As pointed out earlier, nearly 10 per cent of such restaurants in Delhi refused to renew their licences in 2013 for the simple reason that it was difficult for them to recover their licence fees.
2. High interest rates make goods less affordable and therefore reduce the number of transactions. This applies to both manufacturers who borrow money to set up factories and to consumers who buy on credit and have to pay high interest rates on their borrowings.
3. All indirect taxes like VAT or sales tax, excise taxes, service taxes, etc. reduce the difference between the price at which goods can be offered for sale and the price consumers are willing to pay for them. These taxes reduce the number of trasactions that can take place.

When every area of the market is functioning efficiently, the market creates wealth. Improvements in the functioning of the market increase the number of transactions. As more goods are bought and sold in a given time frame, the velocity of money increases. 'The velocity of money (also called velocity of circulation of money) is the frequency at which one unit of currency is used to purchase domestically produced goods and services within a given time period. In other words, it is the number of times one dollar is spent to buy goods and services per unit of time. If the velocity of money is increasing, then more transactions are occurring between individuals in an economy.'[11]

If Jack buys goods for 100 dollars from Jill and Jill later uses the same money to buy other goods from Jack, they have transacted business worth 200 dollars despite having only 100 dollars to start with. The money velocity in this case is 2. If Jack and Jill repeat these transactions every month and if money velocity is measured for a year, the time period assumed unless mentioned otherwise, they will have done business of 2400 dollars, having had 100 dollars to start with, the money velocity would be 24.

The effect of the velocity of money on the GDP of an economy is represented by the following equation:

GDP = Money supply x velocity of money

It is a straightforward equation which tells us that the GDP of a country can be increased by either increasing the money supply or by increasing the velocity of money. However, it is far easier to control money supply than to control velocity of money. Velocity of money is a function of the structure of the entire economy. Indeed most economists take the velocity of money in an economy as a given and focus on money supply to raise the GDP. This chapter, as also this book as a whole, focuses on the structure of the economy and all the factors that would eventually lead to increased velocity of money. Increasing money supply without addressing the structural shortcomings of an economy is always inflationary. The effect of increasing money supply on GDP is thus better represented by a slightly altered equation:

Nominal GDP = Money supply x velocity of money

The difference between GDP and nominal GDP is that nominal GDP ignores the inflation caused by increasing money supply.

Increasing money supply does not result in the structural changes that could result in the increased velocity of money. Increased velocity of money, on the other hand, leads to an increase in non-inflationary money supply as an increase in the number of transactions results in greater aggregate profits in the economy which leads to more taxes to the government, greater spending and more savings. Unfortunately, increasing the velocity of money is not as easy as increasing money supply. A high velocity of money is the outcome of an economy which is working well in all its parts. Indeed it is the outcome of the policies advocated in this book.

Thus far we have looked at the internal market of a country, treated as a stand-alone edifice. We have not looked at the external market or foreign trade which is a different kettle of fish altogether.

Almost every country in the world can produce some goods cheaper or better than other countries. This could be for a variety of reasons, including abundant natural mineral resources, plenty of suitable land and water for agricultural produce, a good pre-existing industrial base with a skilled workforce, enough plant and machinery, an abundant and inexpensive labour force. The list is practically endless and a country can enjoy a wide variety and combination of advantages to process some goods cheaper and better than others. The most sensible course of action would be to buy those cheaper or better goods from the countries that can deliver them and through those lower prices, share some of the advantages of the producing countries. There is of course a constraint in adopting this simple course of action—every country needs to sell something in order to have the money to buy anything else.

Countries vie for goods to sell so that they may have the wherewithal to buy the desired goods of other countries or have the luxury of building up a trade surplus which can be used or hoarded and encashed in the future. While it is true that in the internal market of a country too, every individual needs to sell something in order to be able to buy something else, the difference lies in the fact that profits generated by transactions in the internal marketplace stay within the economy where they contribute to better living standards or to investments which can enhance the competitiveness of the economy over a period of time. The profits generated by buying goods from another country do not remain in the buying country and do not contribute to raising living standards or additional investments within the country. This is a manageable issue when trade is between countries of comparable sophistication and advancement, with each having an advantage in some area of economic activity. Even so, these countries employ high-powered trade delegations to constantly look out for their interests and are usually able to handle trade disputes without too much acrimony so that each country's vital interests are looked after, as per the trade agreements signed.

This is not the case when an economically advanced country trades with a developing country whose main items of exports are raw material, whether mineral or agricultural, and other goods with little value addition. The value addition to those raw materials is carried out in the advanced country, where the profits accrue. The smaller share of the benefit of trade accruing to less developed countries does not come in a steady stream. These countries are far more vulnerable to fluctuating commodity prices and to the vicissitudes of the weather resulting in crop failures or bumper crops which drive down the prices of their agricultural produce. Why do these countries acquiesce to the current system of trade which is disadvantageous to them instead of trying to alter their situation?

I think the main reason is that developing countries lack the intellectual capacity and confidence to challenge the world view of international trade foisted upon them by advanced countries and the institutions controlled by them such as the World Bank, the IMF, the WTO and others, both directly and through the numerous NGOs they fund. It may be wise for the developing countries which host these NGOs to treat the views espoused by them with some scepticism. They may even view these NGOs as potential fifth columnists, for the views they propagate are not necessarily in the interests of the host country. Among the beliefs they espouse is a reliance on David Ricardo's law of comparative advantage and a set of ten beliefs termed the Washington Consensus.

David Ricardo (1772–1823) was a British political economist. His theory of comparative advantage is the cornerstone of the arguments in favour of international free trade. His theory does not refer to one country having an advantage over another country in producing a certain good. It says that if a country produces a certain good more efficiently than it does another, it must produce that good and also export it it for trade while it imports the other good. This theory goes against the idea of import substitution, that is, of trying to manufacture all its needs, a practice followed by some developing countries. Ricardo argued that there is mutual benefit from international trade even if one party is more competitive in every possible area than its trading counterpart and that a nation should concentrate on sectors where it has a comparative advantage while engaging in international trade in order to acquire those products in which it does not have a comparative advantage. He attempted to prove, by using a simple numerical example, that international trade is always beneficial. The example he gave involved two countries, Britain and Portugal, and two products, cloth and wine:

	Unit Labour Cost	
	Cloth	Wine
Britain	100	110
Portugal	90	80

Paul Samuelson, American Nobel Laureate in economics, called the numbers used in Ricardo's numerical example the 'four magic numbers'. From these numbers one can see that Portugal had an absolute advantage over England for the manufacture of both wine and cloth. However, it had a comparative advantage of 30 units in the manufacture of wine as against cloth at 10 units. Similarly England had a comparative advantage for the manufacture of cloth. In Portugal it is possible to produce both wine and cloth with less labour than it would take to produce the same quantities in England. However, the relative costs of producing these two products are different in the two countries. In England it is very hard to produce wine, and only moderately difficult to produce cloth. In Portugal both are easy to produce. Therefore while it is cheaper to produce cloth in Portugal than in England, it is cheaper still for Portugal to produce excess wine and trade that for English cloth. Conversely England benefits from this trade because its cost for producing cloth has not changed but it can now get wine at a lower price, closer to the price of cloth. The conclusion drawn is that each country can gain by specializing in the product where it has a comparative advantage and trading that product for another.[12,13] There is a seminal truth and irrefutable logic in Ricardo's statement of comparative advantage. It is, however, based on certain assumptions.

The assumption that is most detrimental to the interests of developing countries is that Ricardo's analysis can only hold true if the comparative advantage of the different goods stays the same. The theory leaves no room for a country improving its competitiveness. In a critique, British economist Joan Robinson (1903–83) pointed out that in reality following an opening of free trade with England, Portugal endured centuries of economic underdevelopment: 'the imposition of free trade on Portugal killed off a promising textile industry and left her with a slow growing export market for wine, while for England, exports of cloth led to accumulation, mechanisation and the whole spiralling growth of the Industrial Revolution.'[14] If developing countries were to fully rely on the efficacy and virtues of trade along the lines advocated by the theory of comparative advantage and open up unreservedly to free trade, they would perpetually lock themselves into a low-income existence. With time their comparative well-being would decline.

The Singer–Prebisch thesis points in this direction. Raul Prebisch and Hans Singer examined data over a long period of time (from 1876 to 1948), which suggested that the terms of trade for primary commodity exporters did have a tendency to decline. A simple explanation for this phenomenon is the observation that the income elasticity of demand for manufactured goods is greater than that for primary products, especially agricultural goods to which little value addition has been done. Therefore as incomes rise, the demand for manufactured goods increases more rapidly than the demand for primary products, that is, mainly mineral and agricultural produce. The theory implies that it is the very structure of the international market that is responsible for the existence of inequality in the world system.[15]

Countries in the nascent stages of development often follow one of two extreme strategies: they either open up their markets fully to imports, choosing to pay for those goods through the export of primary goods, or severely restrict imports and rely on inept attempts at import substitution. Both strategies are misconceived. With the first the country locks itself into a long-term disadvantageous position and with the second ensures for itself inefficiently produced and shoddy goods that have little chance of improving because the import of capital machinery, intermediary goods and technology is restricted. Further, with no import of superior quality goods there is no impetus to improve the quality of their own products.

There is a third group of countries that has done things differently. These countries thought strategically. They imported what they had to while resolutely protecting their nascent industries behind high tax tariff barriers and by banning certain imports. Protecting their companies in selected sectors from imports, they let them grow and compete in the internal market. This caused some companies to perish while others grew in size and sophistication until they had near-world-class products. It was only then that these countries started dismantling the tariff and import barriers. As a next step they became vociferous proponents of free international trade.

The list is impressive, and includes Britain, the USA, Japan, Germany, Taiwan, China and South Korea. All these countries used protectionist measures to give their industries a chance to become competitive. It was only when their industries were well established that they advocated untrammelled free international trade. These countries also use the IMF, the World Bank and since 1995, the WTO, which they fund and whose policies they control, in opening up the markets of poorer countries. When these countries approach the IMF or the World Bank for loans, the conditions imposed on them include their lowering of tariff barriers, opening up their capital markets to foreign fund flows and investments, privatization of state-owned companies, balanced government budgets and many other conditions that diminish the control those countries have over their destinies. These multilateral agencies in turn fund numerous NGOs and think tanks in the developing world directly or indirectly, with a view to making these countries more amenable to the policies prescribed for them by wealthier countries.

The economist Ha-Joon Chang, in his book *Bad Samaritans* spells out in detail the steps that wealthy nations took to become competitive in the world market and how they now, along with the institutions they control, advocate policies for the developing world that are the exact opposite of the policies they had employed to get to where they are now.

There is no denying that there are benefits to international trade. This is as true for developing countries as it is for developed countries. The question is not whether a developing country should interact with the rest of the world or try and eke out an isolated economic existence. The question is how best a country can integrate with the rest of the world in a way that it is not swamped by the developed countries, that its future course of action is not severely curtailed by concessions made and actions taken or not taken today.

The term 'Washington Consensus' was coined in 1989 by English economist John Williamson at the Institute for International Economics, an international economic think tank based in Washington, DC. It describes a set of ten economic policy prescriptions that were considered the 'standard' reform package for crisis-wracked developing countries by Washington, DC-based institutions such as the IMF, the World Bank, and the US Treasury Department.[16] Please note that this is a prescription for developing countries and not for developed countries. The recommendations are:

1. Fiscal policy discipline, with avoidance of large fiscal deficits relative to GDP
2. Redirection of public spending from subsidies ('especially indiscriminate subsidies') towards broad-based provision of key pro-growth, pro-poor services like primary education, primary health care and infrastructure investment

3. Tax reform, broadening the tax base and adopting moderate marginal tax rates
4. Interest rates that are market determined and positive (but moderate) in real terms
5. Competitive exchange rates
6. Trade liberalization: liberalization of imports, with particular emphasis on elimination of quantitative restrictions (licensing, etc.); any trade protection to be provided by low and relatively uniform tariffs
7. Liberalization of inward foreign direct investment (FDI)
8. Privatization of state enterprises
9. Deregulation: abolition of regulations that impede market entry or restrict competition, except for those justified on safety, environmental and consumer protection grounds and prudential oversight of financial institutions
10. Legal security of property rights

From an economics point of view there can be little argument against the first three points and the last two points, provided that point 9 refers to the internal market of a country and competition within the country. However, we need to examine points 4 to 8 in detail.

4. Interest rates do need to be positive but moderate in real terms. They need supportive actions from the central bank and fiscal discipline from the government. The role of the central bank and government cannot be wished away in achieving desired interest rates which are seldom entirely market driven anywhere in the world.
5. I am not sure what competitive exchange rates mean but influencing exchange rate changes is one of the tools governments of developing countries use to protect their markets. Devaluation of the currency can improve trade balances in the short term by making imports more expensive

and exports more competitive. If Greece still had the drachma instead of being in the Eurozone the value of which it has no control over, it could have used a devaluation to get out more quickly from its current economic crisis. The prospect of cheap holidays would have greatly boosted tourism, one of the main industries of Greece.

6. Trade liberalization of imports is not something that helps a developing country but is rather a step in the interest of developed countries that to export to it.

7. Liberalization of inward FDI is again a step that is more in the interest of developed countries. I hasten to add that FDI is the best way to get capital into developing countries. The money that comes in by way of FDI is for the long term and is not hot money looking to make a quick profit by speculating in stock markets and which can destabilize markets and economies as it rushes in and rushes out even faster. It also brings with it know-how and expertise. FDI is to be welcomed but only where desired. Being forced to let it in indiscriminately in all sectors is another matter altogether and not in the interests of any developing country.

8. Privatization of state enterprises is one of the tenets of neo-classical economic thought subscribed to by most mainstream economists. The main reason for advocating privatization is that private companies can deliver many goods and services more efficiently than governments can, due to free market competition. This is usually true but not always. Take the case of two majority government-owned airlines, Singapore Airlines and Air India. Singapore Airlines came into being in 1972, when it separated from Malaysia Singapore Airlines. Since then it has grown in size and quality of service and today it is one of the world's most preferred airlines and has been profitable every year since its inception. Air India was set up by Tata Sons Ltd in 1932 and is one of the world's

oldest airlines. It earned itself a reputation as an excellent service provider and was profitable every year until it was nationalized in 1953. Thereafter both its service standards and finances started declining. In the year 2012–13 it made a loss of about 900 million US dollars and is today one of the least preferred airlines amongst travellers. While it is apparent that Air India should be sold by the government and privatized, there is no compelling reason for the ownership pattern of Singapore Airlines to be changed.

One compelling reason why developing countries cannot avoid having state-owned enterprises is that their capital markets are not developed enough to fund large ventures with long gestation periods. The requirement by the institutions party to the Washington Consensus that governments do not participate in commercial ventures is detrimental to the growth of developing countries. State-owned companies can at times provide the initial impetus for the growth of any particular sector.

The ten requirements listed in the Washington Consensus are not the end of the story. There are further requirements being added to the list by the developed countries, further limiting the courses of action available to developing countries. An indication of this is seen in Thomas Friedman's book *The Lexus and the Olive Tree*. Friedman is an American journalist who writes extensively on foreign affairs and global trade. He has won the Pulitzer Prize three times and his views probably reflect the thinking of the Washington establishment. In this book, published in 1999, ten years after Williamson's Washington Consensus, he has defined a set of policies he calls the Golden Straight Jacket. According to him, these are the policies every developing country must follow if it is to be successful. The list goes far beyond the Washington Consensus in curtailing the course of action available to developing countries, should they subscribe to this thinking. In that sense the golden straightjacket is really a straitjacket leaving the wearer helplessly trussed up. The policies recommended that are in addition to the ones suggested by the Washington Consensus are as follows:

1. Eliminating and lowering tariffs on imported goods
2. Removing restrictions on foreign investments
3. Getting rid of quotas and domestic monopolies
4. Deregulating capital markets
5. Making its currency convertible
6. Opening its industries, stock and bond markets to direct foreign ownership and investment
7. Allowing its citizens to choose from an array of competing pension options and foreign-run pension and mutual funds

If all these recommendations were to be followed completely by a developing country whose industries have not yet developed to a level where they might hold their own against international competition, it would result in industries that are either manufacturing plants or subsidiaries of a foreign multinational company. Further, savings from within the country would be siphoned away to foreign funds and not be available for investments within the country. A developing country would need to be naive to the extreme to believe that the advice given and conditions applied by the World Bank, IMF or WTO are to its benefit. It is part of an agenda to increase the dominance of the already developed countries. Developing countries should not be looking at these bodies for a fair deal.

It should be kept in mind too, that multinational companies are not truly multinational entities but companies with operations in many countries. The decision-makers of these companies usually belong to the country where the company originated. While their avowed aim is to maximize profits through their multinational operations, when push comes to shove, their decisions will favour their home country. The ultimate interests of multinationals lie within the country where the bulk of the ownership and senior management reside and think of as home.

Against this hostile world environment, developing countries must realize that they alone can look after their interests. In the internal market a government needs only to ensure a level playing field and pursue policies that are conducive to trade, secure in the knowledge that enhanced trade will benefit everyone in the country. In its participation in the international market, every country needs to think strategically. It needs to identify and promote the sectors where it has an advantage and establish those sectors as among the best in the world, while letting its citizens enjoy the benefits of low prices or better goods from those sectors where others have an advantage. International trade is in many ways war through other means and instead of putting on an accountant's cap a developing country needs to don a general's hat, for the advantages it must seek are not current profits but long-term strategic gains that will stay with it for a long time.

For the past few years, there has been a heated but muddled debate in India on whether to allow FDI in retail trade, that is, whether to let companies like Walmart and Tesco set up operations in India.

The reasons given by those opposing the entry of foreign retail chains are:

1. The chains of large stores would adversely impact the viability of millions of small convenience stores that dot the Indian scene
2. The chains would concentrate buying power in the hands of a few and drive down prices for all vendors that supplied goods to them
3. Foreign-owned stores would bring in myriad imported goods, thereby adversely affecting local manufacturers

Those in favour of letting FDI in the retail sector counter these reasons with the following:

1. Large chain stores and convenience stores coexist the world over. The two do not cater to the same needs. While it is true that much of the buying would shift to the larger stores and some convenience stores would shut down, this is offset by the job opportunities that would open up for those who either lack the capital to open convenience stores or do not have the inclination to go into business for themselves.
2. With their larger buying and better negotiating skills, the large chain stores would certainly drive down suppliers' prices and provided there was sufficient competition between chain stores, it would result in lower prices for consumers, thus increasing overall sales and resulting in larger volumes for suppliers.
3. Unwanted foreign goods coming in through foreign-owned chains is not a valid reason to oppose FDI in retail as the government would continue to retain control over the import policy of the country.

Proponents of FDI further argue that foreign chains would invest in a cold transport and storage chain, as in refrigerated trucks and godowns, greatly reducing wastage of perishables including fruits and vegetables. This is true but so would Indian-owned retail chains. If the setting up of cold chains makes economic sense to foreign-owned chains, it will also make economic sense to Indian-owned ones. Astronomical figures ranging in billions of dollars have been put forth as the cost of setting up a cold chain. The proponents argue that India has neither the money nor the expertise to set up cold chains and only large foreign retail chains like Walmart, Tesco, etc. have the wherewithal to set up expensive cold chains.

The argument is preposterous. We did not wake up one fine morning to find a fully grown Walmart or Tesco with their nationwide cold chains in place anywhere in the world. Nor is it going to happen that way in India, whether FDI in retail is allowed or not. Multiple retail outlet chains will roll out sequentially, region by region, along with the required cold chain facilities. As far as technological expertise is concerned, nothing prevents India from shopping for technology or buying components of the cold chain from other countries. It is not my case that India or any other country should try and do everything itself in a frenzy of import substitution. That is the beauty of foreign trade. Every country can benefit from the better or cheaper goods of another country, but every country must nurture those sectors of its economy where it has an advantage. As far as deep pockets go, it does not even make economic sense for every retail company to set up a cold chain of its own. That would result in an expensive duplication of resources. Cold chains should be a stand-alone business with other businesses, including retail chains paying for the use of their facilities.

The arguments made both for and against the opening up of the retail trade to FDI have nothing to do with allowing FDI in the retail sector. They are rather arguments for and against the setting up of large retail chains in India, whether Indian-owned or foreign-owned. Indian-owned retail chains already exist and operate legally.

A discussion on allowing FDI in retail trade in India must have very different parameters. It must focus on whether the budding Indian modern trade industry has the potential to evolve to world standards; whether it should be protected and nurtured in its infancy so that it can grow to a level where it can set up operations in other countries. If, however, it is believed that Indian companies do not have the potential to develop efficient retail operations, then the discussion should be on whether foreign companies should be let in so that both consumers and suppliers benefit from their expertise.

India enjoys several advantages that can help its companies become among the best in the world in retail trade. Some of these advantages may not appear to be as such at first glance but have the potential to make Indian retail companies amongst the most efficient in the world. India is one of the largest markets and has the ability to harbour many competing retail chains. India has amongst the most disparate buying needs, ranging from the needs of people just above subsistence level to the desires of the affluent. This may seem more of a disadvantage than an advantage, but any retail chain that survives the competition will have learned to handle such complexity. Similarly, India has poor infrastructure in terms of roads and electricity. Again the same logic applies. Successful retail chains in India will learn to manage with poor infrastructure. Should government policies encourage fierce competition between retailers, some of them will surely perish, but the surviving retail chains will have acquired skills not readily mastered in other countries. Also, India has strengths in information technology to help it develop systems to manage, at a lower cost, inventories, purchases and deliveries, all of which are part of the core competencies of a successful retail chain. These skills will make it possible for Indian retail companies to set up operations in a wide range of countries.

In my view, India must not, at this stage, permit FDI in its retail trade. It must instead protect and nurture its own retail companies until they mature, removing impediments to their growth and encouraging open competition between them. It must prevent monopolization or cartelization between a few companies, lest they start behaving like rent seekers and increasing prices without reason, which they would in the absence of competition. It is neither important nor necessary that an Indian retail chain should grow to be a behemoth like Walmart. It is only important that it is large enough to meet the needs of consumers and suppliers and reduce wastage.

The thinking that applies to India and FDI in the retail trade is applicable to all countries and all trades. It is especially true for developing countries which have very few areas of strength but need to move up the value chain in at least some areas so that they can finance imports in other areas. Every sector needs to be evaluated and one of three choices made: if it has the potential to grow to world standards it should be protected and promoted by all means available until it becomes internationally competitive and is able to generate export earnings; if a particular sector has no inherent advantages that can be built upon to make it competitive, it would be best to import those goods; if a sector is developed enough that imports would not swamp the domestic industry they should be let in to encourage competition.

Every country needs to think strategically and not be lured into a feeling of inevitability by the platitudes of multilateral agencies and developed countries that maintain that free trade without restrictions is the best way to prosperity. It is not easy to break away, of course, for considerable pressure is brought to bear upon developing countries that do not fall in line and open up their markets. The pressures range from conditions being attached to loans granted by the World Bank and IMF to one-sided trade agreements to inducements of aid packages and even bribes to decision-makers in developing countries. International trade is not a gentleman's game. However, an effort must be made to exercise all of a country's options, for the stakes are high.

The choice is clear. Either a country develops the ability to move up the value chain in some areas or it will be relegated to being a supplier of primary goods with little control over the pricing of its products. In a developing country, the need to sell at least something is often so great that it is ready to accept the most unfavourable prices and trade agreements. Developing countries that grow coffee and cocoa, for example, get little out of it. Most of the profit generated by these crops comes after the stage of the farm, when these primary products are out of the hands of the growing countries.

When a country is mainly a primary goods seller, it is difficult to start moving up the value chain. It is not impossible, though. Most countries that are today developed economies have done the same. I paraphrase the following from Ha-Joon Chang's book *Bad Samaritans* where Chang refers to Daniel Defoe's *A Plan of the English Commerce* (1728). In the book Defoe describes how the Tudor monarchs, especially Henry VII and Elizabeth I, used protectionism, subsidies, distribution of monopoly rights, government-sponsored industrial espionage and other means of government, intervention to develop England's wool manufacturing industry, Europe's high-tech industry at the time. Until then Britain had been a relatively backward economy relying on exports of raw wool to finance imports. Wool manufacturing was centred in the Low Countries (today Belgium and the Netherlands), where most of the profits from this cloth were made.

According to Defoe, Henry VII sent royal missions to identify locations suited to wool manufacturing. Like Edward III before him, in an attempt to establish an English wool industry, he poached skilled workers from the Low Countries. He increased the tax on the export of raw wool and even temporarily banned its export in order to encourage further processing of the raw material at home. As Defoe emphasizes, Henry VII did not have any illusions as to how quickly English producers would catch up with their sophisticated competitors in the Low Countries. The king raised export duties on raw wool only when the English industry was established enough to handle the volume of the wool to be processed. Henry VII then quickly withdrew his ban on raw wool exports when it became clear that Britain simply did not have the capacity to process all the raw wool it produced. Indeed, it was not until 1578, in the middle of Elizabeth I's reign and nearly a hundred years after Henry VII started the effort, that Britain had sufficient processing capacity to ban raw wool exports totally. Once in place, however, the export ban drove the competing manufacturers in the Low Countries, who were now deprived of their raw materials, to ruin.

Without the policies put in place by Henry VII and pursued by his successors, it would have been very difficult if not impossible for Britain to transform itself from a raw material exporter into the European centre of the wool-making industry. Wool manufacture became Britain's most important export industry. It provided most of the export earnings that financed the massive import of raw materials and food that fed the Industrial Revolution.

Defoe's book shatters the foundation myth of capitalism that Britain succeeded because it figured out the true path to prosperity before other countries—free markets and free trade. In reality England prospered and its industry grew precisely because it followed policies that were the opposite of allowing free imports and free trade.

All countries that are industrially advanced today have in the past followed policies that protected and nurtured their incipient industries. America under British rule was given the full British colonial treatment. It was naturally denied the use of tariffs to protect its new industries. It was prohibited from exporting products that competed with British products. It was given subsidies to produce raw materials. Moreover, outright restrictions were imposed on what Americans could manufacture. The spirit behind this policy is best summed up by a remark William Pitt the Elder made in 1770. Hearing that new industries were emerging in the American colonies, he famously said,' '(The New England) colonies should not be permitted to manufacture so much as a horseshoe nail.' After independence, Alexander Hamilton, America's first treasury secretary, submitted to the US Congress in 1791 his 'Report on the Subjects of Manufactures'.

The core idea of his report was that a backward country like America should protect its industries in their infancy from foreign competition and nurture them to the point where they could stand on their own feet.

In the report, Hamilton proposed a series of measures to achieve the industrial development of his country, including protective tariffs and import bans, subsidies, export ban on key raw materials, import liberalization and tariff rebates on industrial inputs, prizes and patents for inventions, regulation of product standards and development of financial and transportation infrastructure. Although Hamilton rightly cautioned against taking these policies too far, they are, nevertheless, a potent set of policy prescriptions. Were he the finance minister of a developing country today, the IMF and the World Bank would certainly have refused to lend money to his country and would be lobbying for his removal from office.[17]

Hamilton's report was not acted upon to the extent he advocated because at that time American politics was dominated by southern plantation owners with no interest in developing American manufacturing industries. They wanted to be able to import higher quality manufactured products from Europe at the lowest possible price with the proceeds they earned from exporting agricultural products. After the American Civil War and the defeat of the Southern Confederacy, Abraham Lincoln raised industrial tariffs to the highest level in American history, which remained at 40–50 per cent until the First World War. It was only when its own industries were well established that America started lowering tariffs and became an advocate of free trade.

Hamilton's views influenced the German economist Friedrich List (1789–1846), who converted from a free trade between nations position to one that was more focused on the interests of a particular nation. List's theory of 'national economics' differed from the doctrines of 'individual economics' of Adam Smith, who said that individuals acting in their own interest would ensure prosperity and economic growth and the 'cosmopolitan economics' of Jean-Baptiste Say who maintained that 'supply creates its own demand.' List was a forefather of the German historical school of economics and is considered the original European unity theorist whose ideas formed the basis for the European Economic Community which has now evolved to be the European Union.

List contrasted the economic behaviour of an individual with that of a nation. An individual promotes only his own personal interests but a state fosters the welfare of all its citizens. An individual may prosper from activities that harm the interests of a nation. List asserted that economists should realize that since the human race is divided into independent states, 'a nation would act unwisely to endeavour to promote the welfare of the whole human race at the expense of its particular strength, welfare and independence.' Contrary to Smith, he argued that the immediate private interest of individuals would not lead to the highest good of society. The nation stood between the individual and humanity and was defined by its language, manners, historical developments, culture and constitution. This unity must be the first condition of the security, well-being, progress and civilization of the individual. Private economic interest, like all others, must be subordinated to the maintenance, completion and strengthening of the nation. As List put it:

I perceived that the popular theory (Adam Smith's) took no account of nations, but simply of the entire human race on the one hand, or of the single individual on the other. I saw clearly that free competition between two nations which are highly civilised can only be mutually beneficial in case both of them are in a nearly equal position of industrial development and that any nation which owing to misfortunes is behind others in industry, commerce, and navigation must first of all strengthen her own individual powers, in order to fit herself to enter into free competition with more advanced nations. In a word, I perceived the distinction between cosmopolitical and political economy.

List clearly understood the disadvantages an underdeveloped country faces when trying to trade on equal terms with developed nations. He was percipient in his observation that free competition between countries could only be beneficial between equals and that the responsibility of bringing itself up to an equal position lay with the country that was lagging behind. He was a realist and under no illusion that developed countries would in any way aid underdeveloped ones. The economically weaker nations must do all they can to catch up and then trade and compete as near equals to the benefit of both countries.

List's argument was that Germany should follow actual English practice rather than the abstractions of Smith's doctrine. He advocated the enlargement of the Zollverein or German Customs Union which was a coalition of German states formed to manage tariffs and economic policies within their territories. The foundation of the Zollverein was the first instance in history in which independent states had consummated a full economic union without the simultaneous creation of a political federation or union.[18, 19]

Almost all other countries that are industrially advanced today have protected and nurtured their nascent industries until they evolved to world standards. Japan and South Korea are fine examples. Among the industries they have nurtured is the automobile industry. Both countries protected and nurtured their automobile industries for about forty years before seeing any significant results. Both countries today have more than one car manufacturer.

Japan's largest car manufacturing company is Toyota. Toyota was a manufacturer of textile machinery and got into car manufacturing in 1933. In 1939 the Japanese government threw out General Motors and Ford from the country. In 1958, twenty-five years after getting into the business, Toyota exported its first car, the Toyopet, to the US. It flopped. The Japanese government had ensured high profits for its car manufacturers through high tariffs and reserved the home market for them. After the Toyopet debacle and twenty-five years of protecting the automobile industry, many argued that Japan should get out of the car manufacturing business and freely import cars. However, the government and the car companies persevered. After a few more years they started exporting cars of acceptable quality and Toyota's top model, the Lexus, is today a top-of-the-line model, the world over.

The Korean car manufacturing story began in 1955 when a Korean businessman, Choi Mu-Seong, and two of his brothers mounted a modified and localized jeep engine on a US military jeep-style car body made with the sheet metal from a junk oil drum can and military junk jeep parts to manufacture the first Korean car. In 1962 the Korean government passed the Automobile Industry Protection Act to protect its infant industry. Foreign automakers were barred from operating in Korea, except in joint ventures with local businesses. The government's efforts encouraged companies that were established in other businesses to enter the automobile industry and also led to several new start-ups. Some new auto companies were formed in 1962 itself while the Hyundai Motor Company was formed in 1968.

The Hyundai Motor Company grew faster than the others by engaging the services of a group of top foreign managers and engineers, a strategy that is open to all countries that wish to compete internationally in any particular industry or business segment. It took just seven years for Hyundai to produce the first Korea-developed automobile, the Hyundai Pony.[20]

Today Japanese and Korean auto companies not only export cars to most of the world, they have also set up production facilities in other countries, either on their own or in collaboration with local entities. Thus they benefit from the repatriation of funds by way of profits and licence fees and by selling key components to the local manufacturer and other means. None of this would have been possible if Japan and Korea had not protected their infant industries and had just imported cars or permitted foreign auto companies to set up manufacturing facilities in Japan and Korea.

India too protected its auto companies from foreign imports for about forty years. Hindustan Motors was launched in 1942 and Premier Automobiles in 1944. They were soon making cars based on the Morris Oxford and Fiat 1100D models respectively and continued to do so for half a century with minor cosmetic changes. Hindustan Motors and Premier Automobiles formed a virtual duopoly for all car production in India. While the Indian government did not permit car imports into the country, it inexplicably hobbled the industry with price and production controls due to which the companies were unable to improve the quality of their cars.

Prevented from raising prices or trying to increase sales, the only avenue left for Indian car companies to safeguard their earnings was to cut costs. This resulted in shoddier versions of already superannuated cars. Indian consumers paid for these policies by having to wait almost ten years after booking a shoddy car to actually get it. The reason the government gave for production controls was that India was a poor country and there was no market for more cars. This was a strange claim, considering there was a waiting period of years to buy a new car. In that period India was producing about 100,000 cars a year. A couple of decades after opening up the market to foreign companies and removing price and production controls, India was manufacturing 4 million cars a year, mostly for domestic consumption. Perhaps this is a validation of Jean-Baptiste Say's Law which maintains that the supply of goods leads to a demand for them. Of the 4 million cars produced each year in India, only a few are designed and produced in India by Indian-owned companies and may be called Indian cars. Much of the profit generated by the manufacture and sale of cars built by foreign companies finds its way out of the country and amounts to a regular transfer of wealth out of the country. Had the Indian government not wilfully stunted its auto companies while protecting them from external competition, the story could have been very different. Indian auto companies would have been exporting their own cars and setting up manufacturing plants in other countries. Needless to say, when imports and foreign companies were allowed in after forty years of protection, Indian companies and the products they had been making stood no chance at all.

It makes no sense at all for a country to protect its industries through import bans or high tariff barricades and then hamper the growth and development of its own industries. It is like paying a steep price for no benefits achieved. If a country sees a possible advantage in a particular sector and wishes to promote that sector so that it can grow to world standards and eventually export its product, it must do all it can to protect and promote that sector until it comes of age. The essential steps to this is to first protect the industry through import bans or high tariff barriers; the second is to remove import tariffs on all inputs of that industry, such as capital goods or essential components that cannot immediately be manufactured locally; third, the government should not try and second-guess the market regarding price and demand levels; and fourth, the government must remove all restrictions on companies and entrepreneurs wishing to enter that sector, thereby ensuring the highest possible degree of competition. Some companies will certainly fall by the wayside but others will prosper and come up with better products. As the industry matures import tariffs should be gradually lowered to ensure gradually increasing competition against best international products. As the next step, tariffs on capital goods and components pertinent to that industry should be gradually raised to encourage indigenous production of those as well.

I am not advocating a version of an import substitution policy. We all stand to gain from foreign trade. No country possesses all the advantages. I am arguing instead that each country must recognize its strengths and build on them and approach the issue of foreign trade pragmatically and not on the basis of any ideology nor on the platitudes or blandishment of bodies like the World Bank, WTO and IMF and their armies of NGOs and panels of renowned economists who are perhaps only propounding the interests of developed countries. The way to handle the often unsolicited advice forthcoming from these bodies is with a pinch of salt, a healthy dose of common sense and an unwavering focus on the interest of one's own country. Countries need to be more focused on their potential areas of strength until they reach some sort of parity in those sectors.

A country can enjoy several advantages that can help it build a particular industry. The endeavour must be to move up the value chain in those areas where it has an inherent advantage. Very often developing countries do not seriously attempt to do so, for had they done so, they would not have remained developing countries. Some advantages are obvious, such as mineral resources or agricultural potential, but they are not always utilized to their full potential. India has the fourth highest reserves in the world of both iron ore and coal, the chief inputs needed to make steel, and yet India was a net importer of steel between 2007 and 2013. The four West African countries, Ivory Coast, Ghana, Nigeria and Cameroon, together produce over two-thirds of the cocoa beans of the world and yet have no internationally known chocolate industry. Similarly, Europe and North America grow no coffee yet the bulk of coffee processing, branding and marketing and value addition takes place there.

Internal demand for particular goods can also be an advantage. India has one of the largest military and paramilitary forces in the world. It is also the largest importer of arms. It ought to have developed at least some sophisticated armaments and been a significant exporter of those. Data published by the Stockholm International Peace Research Institute in 2015 shows that India accounted for 15 per cent of the world's total arms imports over the preceding five-year period.

There is another advantage a country can have: an educated populace, which can enable it to move up the value chain even in sectors where it has no natural advantages. The better the level of education, the greater possibilities a country has. India with its large number of educated, English-speaking young people was able to use this to grow in the information technology sector where it continues to move up the value chain. Individual Indian companies, some of them start-ups, realized this and started exporting software. The Indian government does not appear to have thought strategically and boosted the sector but it has not hampered the sector either, happy with the foreign exchange it brings in. The government needs to be proactive in other areas where it thinks the country has natural advantages and not expect to be as lucky as it has been in the IT sector. Each fortuitous advantage a country enjoys brings with it the possibility but not the guarantee of moving up the value chain in that area.

Every country needs to identify areas where it can move up the value chain and then marshal its resources towards that endeavour. Developing countries often lack the financial resources to undertake large ventures and may need to look outside for capital. Of the many ways of getting capital into a country, the best is through FDI. It is stable money and the fortunes of the investor are tied to the fortunes of the endeavour. Unlike foreign money coming into the stock market it does not cause euphoria or panic as it rushes in and out without directly contributing to industrial growth. In a developing country, the FDI policy must be oriented towards investments that can raise the future competitiveness of local industries through the introduction of new practices or technology.

A developing country has every reason to negotiate for the best terms when letting in FDI, including tariff rates, the number of branches it allows, local content requirement and minimum export requirements. However, once the terms have been agreed upon they must be adhered to. No matter what terms are offered, provided they are reasonable and offer the prospect of future profits, FDI will always be forthcoming. It may not come from the leading companies of the world but instead from companies that seek to grow in an environment that is protected from the world leaders in that field. This is especially true for a large country like India which promises a large future market. What can deter FDI from coming into a country is lack of security for people and property and lack of stable laws and policies.

Among the worst things a developing country can do is to make itself an unattractive destination for FDI by changing the goalposts once the terms have been agreed upon and the project is under way. India did that recently to Vodafone by levying new taxes with retrospective effect. The Indian government may well have gambled that Vodafone was far too deeply invested to pull out and it may have guessed right. As a consequence of this, however, India will find it harder to attract FDI and will probably have to accede to the terms demanded by the companies bringing in the FDI, when they come at all.

The functioning of the domestic market is very distinct from the way in which a country must carry out its external or foreign trade. Internal trade requires openness, non-restrictive trade policies, free competition which may also lead to the redundancy of older industry which is replaced by more relevant new industry. There must be free movement of labour and capital between industries. Foreign trade, on the other hand, requires strategic thinking with calculated give and take. Foreign trade between nearly equal developed countries is protected and promoted by large trade delegations looking out for their own interests. Trade between developed and developing countries normally favours the developed countries which have far more powerful trade delegations and are aided and abetted by international organizations like the WTO. Any attempt to approach foreign trade with the same strategies as internal trade or vice versa will never lead to a satisfactory outcome.

A different set of concerns arises from common markets and free trade agreements (FTAs). An FTA is when two or more countries are bound by treaty to open up their markets to each other's goods without any import duties or other restrictions. For an FTA or a common market to work to the mutual benefit of all participating countries, the countries must be at a similar level of development, both industrially and also as regards their economic policies. There has been intermittent talk of India joining ASEAN, the FTA of Southeast Asian nations. India would be ill advised to take such a step until it has liberated itself from its stranglehold of red tape, restrictive policies and interminable licensing requirements. Else it will discover that it has opened up its markets and that foreign companies, being more free to act quickly, are running circles around the much slower Indian companies.

The European Union is the largest and longest-standing common market till date. On 1 January 1995, to arbitrarily choose a date which nevertheless gives a twenty-year perspective, there were thirteen countries in that common market, of which four could be said to be less advanced. These were Portugal, Ireland, Greece and Spain. Again to arbitrarily choose a parameter, albeit an important one, the unemployment figures as of February 2014, as put out by Eurostat, are revealing. The average unemployment rate of these four countries stood at 20.025 per cent. The corresponding average unemployment rate of the remaining nine countries was 8.044 per cent. The four less advanced countries do not seem to have gained much from the common market. Certainly their GDP has grown. However, much of the new industry which came up is owned by companies in the other nine countries and a considerable amount of the profit is repatriated back to the home countries.

The European common market went further than other FTAs and gave the right to citizens of all member countries to move freely between countries and own businesses and property in any of the countries. The right to free movement of people looks attractive on paper, but in reality people do not readily relinquish the comfort zone of their own country, nor give up their culture and way of life. People from the advanced countries, finding cheap property in the less advanced countries, bought second homes and some even settled there but very few people from the less advanced countries could afford to buy expensive properties in the advanced countries or even holiday there. The limited movement of people was largely in one direction except for the people who, not finding work in their own countries, moved to the advanced coutries in search of work. As a consequence of foreigners buying homes in the less advanced countries, the price of property in the less advanced countries rose manyfold, making it difficult for locals to buy property in their own areas. The less advanced countries had enjoyed an advantage in agriculture largely because of the lower wages that prevail there. In the case of the European FTA, the advantages in agriculture that were enjoyed by the less advanced countries were diluted by large subsidies given to French and German farmers to protect their way of life. I am sure there must be many people in the less advanced countries who wonder how exactly they have benefited from the common market. FTAs and common markets can only work between near equals and their terms of agreement must be carefully thought through.

The potential benefits of foreign trade are not to be underestimated. At the same time foreign trade must be entered into with clarity of mind and dare I say vision. It is no use relying on platitudes and homilies that say foreign trade is good and increases the wealth and prosperity of a nation. It does increase wealth and prosperity and even the quality of life but not necessarily of those nations that enter it without clarity of thought.

REFERENCES

1. http://en.wikipedia.org/wiki/Pareto_efficiency. Accessed on 3 May 2016
2. http://en.wikipedia.org/wiki/Heat_exchanger. Accessed on 3 May 2016
3. http://en.wikipedia.org/wiki/Predatory_pricing. Accessed on 3 May 2016
4. http://en.wikipedia.org/wiki/European_Union_competition_law. Accessed on 3 May 2016
5. http://en.wikipedia.org/wiki/Price_elasticity_of_demand. Accessed on 3 May 2016
6. http://en.wikipedia.org/wiki/Veblen_good. Accessed on 3 May 2016
7. http://en.wikipedia.org/wiki/Giffen_good. Accessed on 3 May 2016
8. http://www.paulrittman.com/EastIndiaCompany.pdf. Accessed on 3 May 2016
9. http://www.foodnavigator-asia.com/Policy/India-damned-by-food-wastage-report. Accessed on 3 May 2016
10. http://www.globalpost.com/dispatch/news/business/120703/business-insider-India-surplus-grain-going-waste. Accessed on 3 May 2016

11. http:en.wikipedia.org/wiki/Velocity_of_money. Accessed on 3 May 2016
12. http://en.wikipedia.org/wiki/Comparative_advantage. Accessed on 3 May 2016
13. http://en.wikipedia.org/wiki/David_Ricardo. Accessed on 3 May 2016
14. https://fixingtheeconomists.wordpress.com/2014/05/01/arguments-against-free-trade-and-comparative-advantage/. Accessed on 3 May 2016
15. http://en.wikipedia.org/wiki/Singer-Prebisch_thesis. Accessed on 3 May 2016
16. http://en.wikipedia.org/wiki/Washington_Consensus. Accessed on 3 May 2016
17. Ha-Joon Chang, *Bad Samaritans*, (Random House Business Books, 2007)
18. http://en.wikipedia.org/wiki/Friedrich_List. Accessed on 3 May 2016
19. http://en.wikipedia.org/wiki/Zollverein. Accessed on 3 May 2016
20. http://en.wikipedia.org/wiki/Automotive_industry_in_South_Korea. Accessed on 3 May 2016

6

LETTING IT ALL HAPPEN—
CULTURE MATTERS

A CERTAIN DEGREE OF TECHNOLOGICAL SOPHISTICATION NEEDS TO be in place before a nuclear power plant can be set up. We need to understand electricity, pumping systems and radioactivity before we can attempt building one. We started understanding radioactivity only at the beginning of the twentieth century and a few short years later were building nuclear power plants for the first time.

A certain degree of sophistication must also be in place before an economic engine can get going. The sophistication required is not technological in nature, it is cultural. This chapter tries to identify those facets of our cultures that are essential for an economic engine to work.

◆

I am aware that I tread on slippery ground when I talk of culture. I hasten to say at the outset that I do not advocate either the imposition or acceptance of any global culture. Indeed I believe a uniform global culture would rob us of our diversity as a species.

It would rob us of different points of view and diminish the cross-fertilization of ideas, for if everyone behaved in the same manner there would be little to pique our curiosities and give rise to new ideas. The world would be a boring place and travel would lose its purpose. In many ways, we would lose our vitality and become moribund.

Our cultures surround and influence us. Our cultures are not so much a part of us as we are a part of our cultures. They act as moulds into which our personas are poured and they dictate the minutiae of our lives in all sorts of mundane and special occasions. Our culture defines much of us and dictates a great deal of our actions without us being consciously aware of it. It takes a great deal of effort to break out of the moulds into which we have been cast and we usually do not make the effort, preferring instead to try and rationalize even those aspects of our cultures that are not appealing with circular logic resting on statements like 'This is the way it was meant to be,' or 'This is the natural order of things.'

Our culture manifests itself in more ways than I could enumerate, from the mundane to the significant. Our culture determines what we eat, how we eat and with whom we eat. It dictates how we woo our prospective mates, if we woo them at all or if we defer that decision to others. It tells us men how to treat the women in our lives. Do we treat them as possessions, partners or friends? Are we open to interacting with strangers or are we insular? Are we inclined to extend a helping hand or do we look away? Are we wedded to tradition even if it makes no sense in changed times and circumstances? Do we put religion before country or is it the other way around? Our cultures determine how strongly we stand up for our rights or how meekly we surrender them. Do we easily bow to authority or do we wish to understand the reason for any directive?

It is our cultures that sometimes allow us to be so browbeaten that we come to believe and act as if we have no rights. Do we object if our governments put irrational obstacles in our way? If we do not learn to stand up for our rights, we will be steamrolled into submission. What is it, for instance, about the citizens of Delhi that they have allowed themselves to be cornered and coerced into a position where government policy and bureaucratic obfuscation make it practically impossible to run a small family-owned restaurant or bistro? What is it about their culture that makes them accept a situation that requires a convenience store selling basics such as milk, vegetables, cereals, bread, eggs and baby food to require a minimum of 29 licences from nearly 20 different authorities?[1]

There cannot both be a high deference to authority and a strong tendency to stand up for our rights. The two stances are at the extreme ends of the same scale on which we can mark our position at one point only. An individual will only take a stand for his or her rights and by extension the rights of every citizen, if he or she can count on the approval of his or her peers in taking such a stand. Does our culture permit this?

It is our culture that determines how we treat ideas that are contrary to ours and our culture that urges us to either suppress those ideas or to consider them, and whether we tend to punish the originators of new ideas or reward them. How easy or difficult is it for us, in our culture, to defend a position that is unpopular and not part of the accepted stand? It is our cultures that dictate how much obeisance we display for traditional thought processes. The greater that obeisance, the greater the resistance to new ideas.

There is more than one way in which we can try and visualize our cultures. I have already mentioned our cultures as moulds which orient us and our worldview. Another way in which I like to think of cultures is as intricate tapestries, every warp and weft of each one of them shaped by random events in the culture's history and the forceful thoughts and actions of some larger-than- life individuals. The intricate designs of all cultural tapestries vary. New experiences and new thoughts build upon existing designs. Old underlying designs rarely vanish from the tapestry, though some do. Because of the random nature of events that shape them, no two cultures can be identical. We and our thought processes are in many ways the detritus of past generations, past centuries and even past civilizations, and many of the strands that go into the weave of our culture are long-lasting.

This does not mean that change is impossible or that we are permanently tied to those aspects of our culture that ought to change. There are instances of many cultural traits changing rapidly under changed circumstances, for instance, when countries are divided and the two parts start living under differing circumstances. Examples include the division of Germany into East and West. Even after more than twenty years of reunification, the differences are discernible and jokes about 'Ossie' and 'Wessie' mindsets are endemic. The westerners are far more individualistic than the easterners. Other examples are North and South Korea, and India and Pakistan. While South Koreans are among the most highly educated people in the world, and are constantly putting innovative products into the world markets, North Koreans are afraid to share any ideas. Rapid cultural change is possible. Perhaps, therefore, it lies within our power to quickly change those few strands of our cultures, if we can identify them, that will facilitate the setting up and perpetuation of our own economic reactors and power plants.

The list of cultural inputs needed to get the economic reactor and engine running is quite small. It comprises just four cultural strands:

1. The first aspect we need to consider is the orientation of the culture. Does it desire economic progress? If a culture is oriented towards a sense of virtue derived from self-denial

and self-abnegation, if it is more focused on rewards in an afterlife arising from shunning material wealth in this life, if it believes that it is easier for a camel to pass through the eye of a needle than for a rich man to pass through the gates of heaven, then it may not want an economic engine that delivers wealth and creature comforts. If the heroes of a culture are not its doers and achievers but people who are content with little, the culture will not inspire its people to achieve. There must be social sanction, even admiration, for those who by dint of effort and through legitimate means improve their lot in life and create wealth. It may seem strange and perhaps unnatural to many of us that a culture could look down on material progress, but there have been many instances in history where the purity of culture or the purity of a revolution have mattered more than growth and progress.

The definers of purity are often self-appointed custodians of the culture, revolution, administration or any existing status quo. Periods of history when the purity of any thought process was the paramount concern of a culture have never coincided with periods of exponential growth of either knowledge or material wealth.

An essential component of growth is risk. If a culture shuns risk it sacrifices growth. Some risks that are taken will pay off while others will not. Does a culture encourage taking risks by providing a safety net, either as family support or through partnerships with shared risks and rewards or by insuring a risky enterprise? Insurance is a practice with a long history in certain cultures. It is mentioned in the Code of Hammurabi around 1750 BCE and was practised by early Mediterranean sailing merchants. If a merchant received a loan to fund his shipment he would pay the lender an additional sum in exchange for the lender's guarantee to cancel the loan should the shipment be stolen.[2] In more recent times, in 1688 CE, Lloyd's Coffee House in London, where sailors, merchants and shipowners met, became an insurance hub for individual underwriters who took on as much risk as they wanted of a large venture to make possible innumerable voyages of commerce and discovery, contributing to England's growth as a maritime power.[3] A culture that evolves methods that encourage risk taking prospers.

A well-functioning economic engine delivers wealth, knowledge, creature comforts and well-being. It delivers its fruits to all but does not do so evenly. Let us look at the combined current population figures for Europe and North America, both having similar cultures and both with an economic engine running since the nineteenth century, imperfectly perhaps, but running nonetheless.[4] We see that since 1800 the population has increased by over five times, all of which on average eat better, live longer, are healthier, work fewer hours and enjoy creature comforts that were unimaginable in 1800. There can be no doubt that the fruits of the economic engine have devolved upon the entire population. However, some have become wealthier than others. That is the nature of the economic engine. It rewards achievers more than the average person. If a culture sets more store by greater equality of wealth than it does by creation of wealth, it might not want an efficient economic engine, for when nobody has much, there cannot be much inequality.

2. The second essential cultural prerequisite for setting up an economic engine is the concept of personal property. The concept of personal property is the lynchpin that supports the edifice of economic progress. Without personal property, economics as we understand it would not exist. The incentive to implement new ideas vanishes. Adam Smith's invisible hand ceases to work. Individuals would cease their efforts to

maximize their gains because if their gains, and hence their personal property, have many claimants or are violable at the will of the state or society at large, it gives an individual little reason to strive. Property belonging to a family group, a tribe or even a state, as in communist countries, is not personal property. A culture that does not endorse the inviolability of personal property and does not set up mechanisms to protect this cannot have a functioning economic engine.

It is debatable whether, 12,000 years ago, it was property rights that encouraged agriculture or agriculture that forced the emergence of property rights. What is clear, though, is that agriculture would not have existed very long without property rights. The first property rights that came into being must have been about land and its produce. Without these rights it is difficult to see how farmers could be persuaded to work the land and tend to their crops if they were not sure they would enjoy the harvest.

Before the advent of agriculture we were hunters and gatherers with no meaningful property, our total wealth comprising what we could carry as we moved from place to place. While it was agriculture that necessitated land and crop property rights, it was the surpluses generated by agriculture which, when exchanged for other possessions, brought about the need for property rights.

We now know that agriculture first took root and flourished in the Fertile Crescent between the Tigris and Euphrates rivers and at the eastern end of the Mediterranean Sea. It was here that barley and wheat were first domesticated as were dates and figs. The large animals that comprise the bulk of global livestock today, namely, cows, goats, sheep and pigs, were all first domesticated in this region. Many reasons have been advanced as to why farming started in this region and include favourable climate, the abundance of grass with the largest seeds, wild varieties of barley and wheat, and the fact that the area was home to the forebears of modern cows, pigs, sheep, goats and asses. All of these are valid reasons but there were other regions on Earth with favourable climates, wild grass and other large mammals that could have been domesticated. Why did the domestication of these plants and animals all take place in the same small region of the world? Some historians have argued that the spread of hunter gatherers into other areas decimated the large mammals existing there. If that is so, why then did not the hunter gatherer forebears of the eastern Mediterranean people, who had a higher population density, decimate the large mammals living in their area?

I believe the early evolution of agriculture in the eastern Mediterranean region is closely linked with the early evolution of property rights there. Amongst the earliest written records in the world is the Code of Hammurabi, who ruled Babylon from 1792 BCE to 1750 BCE. The code clearly recognizes property rights. The code recognizes many ways of disposing property—sale, lease, barter, gift, dedication, deposit, loan, pledge, all of which were matters of contract.[5] Hammurabi was an Amorite. The Amorites were not native to Mesopotamia but were semi-nomadic Semitic invaders from the west.[6] The concept of Semitic people is derived from Biblical accounts of the origins of the cultures known to ancient Hebrews. Those closest to them in culture and language were generally deemed to have descended from their forefather, Shem (Son of Noah of the Flood). The family of Semitic people comprises many subgroups of largely Middle Eastern origin with shared languages and cultural traits.[7]

It is from the same Semitic people, residing in the area where agriculture first took root, that we have another codification of laws, the Ten Commandments, estimated to have been codified somewhere between the sixteenth and thirteenth centuries BCE. The Tenth Commandment reads, 'You shall not covet your neighbour's house, you shall not covet your neighbour's wife, or his male servant, or his female servant, or his ox, or his donkey, or anything that is your neighbour's.' This along with the Eighth Commandment that reads 'You shall not steal' is an unequivocal stand for property rights. It is a separate matter that when the Commandments were codified wives and servants were regarded as property.

We will probably never know how personal property was regarded at the start of agriculture and can only conjecture that there must have been some permanency of possession to enable farmers to labour and grow their crops, and to improve their land, crops and livestock over time. It is likely that there was some concept of personal property which over time evolved into the Code of Hammurabi and the Ten Commandments. It is also likely that with the spread of agriculture to the nearby areas of the Mediterranean lands, the concept of property spread as well.

With the Ten Commandments becoming an accepted tenet of Christianity, the concept of property spread along with the spread of Christianity. Some strands of culture are long-lasting and span not only generations but civilizations as well. It is difficult to see how, in societies professing to be guided by these Commandments, property rights could ever be completely abjured. Perhaps this cultural strand going back thousands of years is the reason we see property rights better defined and adhered to in societies following Judaeo-Christian traditions wherein the Commandments are enshrined. The other ancient cultures of China, India and Egypt did not follow the same concept of personal property and its inviolability.

China, which was contemporaneous with Hammurabi, was then a collection of various kingdoms. However, there is no record of personal ownership of land. The land belonged to overlords who leased it out. A commonly followed practice was the Ching system, where the overlord divided his property into nine squares which were run by eight families, with the central square cultivated for the benefit of the overlord. In the fourth century BCE, Shang Yang, better known as Lord Shang, the powerful adviser to Duke Hsiao of the state of Qin, gave ownership of land to farmers along with the right to buy and sell it.[8] Lord Shang was in no sense a benevolent man. He was focused on augmenting the power of the ruler and the state and gave out land property rights in an attempt to tie the people to the land and to encourage immigration, as farmers had no property rights in other places. His act so enraged the noble classes who had hitherto been the only owners of land that the next ruler, King Huiwen, ordered the execution of Lord Shang and his family on grounds of fomenting rebellion. Lord Shang's experiment with property rights was an exception in China's history. Thereafter, inviolable property rights eluded the Chinese people into modern times.

Ancient India has had two distinct civilizations—the Indus Valley civilization and the Vedic civilization. The Indus Valley civilization is the older of the two and dates back to about 3300 BCE, contemporaneous with the civilizations of Mesopotamia and ancient Egypt. We know that the Indus Valley civilization had evolved into well-laid-out towns but know little else. Though we have numerous seals with markings on them, we have been unable to decipher them. Nor do we have knowledge of their concept of property rights. The second civilization is the Gangetic plains' civilization or the Vedic civilization and is dated variously between 1700 BCE and 1000 BCE.[9] In this period there was no concept of property rights as life was nomadic.[10] When property rights did arise they were a mishmash of rights. Frithjof Kuhnen, Professor at the University of Gottingen, has researched land tenure and agrarian structure in many places. About the Vedic period, he says: 'Thus at an early period already, there were individual and joint rights. But landed property, as known in the West, did not exist at all. The rights were a privilege granting inheritable utilization rights and included social obligations, especially taking consideration of the village community's interests.'[11]

In ancient Egypt too, individual property rights did not exist: 'In theory all the land seems to have belonged to the gods and to the Pharaoh as representative of Horus. It was regarded as communal property administered by the King and was given to his subjects for usufruction ...' Property rights in Egypt began changing almost 2000 years later. 'The traditional approach to ownership appears to have changed by the late period (664 BCE to 332 BCE), and land had become more like any other possession but the state never relinquished all its rights over it.'[12]

It is in the Fertile Crescent and the area surrounding it that agriculture first took root. It was this area that first domesticated plants and animals. It is in this same area that individual property rights first evolved and were codified. I do not believe this was a coincidence.

It is remarkable that of all the world's ancient cultures only one evolved a culture which recognized, respected and codified personal property rights. It would be simplistic to assert that property rights were the only reason why many species were domesticated in that region but it surely facilitated the undertaking of an activity that spanned generations. We do not know how many other species might have been domesticated in other parts of the world from native flora and fauna had suitable conditions prevailed there. Once the plants and animals domesticated in the Middle East reached these other parts of the world there was no incentive to undertake a lengthy and uncertain venture. Had wheat and barley reached America earlier it is unlikely that an effort would have been made to change the unpromising teosinte wild grass into the maize or corn we know today and we would have been one major crop poorer.

Property rights gave an impetus to farming. However, property rights are not only about land. They are about all possessions. Any class of possession that does not have the security of property rights will not have people wanting to possess it or invest in it. Obviously this applies to all material goods such as livestock, precious metal, coins, houses and goods of every description. It also applies to intellectual property. Where there is no protection of intellectual property rights, innovation withers away. Money in the bank is property too. While the phrase 'money in the bank' suggests reliability, security and safety, these days the world over money in the bank is neither a reliable repository of wealth nor is it safe and secure. It is pilfered through inflation. The higher the inflation, the greater the theft and the less the tendency to hold surplus and savings as money, which is readily investable, thereby negatively impacting growth.

While personal property rights must be sacrosanct in the real world, they cannot be absolute. At times a particular piece of land may need to be acquired when no alternate property can serve the purpose, as, for example, contiguous land needed for railways and highways. In such cases the compensation paid for the land must be significantly more, even double the market value of the land. This will ensure that neither personal property rights are ignored nor progress halted. All other properties may only be sold if the buyer and seller can arrive at a mutually acceptable price.

3. The third cultural input needed to get an economic engine going is cultural tolerance and encouragement of new ideas, especially those that go against current beliefs and trends. There can be no progress if we continue to do the same things in the same manner as before. Every instance of human progress is the result of doing new things or doing the same thing in a new way.

   The longer a practice has been followed, the more entrenched it becomes in the culture and the more stakeholders it acquires. The stakeholders are all those who profit from it directly or have learned to profit from it indirectly. They will always resist ideas that propose a change in the status quo, irrespective of whether or not the proposed change is for the overall good of all.

   Kings opposed ideas that questioned their divine right to rule. The clergy of every religion will always oppose ideas that question the existence of a vengeful being, minutely interested in each of our doings and who needs to be appeased and propitiated through the intercession of the clergy. These ideas have often been put down with a heavy hand with measures ranging from book burning to excommunication to execution. Politicians and bureaucracies will oppose ideas that put their actions under scrutiny or question their right to print money. Trade unionists resist ideas that deplete their membership. Crony capitalists oppose ideas that question the existing set-up. Individuals and groups enjoying government patronage, like NGOs, have a good thing going and would not like to upset the apple cart. The list of people who would oppose ideas is quite exhaustive.

This group of interests is sometimes referred to as the establishment or the orthodoxy. The tools these entrenched interests use to deride new ideas threatening their interests are potent. They include appeals to patriotism, the threat of anarchy, accusations of treason or blasphemy along with threats of ostracism for being an infidel, disrespectful of 'our' culture and way of life, a threat to the profitability and viability of existing businesses and disruptive for employment. This array of powerful tools is sometimes used against fairly innocuous targets such as certain genres of art or music, economic theories, the beliefs of small religious sects or individual mores of victimless sexual behaviour, unusual lifestyles and even mores of attire.

Of the cultural inputs needed to get an economic engine running, perhaps a tolerance of new ideas that may in any way upset the status quo is the most difficult to achieve. Some cultures have achieved this sooner or in greater measure. Currently what is broadly referred to as Western culture has achieved this tolerance and openness to new ideas in greater measure than other cultures. In that culture today, there is little fear of persecution for expressing ideas that go against the mainstream in a wide range of topics including science, religion, politics, economics, food preferences, dress codes and relations between the sexes. Many people may oppose a particular idea, but the liberty to express it in safety exists. This is more than can be said of some other cultures. However, the lessons of history teach us that this openness once achieved may not always remain with us.

At many times in our past there have been periods of outstanding achievement against a backdrop of humdrum human existence. Look, for instance, at the engineering marvel of the pyramids 4500 years ago, more than a thousand years before the start of the Iron Age. Then there were the mysterious dwellers of the Indus Valley civilization who, around the same time as the pyramids were going up, built cities of two-storeyed houses with well-laid streets and drainage systems over a very large geographical area. These are only two of the many instances in history where well-being and progress took place for a considerable length of time. I view these periods as those where everything meshed and at least a crude economic engine must have got going. Sadly, we do not know enough about them to speculate upon either their openness to ideas or the reasons for their demise. Some other periods are better recorded and we have a reasonably good idea of the classical Greek period and that of the Abbasid Caliphs who ruled from Baghdad. I choose these two periods because these two civilizations witnessed hundreds of years of flourishing growth of ideas and prosperity over large geographical areas. It is quite probable that a person living in one of these eras would have assumed that this progress would continue forever and life would only become better with time. We have the advantage of learning from history and being guarded in making a similar assumption.

Greek mathematicians and philosophers, starting about 2600 years ago, ventured forth in a quest for knowledge and understanding in a wide variety of fields, and their thoughts still influence us today. It is difficult to say exactly when this quest started but I like to think it was from Thales of Miletus (620–546 BCE) who among his many achievements made an astounding break from the past in seeking natural causes for all phenomenon, and not divine or supernatural causes. Today this may seem a very obvious stand but in a world where every occurrence was attributed to the whims of various gods it was pathbreaking and in many ways Thales of Miletus can be viewed as the true Prometheus who stole the fire of the gods and gave it to mankind. Thales is also credited with using geometry to calculate the distance of a ship from the shore and of having predicted a solar eclipse leading to the end of a war.

Socrates (469–399 BCE) is credited as being one of the founders of Western philosophy. He taught men to pose a series of questions to arrive at an understanding. This is still known as the Socratic Method. Plato (427 BCE–348 BCE) was a student of Socrates and was, among other things, a political thinker with some of his most famous doctrines contained in his works, *Republic and Laws* and *Statesman*. Aristotle (348–322 BCE) was a student of Plato and a teacher of Alexander the Great. His writings cover physics, metaphysics, poetry, theatre, music, logic, rhetoric, linguistics, politics, government, ethics, biology and zoology. His influence in these fields lasted well into the European Renaissance.

In the fields of mathematics and science, great achievements were made by thinkers like Pythagoras (570–495 BCE) and Euclid (around 300 BCE) and Archimedes of Syracuse (287–212 BCE), a mathematician, physicist, engineer, inventor and astronomer and laid the foundations of hydro-statistics, statistics and explained the principles of the lever. Democritus (460–370 BCE) defined the atom by saying that atoms are indivisible and between them lies empty space. These thoughts pre-date the atomic theories of the current era by 2400 years. Eratosthenes of Cyrone (276–195 BCE) was a mathematician, poet, athlete, geographer and astronomer and invented the discipline of geography. He calculated the circumference of the earth and its distance from the sun with accuracy. His calculation of the distance from the moon was not so accurate. He invented the system of latitudes and longitudes and was the first person to prove that the world was round. Then there was Hero of Alexandria (10–70 CE), a Greek from the Roman province of Ptolemaic Egypt who made a steam engine and a wind wheel 1800 years before the Industrial Revolution and whose works included books on pneumatics, automation, mechanics, metrics and methods of measuring lengths.

The Greeks also gave us democracy and ethics and one of the greatest conquerers of all time, Alexander the Great, who extended Greek influence all the way to India. The Greek Golden Age held sway over vast areas for more than 600 years. The Greeks accumulated great knowledge in all the sciences, philosophy, theatre, poetry and art. Surely during their day in the sun no one could have imagined Europe sinking into the Dark Ages. But it happened and a great economic engine of its time slowed down and finally stopped, giving way to the rise of the Romans to be followed by the Dark Ages.

The decline of this period can be traced to the limits on free thought imposed by the Church. Theology superseded reason and heralded the Dark Age of Europe. The curbs on free thought culminated in 529 CE when the Christian Emperor Justinian I, ruling the Eastern Empire from Constantinople, held that Greek philosophy was 'inherently subversive of Christian belief' and closed all the pagan schools of philosophy, including Plato's Academy, which for 900 years had specialized in the teachings of its founder. To fully enforce his ban, Justinian forbade any non-Christian to teach. As a result nobody in the West would have the opportunity to study the achievements of Greek culture for six centuries. As the eminent historian Will Durant observed, Greek philosophy after eleven centuries of history had come to an end. Growth suffered. According to economic historian Angus Maddison, 'Europe suffered through zero economic growth in the centuries from 500 AD to 1500 AD.' Maddison shows that for a millennium there was no rise in per capita income, which was abysmally low.

Let us now look at the period of the Abbasid Caliphs. It is often impossible to date an era as it is a result of the gradual changing of a people's thought process and creeps up almost imperceptibly. In the case of the Abbasid Caliphate, however, we can safely date the start of the intellectual era to the victory in 750 CE of Abu-al-Abbas as Saffah over the Ummayads and the opening up of their society to non-Arab influence, in contrast to the practice of the Ummayads. Shortly after their victory the Abbasids shifted their capital from Damascus to Baghdad; this period, also known as the Baghdad Caliphate, ushered in the Islamic golden age. The Abbasids were influenced by Quar'anic injunctions and Hadith such as 'the ink of a scholar is more holy than the blood of a martyr', stressing the value of knowledge. During this period the Muslim world became the unrivalled intellectual centre for science, philosophy, medicine and education as the Abbasids championed the cause of knowledge. They established the House of Wisdom in Baghdad where both Muslim and non-Muslim, Arab and non-Arab scholars sought to translate all the world's knowledge into Arabic. Many classical works of antiquity from Greece that would otherwise have been lost were translated into Arabic and Persian and later into Turkish, Hebrew and Latin. The Muslim world at this time was a cauldron of cultures which collected, synthesized and significantly advanced the knowledge and learning gathered from ancient Roman, Chinese, Indian, Persian, Egyptian, North African, Greek and Byzantine civilizations. It is written about this period that the 'Arab Muslims now studied astronomy, alchemy, medicine and mathematics with such success that during the ninth and tenth centuries, more scientific discoveries had been achieved in the Abbasid Empire than in any previous period of history.'

Alas, this glorious period of history also came to an end. Since its establishment in 750 CE the Abbasid Caliphate had actively sought out knowledge and ideas from across the known world, collated them and synthesized new ideas and knowledge from them. Barely four centuries later that culture became insular in its thinking and stopped imbibing ideas from outside its culture. The early Abbasid Caliphs followed the sect of Mu'tazili which supported mind-broadness and scientific enquiry. The tenth Abbasid Caliph al Mutawakil (847–861CE) endorsed a more literal interpretation of the Qur'an and Hadith. The tenth Caliph was not interested in science and moved away from rationalism, seeing the spread of Greek philosophy as anti-Islamic. The Abbasid culture never regained its earlier zest for gaining knowledge and understanding and today its heirs are less open to ideas from outside. Innovations from them have slowed down to a trickle.

The fact that there has been a journey from a position of actively seeking ideas and knowledge from across the world to a position that negates everything from outside the borders of its own culture is indisputable. In 1258 Hulagu Khan, grandson of Genghis Khan, laid siege on Baghdad and destroyed the House of Knowledge along with all the other libraries of the city. Although the Mongol invasion is usually considered the sole cause of the sharp decline of Arab scholarship, by the second half of the thirteenth century Baghdad was far from being the only academic centre in the Abbasid Empire so the destruction of the House of Wisdom was not the sole cause of the decay of Arab scholarship.[13]

Perhaps at some point when restrictions are placed on general enquiry leading to the diminishing of new ideas, a tipping point is reached after which the knowledge and ideas of a culture, instead of continuing to spiral outward in an ever-increasing range and depth, start spiralling inward in a decreasing scope that defends the orthodoxy that placed the restrictions in the first place. It does not matter what the orthodoxy is. It could be in defence of a religion or a culture or patriotic fervour for the security of the state or any predetermined 'ism' like socialism or capitalism and is often in an attempt to recapture some golden era. If we are to avoid this, there must be freedom to both propound and criticize any and every viewpoint.

It is worth reiterating that great economic engines can and do go into decline and it is important to understand their workings and make timely corrections at the right places to prevent just such an occurrence in our times.

Is there a danger or even a possibility that the ebullient culture of the West spreading ever outwards in the quest of greater understandings will reverse its direction? I think there is such a possibility and the concern rests on two recent developments.

The first is the manner in which we store our knowledge

and exchange ideas. It has never been so easy ever before to so easily do both. The twin inventions of the computer and the internet have made the retrieval and search for knowledge child's play and the communication of ideas to one or more people practically instantaneous. Indeed it is such an improvement on previous methods of information retrieval and communication that it has almost completely supplanted earlier systems. There are no more bulky paper filing systems being set up nor is the practice of putting pen to paper in wide use. The humble typewriter can now only be found in antique shops.

The gains to efficiency and productivity have been enormous. Hundreds of millions of people have been easily able to access and exchange ideas in a manner that was unimaginable even a few decades ago. These two inventions are a boon to humanity but possess an Achilles heel. This has been brought to sharp focus for me by the curious case of Edward Snowden.

Edward Snowden, an American computer specialist and a former CIA and NSA employee, leaked details of several top-secret United States and British government mass surveillance programmes to the press. The extent of surveillance was extensive. The agency followed what they call a three-hop query, which means that for every individual who arouses suspicion the NSA can look at data not only for the suspect but for everyone the suspect communicated with and then from everyone those people communicated with.[14] Assuming that a person has on average fifty contacts, one suspect can generate over one hundred thousand surveillances. It would not take many suspects to put every individual under surveillance. Though Snowden leaked details of American and British surveillance programmes, it now appears that the practice is more widespread. Probably all countries with the capability of surveillance are either doing so or in the process of doing so and at the governmental level find nothing wrong with it. This is apparent from the lack of response Snowden got while seeking asylum in 26 countries. The plane of the Bolivian President, which would normally enjoy diplomatic immunity, was denied overflight rights by Spain, France and Italy and searched or attempted to be searched by Austria simply because it was suspected that Snowden was on board with the President.[15] He was not. It is interesting that the two countries which have offered Snowden asylum are Bolivia and Russia. Bolivia does not enjoy the best of relations with America and Russia is not a known champion of civil liberties and freedom of speech. We must suspect real 'politik' to be at work here. Internationally the only spirited criticism to this spying has come from the Brazilian President Dilma Rousseff which may be because she herself has been the target of American surveillance. The focus of her criticism as articulated in her speech in the United Nations General Assembly was about one country spying on another but she did mention privacy briefly: 'In the absence of the right to privacy, there can be no true freedom of expression and opinion and therefore no effective democracy.' Perhaps no country considers the surveillance of its people and the suppression of communication to be of any consequence to its well-being.

The information collected by the surveillance agencies is from email, video and voice chats, videos, stored data, VoIP, file transfers, videoconferencing, notifications of target activity, logins, etc., online social networking details and special requests. Apart from when we talk face-to-face and when we put pen to paper, all of these are the means we use to communicate our thoughts and ideas to each other. These are also the means we use to store our information and record our musings and ideas for another day. These are also the ways through which our search for knowledge or idle searches for bits of information are on record and may be scrutinized at will. Our very thoughts are now an open book. George Orwell was astoundingly prescient when in 1949 he wrote *Nineteen Eighty-Four*, long before the advent of the personal computer or the internet, imagining the existence of Big Brother, thought police and thought crime. He may have been off by 25 years but 1984 is today upon us. When the book was first written it was considered a work of science fiction. We were shocked and a little frightened by it but did not really believe that it could come to pass. Surprisingly, now that it is upon us we are sanguine.

Should these developments worry us beyond concern for the loss of privacy and the possibility of harassment or blackmail for some of our views? It is difficult to say. Before the invention of the printing press there were only a few laboriously handwritten copies of any book. These few copies were relatively easy to ban or burn. The printing press made it possible to print numerous copies of any book. Once the book was out and in the hands of many people it became increasingly difficult to seek out and burn all the copies. The banning and burning of a book became largely symbolic. The thoughts in a book, once it was printed and circulated, could not really be lost due to book banning or burning. It is ironic that the twin breakthroughs of the personal computer and the internet which gave the world unprecedented connectivity and the ability to exchange knowledge and ideas could have combined to create a vulnerable jugular vein through the servers of a few internet service providers, which can by one way or another, be accessed and controlled.

The position of the world's governments, and they are all in this together, as evidenced by the lack of any support for Edward Snowden or lack of any criticism for the act of the US government spying on American and other citizens appears to be: 'You have freedom of speech but we will eavesdrop on what you have to say or wish to hear and record it forever. If need be we can go back to it. However, we are nice people and we will not use your recorded words against you unless you do something really bad, which of course is something we will define.' This is not a very reassuring statement for those who use the internet for the exchange of ideas.

Regardless of the intentions of any government, we are creating the ability to hamper the access to stored knowledge and the flow and exchange of ideas. Seldom if ever have capabilities been created and not used. All it needs is a few cases of persecution of people with unpopular ideas for confidence in the system to dwindle and for the exchange of ideas to slow down. When we exchange ideas we do so with confidantes and do not broadcast them until we are ready. Should we come to believe that ideas, which we wish to exchange with a specific person, could become common knowledge for anyone, the exchange of ideas will diminish. New ideas come from anarchic thought processes, in the sense that they break from the status quo and have the potential to upset vested interests.

The openness to new ideas that diverge from existing beliefs and practices is not a very common aspect of cultures. It has only managed to emerge at a few times and places in all of human history. It is a flame that is not only difficult to light but is also easy to snuff out. Just as the culture of the Abbasid Caliphate had turned inwards after centuries of growth and discovery and started rejecting ideas from outside, the same thing happened in Europe centuries earlier. With the Church gaining influence in Europe and projecting its beliefs forcefully, theology superseded reason, heralding the advent of the Dark Ages of Europe.[16]

The Greek period and the Abbasid Caliphate, eras of great human growth of knowledge and living standards, each lasting centuries, both came to rapid ends. The chief reason in both cases was an intolerance of ideas from outside the accepted way of thinking and the consequent stifling of the flow of ideas. The Graeco-Roman period of growth lasted 1100 years and the Baghdad Caliphate period of growth lasted 400 years. Our current period of growth has lasted 500 years if we measure it from the start of the European Renaissance and 200 years if we measure it from the start of the Industrial Revolution. If we put impediments in the flow and exchange of ideas, could our period of growth also come to a relatively quick end? I do not know. It is not my contention that we can afford to ignore security issues that threaten our well-being but we need to be careful not to impede the flow and exchange of ideas. A Big Brother society is not one that encourages this.

We must be careful to not throw out the baby along with the bathwater. The surveillance of our communications was prompted by the events of 9/11. It would be tragically ironic if in response to these events we ensured that the perpetrators of 9/11 turned out to be wildly more successful, in their attempt to destroy a way of life that was open to ideas and irreverent to dogmas, than they could ever have imagined. Their target was not the buildings they destroyed and the lives they took but it was the very existence of a culture that held no brief for unquestioned beliefs, and which was an affront to them and something quite alien to their own set of beliefs. Could our response to the events of 9/11 lead to the snuffing out of open thought processes?

Ours is not yet a world that is completely intolerant of new ideas. Many countries and cultures like to think of themselves as open societies where any set of beliefs may be expressed but almost every culture is in the process of creating shibboleths that may not be challenged. Some of these shibboleths are more common to certain cultures than to others. They include the notion that governments can keep spending more money than they possess for prolonged periods with impunity and without adverse consequences, the idea that a welfare state which increasingly tries to subsidize all aspects of our existence is the only way forward, the belief that we lack the wisdom to look after ourselves and must be protected from ourselves by a paternalistic state, the conviction that it is wrong to criticize another's beliefs even if we find them harmful for fear of offending and that political correctness is always a virtue.

These and other shibboleths do not point towards a tolerance of new ideas. It does not point to a situation where ideas are constantly being exchanged and triggering new ideas in turn. It is the idea reactor that is the heart and the mainspring of the economic engine. Without this driving force the engine will stop. The last couple of decades may turn out to represent the last bright flare before the candle of creativity flickers out. A greater fear is that in this interconnected world, if the flame dies out it will die out everywhere. In the past, when the flame died out in Europe with the onset of the Dark Ages, it was rekindled in the Middle East of the Baghdad Caliphate, where it burned brightly for centuries and eventually helped reignite the same flame in the West. The happenings in Europe and the Middle East did not affect faraway China, which continued along its own path. Today there are no faraway places. What happens anywhere in the world, especially in the dominant or more creative parts of it, affects the rest of the world. For good or for bad.

The fourth cultural input required for an economic engine is a desire to understand the world. Each of the three well-recorded periods of history, including the present, that witnessed prosperity and growth of knowledge lasting hundreds of years, started with an effort to understand the world in rational terms. Thinkers like Thales of Miletus who sought to explain the world without reference to mythology and Socrates who questioned everything set the tone for the Graeco-Roman period. The Abbasids who actively sought knowledge and understanding from every known source set the ball rolling for the Islamic Golden Age. Both cultures regressed when they became insular and reverted to orthodox thinking.

Our own current period of growth started with the Renaissance, when long-accepted dogmas started to be questioned.

More faith was reposed in experimentation and rational thinking than in handed-down wisdom, whether from the Church or ancient texts. It will be for future historians to write about what will happen with our period of growth. We can, however, be forewarned by history and continue to rejuvenate our culture by keeping it open to the generation, release and implementation of new ideas.

With these four cultural strands in place, namely, social sanction for individual prosperity, respect for personal property, openness to new ideas and developing an ability to objectively evaluate new ideas, the economic engine will start functioning.

How long and how smoothly the economic engine functions depends on just one other cultural input which I will come to after we have examined what happens after the economic engine is running. Once the economic engine starts functioning, wealth will be created. While the whole community benefits from the wealth created by the economic engine, the wealth is not evenly spread. There is an uneven agglomeration of wealth, a significantly different situation to ancient hunter gatherer societies which had no wealth and hence no uneven distribution of wealth. This was also largely true at one time of rural farming villages where, apart from their dwellings, the villagers all had meagre belongings. All cultures have stories of the good old times when there was no need to lock the door if one went out. The reason for that, I suspect, was less the sterling moral fibre of the neighbours as the fact that there was little temptation. In nature, wherever there is an agglomeration of assets, predators emerge. This is true of the microbial, plant and animal worlds. It is true for economic assets too. If disproportionate gains can be made with little effort and by running a small risk, the risk will certainly be taken. It does not matter if the actions of those who would usurp the fruits of the economic engine for themselves are legal or illegal, ethical or unethical. That is of secondary importance. What matters is how we respond and how we augment the risk for those who would subvert the workings of the economic engine by appropriating its fruits and eliminating the incentive to prosper. There are two classes of people who could try and subvert the economic engine—non-state players like individuals, companies or other economic entities and state players, including governments and their bureaucracies. There is one big difference between the two. Non-state players usually break laws as they try and take unethical advantage of the system. State players seldom break laws as they are the ones who make the laws and they make laws that facilitate their purpose. Our responses to both sets of players need to be different.

Let us first consider non-state players who seek to take advantage of the system. Imagine a culture that has achieved universal adherence to ethical behaviour. In this society every individual and entity behaves ethically and within the ambit of the law and expects everyone else to do the same. Trust within this society is high and transaction costs low. Should a single individual or entity decide to take advantage of the trust reposed in the system, the returns to that individual or entity will be high and at the cost of others. If the party breaking the law does not have to bear any adverse consequences for its unlawful behaviour, it will induce others to emulate its behaviour and the system, based on universal trust, will rapidly break down. A system based solely on the good intentions of all is unstable. If there are consequences to bear for unethical behaviour, such behaviour is less appealing and diminishes.

In modern societies, consequences imposed upon those who seek to take advantage of the reposed trust and break the law or accepted practices are delivered through the justice delivery system. The factors that matter in determining the efficacy of any punishment as a deterrent to unethical behaviour are the probability of punishment, the speed with which that punishment is meted out and the extent of punishment. There is an inverse correlation between these factors and the frequency of unethical behaviour. The higher the probability of punishment, the greater the speed at which punishment is implemented and the more measured the punishment, the less the frequency of the laws broken. While crime may never completely stop, with any of the above three factors in place only a certain level of crime will exist. For potential law breakers under a particular set of conditions for each of these factors, an Evolutionary Stable Strategy (ESS) for breaking the law will evolve. If the environment for any or all of the above three factors changes, so too will the level of crime.

ESS is a concept expressed by John Maynard Smith in 1972 using the branch of Mathematics known as Game Theory. ESS was first used to understand animal behaviour and has since been widely used in behavioural ecology and economics and has also been used in anthropology, evolutionary psychology, philosophy and political sciences. ESS is defined as a strategy which, if most members of a population adopt it, cannot be bettered by an alternative strategy. Selection will penalize deviation from it. One of Smith's hypothetical cases is with regard to aggression and the fighting strategies of individuals within a species. He termed the two strategies hawk and dove. (The names refer to conventional human usage and have no connection to the habits of the birds from which the names are derived. Doves are in fact rather aggressive birds.) Hawks are aggressive and always fight when they encounter another individual. Doves run away in the face of any aggression. When a hawk encounters a dove, the dove runs away and the hawk wins. When a hawk encounters another hawk both fight and are both injured. When a dove encounters another dove neither will fight but both posture threateningly until one gives up, resulting in loss of time for both and victory for one. While an all-dove population is better for the average individual than an all-hawk population, neither condition is evolutionarily stable. In an all-dove population a single mutant hawk that arises will gain great advantage and multiply. In an all-hawk population the cost of fighting will be so great for the fighters that a single mutant dove will gain by avoiding injury and it will multiply.

Smith examined other strategies too. A more complex strategy is called Retaliator. A retaliator plays like a dove at the beginning of every fight. That is, he does not mount an all-out savage attack like a hawk but engages in a conventional threatening match. If his opponent attacks him, however, he retaliates. A retaliator is a conditional strategist. His behaviour depends on the behaviour of his opponent. In other words, a retaliator behaves like a hawk when he is attacked by a hawk and like a dove when he meets a dove. When he meets another retaliator he plays like a dove.

Another conditional strategist is called the Bully. A bully goes around behaving like a hawk until somebody hits back. Then he immediately runs away.

Yet another conditional strategist is the Prober-retaliator. A prober-retaliator is basically like a retaliator but he occasionally experiments in a brief escalation of the contest. He persists in his hawk-like behaviour if his opponent does not fight back. If, on the other hand, his opponent does fight back he reverts to conventional threatening like a dove. If he is attacked he retaliates just like an ordinary retaliator.

If all these five strategies are turned loose upon one another in a computer simulation, only one of them, the Retaliator, emerges as evolutionarily stable.[17]

These strategies apply as much to animal as to human strategies. A retaliator lives peacefully without attacking anyone until attacked upon which he counter attacks forcefully. In today's world we do not generally go about physically attacking other people but we do attack through economic and legal means. If we are to ensure the continued running of the economic engine, we must, as a culture, aim for a set of sensible laws that balance crime with punishment. We must have effective policing capability enabling us to retaliate and ensuring that those who attack us are brought to book. We must ensure that we have sufficient courts with procedures that enable the speedy delivery of retaliation. Justice delayed is justice denied may well be true but a more pithy statement could be: 'Justice delayed is simply not a good enough deterrent.'

Let us now consider state players and how they can jeopardize a working economic engine. Let us start at the very beginning. Before the start of agriculture when we were all hunter gatherers, we were an undifferentiated society and we were all pretty much equal. The size of our bands was a few dozen people, related by birth or marriage. If there was a leader, it was not someone who had come to it based on heredity, but rather on the basis of personal attributes of strength, intelligence and personality.

Decision-making and conflict resolution within the band was by mutual discussion. Probably all humans lived in bands until at least 40,000 years ago and most continued to do so until as recently as 11,000 years ago, when agriculture was established.

As the bands grew in size and became tribes, numbering in the hundreds and probably centred round a fixed village, their leadership pattern was still largely unchanged and egalitarian. Perhaps decision-making devolved upon an informal group of elders or heads of individual family units. There was no centralized or hereditary leadership yet, nor bureaucracy or taxes. The next stage in the growth of communities was from tribes to chiefdoms numbering in the thousands. Apart from a few places that were abundant in natural resources like rich fishing grounds or teeming animal life, this was only possible with intensive farming which yielded ample surplus. This stage led to many changes in the structure of the community. For the first time in human existence not everyone needed to be directly involved in food production, either through hunting-gathering or through subsistence farming. A division of labour became possible. The growers of food willingly exchanged some of their surplus for better tools, weapons and clothes than they themselves could make. They also exchanged their surplus for other artefacts including jewellery and objects of art and, who knows, perhaps even a song or a dance, enriching all their lives.

There were other claimants to the surplus too. First there were the chiefs who promised to protect the farmers but needed some of their surplus to feed themselves and the soldiers they employed. Then there were storytellers who told bewildering tales of ghosts and evil spirits and ancestors' spirits that needed to be placated and rain gods and fertility gods and war gods that needed to be pleased all through the intervention of storytellers. Once the chiefs had been accepted by the community their bargaining for surplus quickly turned to coercion. The storytellers continued to confound with stories of increasing detail. The chiefs and the storytellers realized they were natural allies. The storytellers legalized the position of the chiefs by indicating that this was the way the gods wanted it and the chiefs in return gave gifts to the storytellers. The positions of the chiefs and the storytellers, both being lucrative, soon became hereditary.

The changes to social structure during the period when chiefdoms existed were seminal and set the tone for the future. Decision-making became centralized and hereditary. Bureaucracy came into existence and enforcement of laws and conflict resolution were centralized while laws were centrally promulgated. Taxes by way of tribute started being levied and forcibly collected. The chief and those closely associated with him started living better than the rest and luxury goods began to be produced for the elite. Organized religion came into being and justified the kleptocracy of the leadership. Division of labour became possible and artisans and craftsmen started making a living without having to farm. Ironically, the farmer who first made the growth of population in a limited area possible and generated the surplus which led to the division of labour (the chieftains, the priesthood, the bureaucracy) and creation of luxury goods all possible, did not find himself anywhere near the top of the social dispensation. These changes must have taken place over several generations and the sequence of events leading to them probably varied from tribe to tribe. However, the fact that these changes took place is inescapable. I came across these thoughts on the evolution of bands to tribes to chiefdoms in Jared Diamond's book *Guns, Germs and Steel*, and was struck by the plausibility of his conjecture.

As the population of the chiefdoms increased from the thousands to hundreds of thousands located in many centres of population in towns and cities in addition to the original villages, chiefs became kings and kingdoms and the state came into being. The states were mostly ruled by kings and decision-making was centralized, the average householder having no say in matters that affected him. Bureaucracy increased and a monopoly of both force and information was now wielded by the state. Taxes were established as an essential part of life. A large consideration in judging whether a king or government was good or bad was if the taxes they levied were considered reasonable or excessive. Grandiose public architecture, including palaces, to which the common man had limited if any access, and better than average residences for the functionaries of the state became common.

The division of labour was complete and starting with the upper layers of society, which most rewarded its members, such as kings, politicians and bureaucrats, vocations became largely hereditary, resulting in the stratification of society. A search for political families reveals a list comprising virtually every country in the world from Albania to Zimbabwe and including every hue of political dispensation from dictatorship to democracy.[18] I have not been able to locate any list of either bureaucratic families or senior service families but anecdotal evidence leads me to believe that these offices too, if not directly hereditary, were largely shared by members of a ruling class.

When in any country political families, influential bureaucratic families and wealthy business families coalesce and morph into one elite entity, liberty and freedom may be at an end and any existing set of affairs beneficial to the elite perpetuates itself. It would seem, in the upper echelons at least, the much reviled Indian caste system is alive and thriving the world over and has been so for a very long time. This caste system may not be completely impermeable and does allow rank outsiders to ingress from time to time but it is followed often enough for us to recognize it as one. Perhaps just enough ordinary folk were able to join the elite to maintain the illusion that the position was not hereditary.

This may be the natural order of things, in the sense that wherever in nature there is abundance, organisms evolve and multiply to take advantage of it. The abundance that the ruling classes thrived upon was first the surplus produced by the farmers and later the surpluses generated by trade and industry. This is not to imply that the rulers did nothing in return for the producers. Indeed the producers could not have prospered without the rulers, who provided, among other things, protection from outsiders, whether brigands or other states, and the necessary administrative functions including law and order. It was in many ways a symbiotic relationship.

Symbiotic relationships are very stable relationships until one of the partners starts growing excessively to the detriment of the growth or survival of the other partner. When that happens the symbiotic relationship becomes unsustainable leading to the collapse of the system within which the relationship exists. Our bodies are host to millions of microbes of many strains, the workings of many of which are not yet fully understood. It is estimated that there are ten times as many microbes in and on our bodies as there are cells comprising our bodies. We have symbiotic relationships with many of these microbes.[19] When any of these microbes start growing uncontrollably and consume most of the nourishment available to the system, the body falls sick.

In human societies too, when too many resources are cornered by the ruling or administrative class, leaving little for producers and consumers, the system ceases to function. Dictatorships and communist regimes where most of a country's resources are mobilized by the state are examples of this. This eliminates both the ability and the incentive for their citizens to pursue ideas. As a result no communist economy thrived until China reintroduced personal property.

There are 195 countries in the world (by one reckoning). It is impossible to make any statement about them that would be true for all. However, it is possible to make general statements that are in keeping with the flow of history and are representative of most if not all countries. As the size and complexity of societies grew from chiefdoms to kingdoms and the state, the rulers assumed greater power over the lives and activities of their citizens than the chiefs had. Ownership of all unutilized land passed over to the state. Taxation, over which the average citizen had little say, was enforced through a multilayered bureaucracy and a monopoly of force by the state. The ideology of the state was enforced largely through neuro-linguistic programming and selective use of history. The state with its current ideology was itself made an object of veneration. Objectivity became a victim, as witnessed by the acceptance of completely opposing ideologies whether about economics, religion, morality or the interaction between the sexes, by large populations of different countries—all with equal fervour, as we can easily see by studying them.

Even as the power of the kings grew and increased its stranglehold over the general population, a cultural strand from ancient Greece resurfaced and attempted to change the order of things. Democracy, which had earlier been practised in ancient Athens and some other parts of the Greek world and in Rome until the Republic gave way to emperors, starting from Augustus in about 27 BCE, came back as an idea to be taken seriously. Events such as the signing of the Magna Carta in 1215 CE, the Bill of Rights in 1689, the American Declaration of Independence in 1776 and the French Revolution in 1789–92 weakened the idea of the absolute power of hereditary kings and their divine right to rule. These were acts of courage against legitimate but oppressive rulers and point towards courage as an essential cultural strand in maintaining the freedoms that permit the setting up of an economic engine.

The kings have all gone now and where they remain they are merely figureheads personifying the state. They have been replaced by politicians. The rest of the system remains much the same. It is now the politicians along with their bureaucracies who have the right to tax us as they see fit and enjoy a monopoly of force. This new dispensation is very recent in terms of cultural evolution and is still evolving, hopefully in the direction of a more stable and egalitarian system. It is interesting to note that even a century ago kings were important enough for the assassination of Archduke Franz Ferdinand of Austria, in 1914, to trigger the First World War.

Another casualty to the change from divinely ordained kings to democratically elected politicians has been the decline in the fortunes of priesthoods. Politicians, unlike kings, do not need to pander to priests for their endorsement of a divine right to rule. They need to pander to their electorate who will vote for them. In the few countries where the rulers are still beholden to the clergy for their legitimacy, the clergy is still influential. Saudi Arabia and Iran are two countries that come to mind.

In democracies, we have been seduced. We have neglected to teach ourselves and our children about economics. I dare say most of our elected representatives know little better than us and when they make extravagant promises, they actually believe they can deliver on those promises by more deficit financing. And we, thinking they know better than we do, vote them into power. We tend to vote for the candidates who tell us the most alluring tales. The painful fact is that with inflation induced by deficit financing driving up the price of everything, the poor are made poorer still and the rich made richer because they own assets, other than money, which often appreciate more than the general rate of inflation. Most of us have to work harder and put in longer hours to try and maintain our standard of living. At times we hearken back to gentler times when leisure was more common, to a time of single-income families when one salary was enough for a family. We bemoan the passing of an era when we had more time for social interaction, without understanding the reasons for the change. A large part of the change can be attributed to inflation, when no amounts of savings ever seem enough and we constantly strive for security. We often buy on debt, fearing that, with rising prices, should we wait for our savings to accumulate, we may not be able to later buy what we desire. Inflation stoked by deficit financing has put all of us, except the very rich who profit from inflation, on a treadmill, where we need to keep running to stay where we are or we may slip into impoverishment.

I do not in any way wish to be disparaging of democracy. It is probably the best and the most empowering way to govern ourselves. However, having the power to govern ourselves wisely or not so wisely, rationally or irrationally, we must be careful. We need to keep our wits about us.

Compared to the period under monarchies, the period under politicians has seen a vast burgeoning of the bureaucracy. This is not surprising. Politicians at various levels are far more numerous than any royal family and consequently need more bureaucrats to look out for them and their interests. Their interests include rewarding themselves through high salaries and perks of office, exercising power beyond the pale of the law and accepted behaviour, and retaining office by trying to get re-elected by pandering to different categories of voters. They are unmindful of the resentment they cause and the resulting divides in society. Indeed, perhaps these divides suit their purposes for they prevent the citizenry from getting together and seeing through their machinations.

The bureaucracy is a willing handmaiden to politicians. He who pays the piper calls the tune, and politicians pay the piper. They are the ones who create the jobs by creating ever-increasing ministries, agencies and departments and woe betide the bureaucrat who does not toe the line; his or her career does not proceed smoothly after any show of dissidence from the political stance, whether that stance is made public or not. Politicians have also created a class of quasi bureaucrats by appointing consultants, commissions, contractors and NGOs that are usually funded directly or indirectly by the government. In cases in which NGOs are funded totally or partially by governments, the NGO maintains its non-governmental fig leaf by excluding government representatives from membership in the organization. Quasi bureaucrats are even more pliant than regular bureaucrats. Today in most countries while it is not very easy for a government to fire an uncooperative bureaucrat, it is very easy for it to cut off funding to an inconvenient consultant or NGO. In 2009, India was estimated to have around 3.3 million NGOs, just over one NGO per 400 Indians and many times the number of primary schools and primary health centres in the country.[20]

The relationship between the political class and the bureaucracy is a symbiotic one. Working in tandem, they both thrive, increasing in number and in power at the cost of the common citizenry. The cost to the citizenry is twofold. The first is that the monetary cost of maintaining the increasing number of politicians and bureaucrats reduces the money available for other needs. The second is the need of the politicians and bureaucrats to emphasize their power by increasing the complexity of all procedures, often for no good reason. Given the fact that almost every country maintains a vast army of politicians, bureaucrats and quasi bureaucrats, I think we might benefit greatly if we agreed to continue maintaining them, provided many of them stayed home and did nothing. That should ease the complexity of often unnecessary procedures. Of course it would be better if we employed fewer of them in the first place. I do not say this either in jest or with sarcasm. All of us can think of some functionaries of the state who serve little purpose other than complicating procedures and generally hampering us with no benefit to anyone. However, they are unlikely to agree with this. It is necessary for them to project power. This can best be seen in India where even relatively minor minions of the state, both politicians and bureaucrats, strut about in cars with beacon lights, much like police cars or ambulances, generating awe among the common citizenry.

With the ever-increasing concentration of resources and power with the state, is it inevitable that the politician–bureaucrat combine will continue to grow and increasingly tie up the economy in so much red tape that growth will cease and the vast majority of people will see a depletion of their little fortunes and a decline in their standards of living? Is it inevitable that cultures that were once exuberant, giving continuous rise to new ideas and ventures, will simply grow old and wither away? Is the untrammelled growth of the state a precursor to the stagnation and decline to follow? It is difficult to see how in a situation in which savings and hence investable capital are continually depleted through inflation and the state tries to control the thought processes that lead to ideas, anything else could possibly happen.

Perhaps the process of an overreaching state leading to a collapse of the economic engine is not entirely inevitable. My measured optimism is based on some relatively recent developments in most of our societies. There are three such developments which when considered together hold the possibility of restricting the state.

The first is that instead of justice being dispensed by the chief or king, it is now dispensed by salaried judges acting according to the laws of a constitution or a body of common law. The judiciary is a major line of defence against an encroaching state and we as citizens need to strengthen the judiciary by ensuring its independence from the politician–bureaucrat combine. It must not, however, be shielded by any 'Lese Majeste of the Law' rules and we must not let any contempt of court rules prevent the reporting and criticism of judgements. The judiciary must be free and independent and not dependent on funds from the government for its functioning. But it must be accountable to the citizens of the country.

The second development is the emergence of a free press. The freedom of the press varies from country to country and nowhere is it completely free from the control of the powers that be. During the period when we were ruled by chiefs and kings, two of the instruments they employed to exert their control over us were a monopoly of force and a monopoly of information. States still maintain an effective monopoly over force but their monopoly over information has begun to unravel.

The unravelling began with the private publishing of news. It grew with international newspapers where one country's secrets could be safely published in another country and was aided by investigative reporting and insightful interviews on television and finally speeded up with the advent of the internet and easy dissemination of news and information that would earlier have been suppressed by the state. Julian Assange and Edward Snowden are certainly not the last people who will reveal embarrassing details about different governments and countries.

Currently a war for the control of information is under way. America is doing everything it can to get custody of Assange and Snowden with the intention of meting out exemplary deterrent punishment to them both. America just happens to be the country that was exposed, but it is certainly not the only country which would like to keep things secret from its own citizens. America also happens to have one of the most elaborate security procedures in place and yet could not prevent the leakages. Such exposés are likely to occur in other places too. Every such exposure weakens a government and forces it to change some practices and make further concessions to its citizens. Governments are responding by putting whatever restrictions they can on the material being put out on the net and sometimes even access to it. This war for the control of information is as important a war as any that has been fought. For the first time since chiefdoms came into being about 7500 years ago in the Fertile Crescent, there is a possibility that most information will be accessible to those other than the ruling elite. Depending on which way this war goes, we could have either a more egalitarian society with a well-functioning economic engine or a more totalitarian society with a stalling economic engine. Governments all over the world will try to curb access to information on any grounds they can think of, ranging from morality to cultural identity to patriotism and we as citizens should be wary of this.

The third development that may work towards a more egalitarian society is the movement towards universal education. As recently as 1900 CE only a few countries in Western Europe and Australia had a 90 per cent literacy rate. The USA and Canada had a literacy rate between 70 per cent and 90 per cent. Eastern Europe had rates between 50 per cent and 70 per cent. The rest of the world, including Asia, Africa, Mexico and most of South America, had literacy rates below 30 per cent.[21] Today, with a few exceptions, literacy rates the world over are in excess of 80 per cent.[22] But the quality of education leading to these literacy rates is patchy. As discussed in Chapter 3, a meaningful education is one that makes us think and understand and lets us access and evaluate information and new ideas. Just a couple of centuries ago, education and literacy were the preserve of the elite. A universal good education cannot but open up other preserves of the elite, leading to a more egalitarian society.

While these three relatively new strands of development, namely, an independent judiciary, a free press and universal education, may tend to work towards limiting the growth and power of the politician-bureaucrat combine, there is a cultural thread needed to tie these developments together. It is courage. The courage to stand up against the erosion of our liberties, the courage to stand up against being steamrolled by a powerful state into a subservient position, the courage to protest against unreasonable laws, the courage not to cede our freedom to act in our interest in exchange for an overprotective government which will try and make us dependent on it, the courage to be counted with our fellow citizens when they take a stand with which we agree. As with all organisms, it is the natural tendency of the politician-bureaucrat combine to grow as much as it can and it should be our endeavour to restrict that growth to sustainable or desirable levels.

In nature the growth of all organisms is limited in two ways. The first is when organisms are attacked by other organisms and their numbers kept down. An organism's position in the food chain will determine the number of predators it faces. If an organism is at the top of the food chain it faces no natural predators. A lion in the savannah faces no natural predators. The second way organisms are limited in growth is by the food available to them. The reason why the savannah is not crawling with lions is because there are only a limited number of gazelles and other wildlife for them to eat and those in turn are limited by the grass and water available to them.

For millennia, the chief, the king and now the politician–bureaucrat combine have been at the top of the food chain. With monopoly over both force and information it has had little to fear from others in society. It is only recently, with the loosening of the information monopoly, that politicians have begun to be a little wary. However, the only choice a voter has is between electing one set of politicians over another. There is often little to differentiate the two. Their policies are often quite similar. They treat the elections as a game of musical chairs, patiently awaiting their turn in government. Their monopoly over force remains.

The constraint of a limited food supply was once applicable to the growth of the politician–bureaucrat combine. What they could spend on themselves and on the promises made to voters was limited by the amount of taxes they could collect. True, some countries did at times resort to deficit financing, but they acted alone and soon suffered the consequences of their indiscretions. Their currencies devalued, inflation grew while exports became competitive, rising wages and the cost of expensive imports pushed up prices and unemployment increased. The resulting hardship induced one of two behaviours in governments. They either set about putting their economic affairs in order by implementing austerity measures and liberating the economy from impediments such as trade unions (the UK in the 1980s) or the bureaucracy (India to an extent in 1991) or went in the opposite direction by printing more money, hoping to somehow revive their economies and ending up with high or hyperinflation. While the first approach worked and the second did not, the point to take away is that countries acted alone and bore the consequences of their imprudence in a world that was basically prudent and believed in balanced budgets, if not every year then at least over a business cycle spanning good and not-so-good years. The deficit in the bad years is called a cyclical deficit. When a country runs a deficit even in good years when growth is high, it is known as a structural deficit and is always unsustainable, resulting in a constantly worsening debt to GDP ratio and an increasing inability of a country to pay off its debt.

From a situation in which the golden rule for the economic behaviour of governments was a balanced budget to the present when hardly any government seriously considers this as an option has been a long journey over a short period of time. There have been three important events along the way which brought us to where we are. The first was in 1971 when America went off the gold standard completely and the rest of the world followed as the US dollar was already the reserve currency of the world. All money in the world became fiat money and all constraints to printing money were removed. The second was in the late 1990s when the Eurozone was negotiating its Stability and Growth Pact for the creation of its common currency, the euro. They mandated the maximum government deficit for any country to be 3 per cent of GDP and the maximum accumulated debt to be 60 per cent of GDP. Somehow, perhaps because of the wide publicity it received, the 3 per cent deficit figure became accepted by governments and lay citizens alike and it came to be accepted that governments would spend 3 per cent of GDP more than their collections. Some even started considering it a desirable figure. There was no rigorous reasoning behind the adoption of the 3 per cent figure other than that it appeared to be reasonable. The new norm shifted from balanced budgets to continuous deficits of about 3 per cent. As a consequence accumulated debt grew too and unsurprisingly started breaking the 60 per cent limit.

There was still a semblance of discipline in government spending. If any country greatly spent over the new norm of 3 per cent GDP more than its collections, it suffered a weakening of its currency against other currencies and an outflow of its money to more reliable currencies and a consequent slowing down of its economy. The economic crisis of 2008 and the response to it by most governments changed that. The major economies all started printing money in a Keynesian attempt to stimulate their economies. While the results of the stimulation were sketchy at best, with GDPs barely rising for over seven years, there was another, perhaps at first unintended, result. With all countries indulging in excessive deficit financing, currency rates did not change much against each other. In fact, the countries that held back and did not try to inflate their currencies suffered. The comparative value of their currencies surged, making their exports more expensive and imported goods cheaper, depressing the demand for locally produced goods, both at home and abroad. These countries soon capitulated, with Japan being the last major economy to undertake aggressive quantitative easing in 2013, resulting in the devaluation of the yen. With this, currency wars came effectively to an end. According to Guido Mantega, the Brazilian Minister for Finance, a global currency war broke out in 2010. It now appears to be over with an armistice having been achieved through the good offices of the G-7 and the G-20. The terms of the armistice are not that all countries will exercise prudence and not get into competitive devaluation, letting their currencies retain their buying power. It appears instead that all countries will devalue their currencies in tandem.

Is all well with the world then? The ghost of Keynes has been propitiated. Printing presses are being thrown into battle against low growth and low confidence, the currency has not been devalued against other currencies, asset prices are rising and stock markets are at or near all-time highs despite sluggish growth. While it is true that we have taken on loans to be able to do this, it is mostly a long-term debt to be paid at some time in the future and most of it by future generations. Our money does buy us less but we now have plenty of it. There is now enough money to pay for a greater political and bureaucratic role in our lives and their numbers will increase.

Having overcome the first constraint to unlimited growth by eliminating predators through a monopoly over force, the politician–bureaucrat combine, along with those who benefit from government largesse and from inflation, have now overcome the second constraint to their unlimited growth by having discovered an unlimited source of funds. They have finally discovered the philosopher's stone that medieval alchemists sought which could change base metals into gold. They don't even need base metals. All they need is to persuade the rest of society that taking on debt is natural and good. Unfortunately, it is neither.

While deficit financing and the consequent accumulation of debt works very well for a small group of people, a tiny percentage of the general population of any country, how does it work out for the rest of the population? Not well at all. They take on debt to feed the beast that preys upon them. Their children and their children's children will not be born free men and free women; they will be born into serfdom. Their overseers will not be brutes who will fetter them physically but they will be fettered nonetheless by people who will seek to control every facet of their existence and restrict and dominate them, imposing rules, regulations, laws and directives and trying to curtail and control their very thoughts. The tithes that will be collected by way of taxes and the diminishing of wealth caused by inflation will be far greater than the tithes collected in the past by kings and clergy. Some of the usurped wealth will be used to pay the interest promised on loans taken ostensibly on their behalf. The loans were taken partly to seduce them to vote in a particular manner and partly to pay for the size and luxuries of the new nobility.

The bribes given to voters by way of subsidized goods and

services are a fraction of the losses imposed on them through inflation. These losses are in addition to the restrictions imposed by the dominating politician–bureaucratic combine, further impeding their efforts to grow and prosper. It is a Faustian contract. The further tragedy is that even this Faustian promise cannot be honoured.

Through the deficit financing that our governments undertake, especially for expenditure that is not for the purpose of enhancing efficiency, competitiveness and growth, we are condemning ourselves to a perpetual cycle of extravagant spending followed by belt tightening and finally reneging on debt and setting up a new dispensation, which is never really new as it is not required to eschew deficit financing. Please note that during the belt tightening phase we are required to give up most of the goodies that were given to bribe us into voting in a particular manner. The Faustian contract is incapable of being kept, not from a lack of good intentions or good faith but because of the laws of economics. The basic tenet of economics is that there is no free lunch and this is as inexorable as the physical laws of the conservation of energy and matter. Wealth can only be created through human enterprise. It cannot be printed and given away. Wealth that is seemingly created out of nothing is eventually paid for by someone else or by everyone, through a balancing poverty created by the resultant inflation.

During the phase of belt tightening there is seldom any meaningful pruning of the bloated political and bureaucratic elite. Indeed a new layer of bureaucracy may even be imposed to deal with the calamitous situation by way of more tax collectors or law enforcers to stem the social unrest and to execute the new 'temporary' laws that have been put into place. I do not wish to imply that politicians and bureaucrats are evil men and women who consciously seek to grow and proliferate to the extent that the normal functioning of society and economic growth become unviable. Any organism in nature grows rampantly not because it is evil but simply because existing conditions let it do so. Politicians and bureaucrats, like everyone else, seek to grow and prosper in what they are doing. In their legitimate functioning they seldom transgress the law. It is a separate matter that they have made the laws that facilitate their own growth and enhance their power. The onus of limiting their unchecked growth does not lie on them but on the rest of society. In no other ecosystem do we expect an organism that is growing rampantly to curb its growth on its own, irrespective of whether its growth endangers or destroys the ecosystem. We do not expect a cancer to stop growing because the entire body may be imperilled. It is for the rest of the body to fight it in whatever way it can. So it is with every organism in any ecosystem. If an organism finds conditions conducive to its rampant growth, it will grow rampantly. It is for the rest of the ecosystem to control it.

Politicians and bureaucrats have a role to play in society as do farmers and weavers and teachers and myriads of other professionals. The inherent advantages of the division of labour mandate this. Just as we cannot individually spin yarn, weave clothes, smelt metals and so on we are not able individually to assume the roles of politicians and bureaucrats in attempting to run a nation state. The issue at hand is not about the utility of politicians and bureaucrats. They are required and we cannot do without them. The issue is about curtailing their rampant growth.

An entity which has monopoly over force is not easy to control or limit. Perhaps we can instead curtail the inexhaustible supply of funds that permits the rampant growth of the state and lets it impede our liberties, our enterprise and our growth. Perhaps we can deny our governments the right to take on debts on our behalf. Perhaps we can deny our governments the right to indulge in deficit financing. Should we be successful in doing so, our governments may need to resort to higher taxation but even that is preferable to giving the state unlimited resources and strangulating our economies in excessive red tape and high inflation which unevenly penalizes the less well-off amongst us. Taxation and government expenditure too may come down to moderate levels with competition at the ballot box. It will, at the very least, force our governments to think carefully about spending our money.

We may possess some tools to enable us to change things. These include a democratic set-up where we have the ability to vote governments out of power and a newly acquired ability to communicate seamlessly and speedily. But more important than these, we must possess the courage to stand up for ourselves. The nobles, when they took a stand against King John in Runnymede and forced him to sign the Magna Carta had neither democracy nor mass communication but they had the courage to take that stand. The politician–bureaucrat combine will attempt to blunt our tools. They blunt democracy by giving us choices of government that are largely indistinguishable from each other and differ mainly by trying to bribe different sets of voters. They blunt our communication with each other by banning publications or spying on our communication. We need to be aware of this and resist.

We often rue the fact that the system we live under is unfair and that our governments lack a sense of fair play. I do not think that a sense of fair play arises out of the magnanimity of those in power. It makes no evolutionary sense for those wielding power to willingly relinquish it. Fair play arises from the cost involved in not being fair and the resultant resistance and retaliation that unfairness generates. It is up to us to instil this sense of fair play in our governments.

At the close of this somewhat meandering chapter I would like to recapitulate the few cultural strands that are crucial for the setting up of an economic engine and its continued running.

These are only a few strands out of the myriad strands that comprise each of the many cultures that flourish around the world. There is little danger that any consensus upon these four traits would impose cultural uniformity in the world or lead to the hegemony of any one culture.

1. The desire to prosper individually along with the social sanction to freely work towards it.
2. The concept of personal property along with societal respect for every individual's property.
3. A tolerance of new ideas, especially those that run counter to our current beliefs and understanding, along with a willingness to fight any attempt to suppress these ideas.
4. A desire to understand the world around us. This involves questioning untested beliefs. It also involves the jettisoning of beliefs that attribute unnatural causes for what we see and experience. Our education system must reflect this desire.

These four cultural attitudes are the prerequisite conditions that must exist before a self-sustaining economic engine can evolve. They do not in any way negate or reduce the importance of the different parts and components of such an engine as this book has described.

Once the economic engine is going it will generate wealth in the hands of those who participate in its functioning, whether as great achievers or ordinary wage earners, and also raise standards of living. This is both the reason why we need an economic engine and the reward for having one. If the rewards are elusive or easily taken away the reason to participate disappears, leading to a slowing down of the engine and its eventual collapse. To prevent this, we need two cultural behaviours which are underpinned by a common cultural trait.

1. The willingness to defend one's individual rights and properties against those who would usurp it either by force

or breach of accepted behaviour or breach of contract. This is best done through an efficient justice delivery system.
2. The willingness to defend everyone's rights and properties from an encroaching state which would abrogate rights and liberties and usurp property and wealth directly or through induced inflation. This cannot be done through the justice delivery system alone and needs a majority to make common cause and work against it.

Both these cultural behaviours are acts of courage. This is a cultural trait that allows us to resist those who would usurp what we have earned, including our freedom, whether they are non-state players or the state itself. This is the trait that ensures that once the economic engine is running, it keeps running. It has been said that it takes courage to build a civilization. It takes greater courage to preserve civilizations.

Alexander Fraser Tytler Lord Woodhouselee (1747–1813) was a Scottish advocate, judge, writer, historian and a professor of universal history at the University of Edinburgh. The following quotation is attributed to him: 'A democracy is always temporary in nature. It simply cannot exist as a permanent form of government. A democracy will continue to exist up until the time that voters discover that they can vote themselves generous gifts from the public treasury. From that moment on, the majority always votes for the candidates who promise the most benefits from the public treasury, with the result that every democracy will finally collapse due to loose fiscal policy, which is always followed by a dictatorship.'

He further observed that the average age of the world's greatest civilizations is about two hundred years and that nations have always progressed through a particular sequence. This sequence is commonly known as the 'Tytler Cycle' or the 'Fatal Sequence' and he identified the sequence as: 'From bondage to spiritual faith; From spiritual faith to courage; From courage to liberty;

From liberty to abundance; From abundance to selfishness; From selfishness to complacency; From complacency to apathy; From apathy to dependence; From dependence back into bondage.'[23]

Is it possible that we are well into the stage of loose fiscal policy on the one hand and as a result stepping from apathy to dependence on the other? If we are to prevent the collapse of this period of growth and prosperity, we will need to be courageous. Can we indefinitely prolong the state of 'From liberty to abundance'? It is certainly worth trying.

REFERENCES

1. '"Speed Money" Puts the Brakes on Retail Growth Amid Thin Margins', *The Economic Times*, 6 May 2013
2. http://en.wikipedia.org/wiki/History_of_insurance. Accessed on 3 May 2016
3. http://en.wikipedia.org/wiki/Lloyds_of_London. Accessed on 3 May 2016
4. en.wikipedia.org/wiki/World_population. Accessed on 3 May 2016
5. http://avalon.law.yale.edu/ancient/hamframe.asp. Accessed on 3 May 2016
6. http://en.wikipedia.org/wiki/Babylon. Accessed on 3 May 2016
7. http://en.wikipedia.org/wiki/Semitic_people. Accessed on 3 May 2016
8. *The Book of Lord Shang*, translated from the Chinese by Dr J.J.L. Duyvendak, the Law Book Exchange, Ltd, Clark, New Jersey, 2003 http://classiques.uqac.ca/classiques//duyvendak_jjl/B 25_book_of_lord_shang/duvvlord.pdf. Accessed on 3 May 2016
9. http://en.wikipedia.org/wiki/Rigveda. Accessed on 3 May 2016
10. http://en.wikipedia.org/wiki/Vedic_period. Accessed on 3 May 2016
11. http://www.professor-frithjof-kuhnen.de/publication/man-and-land/2-1-1.htm. Accessed on 3 May 2016
12. http://www.reshafim.org.il/ad/egypt/economy/land.htm. Accessed

on 3 May 2016
13. http://en.wikipedia.org/wiki/House_of_Wisdom. Accessed on 3 May 2016
14. http://en.wikipedia.org/wiki/PRISM_(surveillance_programme). Accessed on 3 May 2016
15. http://en.wikipedia.org/wiki/Edward_Snowden. Accessed on 3 May 2016
16. http://www.theobjectivestandard.com/issues/2006-winter/tragedy-of-theology/. Accessed on 3 May 2016
17. Richard Dawking in *The Selfish Gene*, (The Scientific Book Club, 1978, pp. 74-80)
18. http://en.wikipedia.org/wiki/List_of_political_families. Accessed on 3 May 2016
19. http://en.wikipedia.org/wiki/Human_microbiota. Accessed on 3 May 2016
20. http://.wikipedia.org/wiki/Non-governmental_organization. Accessed on 3 May 2016
21. Users.erols.com/mwhite28/literacy.htm. Accessed on 3 May 2016
22. http://en.wikipedia.org/wiki/List_of_countries_by_literacy_rate. Accessed on 3 May 2016
23. http://en.wikipedia.org/wiki/Alexander_Fraser_Tytler. Accessed on 3 May 2016

7
HAPPINESS

In this book we have followed the workings of the economic engine from the emergence of an idea, which is the starting point of any new economic activity. We have gone backward from here and looked at the factors that encourage the birth of new ideas as well as those that cause them to be suppressed. We know that it is the capital lying in the savings of a community that permits ideas to be converted into workable and marketable products and services and we have seen how that capital can be eroded through inflation and how its ability to take ideas to the marketplace may be compromised through red tape, corruption and taxes levied on anything other than profits. We have looked at the marketplace and seen the practices that make the offering of new products or services easier or more difficult. We have seen how a few strands of our cultures, most importantly, a respect for the property of others, a tolerance for ideas, especially those that run counter to accepted wisdom, beliefs and practices, along with a willingness to stand up for our rights, can promote progress and prosperity.

Having followed the workings of the economic engine and having understood what makes it work more effectively, we have to ask the most obvious question: what is the purpose of a well-running economic engine? Is it to keep increasing economic activity and the number of transactions carried out and constantly endeavour to bump up a number called GDP? Is that all we ask of a smoothly working economic engine? What about happiness? What about the things that make us feel good?

The term 'Gross National Happiness' was coined in 1972 by Bhutan's fourth Dragon King, Jigme Singye Wangchuk. He used the term to signal his commitment to building an economy that would serve Bhutan's unique culture based on Buddhist spiritual values.[1] The concept of measuring and working towards happiness has since gained worldwide acceptance. Many measurements of happiness have been proposed. For me the most comprehensive is that proposed by the Legatum Institute. The Legatum Prosperity Index measures 89 variables, spread across eight sub-indices.[2]

I have my own list of things that bring happiness, which is not as exhaustive as that of the Legatum Institute but covers most areas. Of the things that make us feel good, some can be laid at the door of economic policies and practices, some at the door of cultural values and some are a result of wealth created due to a nation's economic success. I have accordingly broken up my list into three lists. Of course, no list, neither economic policies nor cultural practices nor even prosperity, can guarantee happiness. A great deal depends on the individual and who he interacts with. Good economic and cultural practices reduce many sources of unhappiness and make it more likely that we will be happy more often and for longer periods. That in itself is to me a worthy objective. I will limit myself to examining the reasoning behind only the list dealing with the economy-driven inputs of happiness as I feel the other two are self-explanatory and beyond the scope of this book.

Before I proceed I wish to point out that the lists pertaining to the economic and cultural inputs of happiness are not in isolation. As we have seen in the previous chapter, there are strong linkages between certain cultural aspects and a thriving economy. Some cultural strands which make a thriving economy possible also give rise to happiness directly. For example, the first point of happiness in my list of cultural inputs is the rule of law. This is an essential ingredient for both a thriving economy and a state of happiness. In a sense these two lists are in a symbiotic relationship. Having said that, the separate lists will help us focus our minds on what can be done.

A list of what can make us happy and can be delivered by economic policy:

1. A degree of egalitarianism giving rise to feelings of fraternity and fellowship
2. Gradually rising living standards
3. Adequate food
4. Adequate shelter
5. Basic health care
6. Savings that are safe in banks, with nil or extremely low inflation
7. Expectation that a living can be earned
8. Environment conducive to entrepreneurship including the ease of setting up a new business.

A list of cultural strands conducive to happiness:

1. Rule of law
2. Confidence in the justice delivery system
3. Enough social capital to impart the confidence that the likelihood of being cheated or stolen from is low and if it does happen, the justice delivery system will quickly set things right
4. Safe walking alone at night
5. Minimal interference by state and society regarding personal choices

6. An intolerance of corruption
7. Equality before the law, regardless of ethnicity or gender
8. Equality of opportunity, regardless of ethnicity or gender
9. Respect for and efforts made to impart a good quality of universal education
10. Societal willingness to spend on primary healthcare
11. Freedom of choice in choosing a spouse, a religion or a livelihood
12. An ability to express political opinion fearlessly
13. A cultural encouragement to interact and help strangers for we are all strangers at some time and place
14. Legitimacy of enjoying and participating in sport, art, music, dancing or any other leisure activity that does not harm a third party. Availability of enjoyment opportunities is also an incentive to work hard. Money is not the only incentive for working hard

A list of what makes us happy arising out of prosperity:

1. A comprehensive safety net of medical care for health problems
2. Progress of financial security in old age
3. Increase of leisure
4. A corresponding increase in available leisure activities
5. Increase in environment preservation
6. An increase in ability to donate to or volunteer for a perceived good cause

Before I go on to examine the sources of happiness arising out of economic practices, I would like to draw attention to a very important quality of a well-functioning economy, namely, the stability of the economic system. An economy that oscillates between cycles of boom and bust is not conducive to human happiness. The sweet fruits of a boom period are shared disproportionately with the bulk of the rewards going to a few, mostly shareholders of companies, bankers and top management. A few top managers manage to acquire superstar status, commanding stratospheric salaries and bonuses, way out of proportion to their contribution to the rise in the fortunes of their companies. The companies pay them well, partly to enhance the status of the company and partly to prevent their migration to other companies. They become in effect Veblen goods, desired by many, affordable by a few and of questionable utility. The bitter fruits of a bust period, on the other hand, are shared predominantly by those lower down the economic pecking order, initially through job losses and pay cuts. When governments and central banks, following standard Keynesian operating procedures, start printing money and spending money they do not have, they worsen the situation for those with little. It may take years to create jobs but the cost of living rises fast. The combination puts pressure on savings and induces distress sales of capital assets such as shares in companies, real estate and jewellery, which are bought at low prices by those who can afford them. Every cycle of boom and bust transfers wealth from the lower percentiles to the upper percentiles of wealth owners.

In the current scenario of repeated financial crises and recurrent boom-and-bust cycles, it is hardly surprising that the gap between the wealth of the upper 1 per cent, 10 per cent or 20 per cent of the people, and the lower 1 per cent, 10 per cent or 20 per cent of the people, is widening. This does not promote egalitarianism and good fellowship.

Until about the end of the eighteenth century, economics did not exist as a separate discipline. Any decisions made on what today are called economic matters were made based on common sense. Economic thinking was a minor branch of philosophy. Later, thinkers on economic matters, perhaps influenced by the breakthroughs in scientific thought and methodology in the hard sciences of physics and to a lesser extent chemistry, tried to make economics more precise. They adopted the methods employed in physics and came up with theories and models which they tried to validate through observations of the world around them. Unlike in physics, it was not possible for them to conduct experiments. It must be remembered that physics then was still the old physics dealing mostly with mechanics and heat. It had yet to fully comprehend the intricacies and uncertainties of complex systems. While positive and negative feedback loops were not fully understood, a negative feedback loop was designed for steam engines in the form of a governor. It was noticed that even a relatively simple system like a steam engine was subject to random perturbations which could cause it to speed up destructively. The governor, invented by James Watt in 1788, progressively cut the supply of steam as the engine speeded up, thereby reducing its speed to the desired equilibrium. Positive feedback loops on the other hand amplified the initial small perturbations caused by randomness or individual actions. A good illustration of this is when a few cows in a herd start running for any reason, spooking a few more that also start running, thereby spooking yet more cows, resulting in a stampede. A bank run is another example. Normally started by a rumour that may have a grain of truth, it prompts wary depositors to queue up to withdraw their money, encouraging others to do the same, until the bank can no longer cope with the rush of withdrawals and goes under.

The complexity of a system depends on the number of parts in it and the number of different ways they interact with each other. The more complex a system, the greater the chances of disturbances, causing the system to move away from an equilibrium. The economy is a very complex system indeed. Adam Smith contended that the invisible hand gave rise to prosperity through the actions of rational men working in their own rational self-interest. His theory implies that men ceaselessly calculate the odds and their own interests every step of the way. But that is not the way we are. We are swayed by rumour and by superstition. We are at times apprehensive about improbable events taking place and at other times ready to stake everything with the odds overwhelmingly stacked against us. We can be parsimonious with pennies and reckless with a lifetime's savings. Unlike Adam Smith's rational man our actions are often guided by the opinions of others and we easily give in to herd behaviour. There are millions of us in every economy and we act rationally at times and irrationally at other times. Sometimes we act alone and sometimes in herds. Often we work at cross purposes.

The economy of any country is complex and hence frequent perturbations in the economy must be expected. I doubt that we can ever devise an economic system that will protect us from ourselves and our follies. The best we can hope for is an economic system that will dampen and mitigate the effects of our occasional irrational behaviour. The irrational exuberance of the markets that Alan Greenspan spoke of is sadly all too frequent an occurrence. Economies need to be designed with negative feedback loops. Instead they have functioning positive feedback loops.

The financial crisis of 2008 was the worst perturbation in the world economy since the crash of 1929 and the Great Depression that followed.

The crisis started with the building up of a housing property bubble in America. Where did the money that fed the bubble come from? The US Fed was not printing money recklessly then. Printing money is not the only way money supply is increased in an economy. When large banks and other financial institutions leverage the already large amounts of money by loaning out many times the money than they actually have, an increase in the supply of money effectively takes place. By some accounts the bigger lending institutions, including big banks, were leveraged as many as 30 times. The banks willingly lent out increasing amounts of money to anyone who would buy a house without any due diligence regarding the prospective buyer's ability to service the debt. They thought they were covered in two ways. First, they had a lien on the property they were financing and with rising property values they believed they were well covered. Second, they insured the loans they gave out against default with AIG, the biggest insurance company in the world, and with other large insurance firms. The insurance firms went by the historical data which said that defaults on housing loans were below 2 per cent, a figure they took into their calculations in determining the insurance premiums. The agents who brought the business from the banks to the insurance companies and the managers who approved the insurance policies made handsome commissions and bonuses. The banks then spread some of the risks away from themselves by randomly bundling up individual loans together and selling them, passing on the loans to other banks and financial institutions for a commission, as secure loans underwritten by AAA-rated insurance companies, on which the buying banks would earn interest, thereby spreading the contagion. (These ratings, which can be done of any entity, including countries, for their credit worthiness and probability of default, are done by specialized ratings agencies such as Moody's and Fitch. An AAA rating is the highest that can be given.) The bundling up of loans made it impossible to evaluate the quality of any particular loan or of the loans overall.

But nothing keeps rising forever and every bubble eventually bursts. After years of a giddying rise, housing property prices crashed. Borrowers found themselves saddled with loans that were well in excess of the value of their properties. As a result, they simply mailed the keys of their new properties back to the banks. The insurance companies could not cope with the deluge of claims being made. The banks, mortgage companies and insurance giants were on the verge of collapse when the central banks and governments—for the contagion had spread to other countries too—stepped in to save the 'too big to fail' institutions. They started printing more money, much of which went to shore up the banks and institutions. The banks being already overleveraged and being further hemmed in by new norms like Basel 2 and Basel 3, which are mandated prudence norms for banks, were in no position to lend money to small-and medium-size business ventures which could have generated both jobs and growth. This in many ways was like shutting the barn doors once the horse had bolted. The damage had already been done. Also, with people having lost wealth due to the collapse of the housing bubble, buying was reduced, giving businesses little reason to borrow money to enhance capacity.

In hindsight, had one of the many possible negative feedback loops been in place the bubble would not have grown to anywhere near the size it did. With rapidly rising property prices, banks could have asked for progressively higher down payments or, sensing increasing risk, charged higher interest rates on loans. Had either of these approaches or a combination of the two been followed, it would have deterred speculative purchasers and prevented the bubble from forming. In any case there should have been better scrutiny of a loan taker's ability to service the loan, both for interest payments and loan repayment. The negligence of the loan giving institutions to do something as basic as that seems to have risen from the confidence that while they could make easy money when the going was good, somebody else would hold the baby if things went wrong. As events went on to prove, they were right. No government can risk having its major financial institutions collapse. If they did, no one really knows what would happen. Would there have been a collapse of all business activities? Would there have been anarchy? Whatever the possible outcomes, we can safely say they would have been calamitous. Accordingly, a rescue-and-salvage operation was launched by governments. Vast amounts of money were printed in an attempt to prop up these financial institutions. While some went bankrupt others were saved.[3] More than seven years after the event, financial systems the world over are still limping back to normalcy. Unemployment rates are higher and GDP growth rates lower than before the bubble formation started. A great many people have paid a heavy price for the recklessness of a few financial institutions.

To prevent a recurrence of the events that led to this crisis, there are two possible approaches. One is for banks to be strictly regulated and monitored to prevent them from being reckless. Towards this end, the Basel Committee on Banking Supervision was set up in 1974 which among other things provides guidelines for the international standards on capital adequacy, the Core Principles for Effective banking supervision and the Concordat on cross-border banking supervision. This came to be known as Basel 1. This was followed in 2004 by Basel 2. This was intended to create an international standard for banking regulators to control how much capital banks need to put aside as a safeguard against the financial and operational risks banks (and the whole economy) face. Advocates of Basel 2 believed that such an international standard could protect the international financial system from the problems that might arise should a major bank or a series of banks collapse.[4] It did not work as intended for had it worked the banking crisis of 2008 would not have occurred nor spread to other countries. The banking crisis was caused mostly by credit default swaps, mortgage-backed security markets and similar derivatives. As a response Basel 3, with more controls, is being put into place. This is not easy and the implementation date for Basel 3 has been moved from 2013-15 to 2018. Even when Basel 3 is finally implemented, keeping in mind the innovative new derivatives and trades being created regularly, it is difficult to believe with any equanimity, that regulators will be able to effectively police banking and prevent another crisis. It will become a case of regulators trying to catch up with bankers. All we may end up getting through this approach is another layer of bureaucracy.

The second approach is to create a core banking and financial system and fence it from investment banks and other speculative players like securities firms, ones that deal with highly leveraged securities instruments. This is not a new idea but had been put into place in 1933 after the Great Depression with the Glass–Steagall Act. Amongst its other provisions the Act was chiefly referred to for its provision to limit the securities activities of commercial banks. It segregated the activities of commercial banks and securities firms and restricted affiliations between them. Bankers tried for years to have the Act repealed as it restricted their desire for innovative banking and greater profitability. Even before the Act was repealed it was already being breached, most notably by Citi Bank's 1998 affiliation with Salomon Smith Barney, one of the largest US securities firms, without opposition from regulators. The key provisions of the act were repealed by the Gramm–Leach–Bliley (GLB) legislation signed into law by President Bill Clinton in 1999. Banks were now free to use depositors' money and put it to use in a more risky manner with their investment bank branches.

Many believe that the Act directly caused the 2007 subprime mortgage financial crisis which led to the financial mayhem of 2008. President Barack Obama has stated that GLB led to deregulation that allowed the creation of giant financial supermarkets that could own investment banks, commercial banks and insurance firms, something that had been banned since the Great Depression. Its passage, critics say, cleared the way for the creation of companies that were too big and intertwined to fail.

Mark Thornton and Robert Ekelund, economists who follow the free market Austrian school, have also criticized the Act as contributing to the crisis. They state that in a world regulated by a gold standard, 100 per cent reserve banking and no Federal Deposit Insurance Corporation deposit insurance, the Act would have made perfect sense, but under the present fiat monetary system it 'amounts to corporate welfare for financial institutions and a moral hazard that will make tax payers pay dearly.'

Another Austrian school economist, Frank Shostak has argued that GLB actually gave more regulation over the banking sector. He argues that with the existence of a central bank, competition among banks led to increased inflation and 'rather than promoting an efficient allocation of real savings, the current "deregulated" monetary system has been channelling money created out of thin air across the economy.'

In an article in *The Nation*, Mark Sumner asserted that the GLB Act was for the creation of entities that took on more risk due to the fact that they were considered 'too big to fail'. Other critics too assert that proponents and defenders of the Act espouse a form of 'eliteconomics' that has, with the passage of the Act, directly precipitated the current economic recession while at the same time shifting the burden of belt-tightening measures onto the lower- and middle-income classes.[5]

In my opinion, not only should the GLB and similar acts and practices be repealed, the solution lies in going far beyond the provisions of the Glass–Steagall Act of 1933. If the desire for a stable economy with a steady if perhaps slightly slower growth rate is to be realized, countries need to establish not just a core banking system but also a core financial system, including insurance companies and pension funds.

This core financial system must be shielded from the far riskier and highly leveraged activities of investment banks and securities firms. The banks within this system must be forbidden from making investments in investment banks and securities firms, and there should not be any cross holdings or common directors and employees between them. Indeed the mindsets of the two sorts of bankers are so different that experience in one should automatically disqualify a banker from getting a job in the other. Insurance firms within the core financial system must not be allowed to offer insurance products to investment banks and securities firms. Pension funds too must not be allowed to invest money in investment banks and securities firms. Any deposit insurance that a government offers depositors must only be extended to depositors in the core banks.

The function of the core bank system is for it to be a safe repository of a nation's savings, enabling secured loans to be made to businesses and consumers. The function of a core insurance sector is to extend insurance cover to normal businesses and personal concerns without extending cover to risky investment banks and securities firm operations, thereby putting their own survival at risk The function of pension funds is to provide financial security for when one cannot work or can work little. The paramount need for security precludes testosterone-driven risk taking. If a country can put together this core financial system, it cannot be held to ransom by large investment banks and securities firms. They will not be too big to fail nor will they be important enough for the financial security of the country to be put at risk by bailing them out with taxpayers' money.

Bankers are not likely to be in favour of such a dispensation, but that is to be expected. Investment bankers would be denied the use of the country's savings for their gambles. Commercial bankers would be denied the opportunity to make a quick profit as they tried to do when they bought the bundled up subprime loans put out by investment bankers which were duly insured by giant insurers such as AIG. However, a country's financial security is far more important than bankers' profits and bonuses.

If countries can establish safe core financial systems, their investment banks, securities firms and other players who are not part of the core system need not be subjected to the complexities of Basel 2 and Basel 3. They need only be subject to the norms of ethical behaviour applicable to all businesses. Fraud and misleading inducements to investors will need to be put down with a heavy hand. Their scope of financial damage will be limited to that of willing participants, as in the case of casinos and race tracks. It is imprudent to gamble the financial security of a country at the races.

Having established the desirability of a stable economic system and having made suggestions as to how this might be achieved, let us look at how certain aspects of economic policy can impact the pursuit of happiness. It was necessary to first touch upon the stability of the economic system, for whatever other virtues an economic system may possess are all quite meaningless if the economic system itself is fragile and subject to periodic bubble formations and collapses.

Before I examine those aspects of our happiness that are dependent on economic policy, I must confess that the list is subjective. There is to the best of my knowledge no widely agreed upon list that attributes certain aspects of happiness to specific economic policies. The basis of this list is subjective feelings of well-being and happiness. The basis of this list is not economics. Economics and economic policy are but tools to help us move closer to that subjective happiness.

1. A degree of egalitarianism, giving rise to feelings of fraternity and fellowship: There are two ways in which this can be improved. One is the removal of all taxes linked to consumption, like sales tax or VAT, because the less well-to-do spend a far greater portion of their income on life's necessities than richer people do, resulting in a higher tax rate for them. The second is to treat all sources of income in the same manner for tax purposes. There is no reason to

tax capital gains or money made in the stock market any differently from the way we tax salaries. Of course, indexation should be allowed for capital gains, but with nil or very low inflation rates the benefits accruing from indexation will be negligible. Warren Buffett, one of the richest people in the world, has claimed that he pays taxes at a lower rate than his secretary. This is anathema for any feelings of fellowship among the different strata of society. Tax rates need to be progressive but only to an extent. Confiscatory taxes for the rich, such as French President Francois Hollande has proposed—a top rate of 75 per cent—are equally divisive of society. In this way it is the rich who would be alienated from the rest. The rich being more resourceful would likely shift much of their money out of the country and out of the reach of confiscatory taxes. Worse, they would possibly become less keen to pursue growth.

2. Gradually rising living standards: A spirit level is a spirit-filled tube with an air bubble in it. It tells us if a surface is level or sloping upward or downward. I believe we each have a spirit level built into us which tells us if our lives are level, indicating acceptance and peace of mind, or sloping downward, indicating despair and despondency, or sloping upward, indicating bliss and cheer and yes, high spirits. It does not really matter if the slope is gentle or more inclined. What matters is the direction of change. Money does not equate directly with happiness. If you have just put your second million in the bank, you will not be twice as happy as when you put your first million in. We are happy if we expect our tomorrow to be better than our today. We are happy if we can expect our children's future to be better than ours. If there is a trade-off between slow, gentle and inclusive growth and volatile patchy growth, it is the former that contributes more to happiness. A core stable financial system, unaffected

by the vicissitudes of greater risks is what leads to stability. Growth may be slow but it will be consistent, giving rise to greater overall happiness. We have to acknowledge, though, that we are not all the same nor does each one of us think in the same way all the time. We will be more predisposed in varying measures towards risk taking. If that is what makes us happy, we are free to do so in the coexisting economy of investment banks and securities firms and gambling casinos. The core economic system, shielded from our riskier actions, will continue to deliver slow but constant growth and will ensure that our spirit levels point towards happiness.

3. Adequate food: Ever since life began, the struggle for food has been the chief concern. With the advent of farming and the ability to store surplus staple foods for future use, the immediacy of the struggle for food diminished for large portions of the human race. With modern storage and processing capabilities, most food can now be stored for future consumption. The resultant food security contributes in a major way to less stress and greater happiness and frees people's minds for other pursuits. Unfortunately, this is not the case in many parts of the world. Famine, caused by drought or floods or war, is still an imaginable possibility. When famine strikes, people can perish in millions, simply because they have nowhere to go and no people near them whom they could fight with for food. They are cut off and helpless. If in the same area some people have food security and others do not, the situation is different. Fights over food and thefts will occur. Social harmony will disintegrate. It is not enough if the aggregate food supply in a country is equal to or exceeds the aggregate need for food. Adequate food must reach the poorest of the poor. Food security is a double-edged sword. If it is available to all, it contributes greatly to happiness and if it is not, it leads to bitter strife and fissures within a society.

Societies at different levels of prosperity have different concepts of what adequate food is. It is possible that what a rich country considers adequate food is far more than what a poorer country can ensure to its people. Having said that, there are clear common-sense lower limits for what is considered adequate food intake. There can be two levels of adequate food intake that a country can strive for. The first is to ensure adequate calorie intake to enable life and the energy to work. The second is to ensure the consumption of nutrients to enable greater longevity and long-term health.

Some of the ways in which economic policies can help bring about food security for all and the resultant happiness are:

- Minimize wastage by incentivizing food storage and processing.
- Eliminate taxes and restrictions of trade on foodstuff, including processed food, to make it affordable to more people.
- Help for those who still cannot feed themselves in the form of money transfers and food kitchens. Food coupons are not the best idea as they limit a recipient's buying to a specific range of products and preclude a search for alternative sources of nutrition, including growing a little food on their own. The food kitchens could be run by the active involvement of or donations from the well-off provided they are not taxed on these expenses and are given public acknowledgement for their contributions. This will have the additional benefit of bridging the social divide and instil a sense of community among all sections of society.

4. Adequate shelter: As with food, there are different concepts of what constitutes adequate shelter among richer and poorer nations. After food, the most primal of life's urges

is to procreate. To do so in a meaningful way, shelter is indispensable. The minimum requirement of adequate shelter is that it must provide protection from the elements and privacy from the rest of the world. It greatly enhances happiness if one has ownership rights or medium- to long-term tenancy rights over one's dwelling. The Peruvian economist Hernando de Soto Polar has written about benefits to the economy if poor people, who form the bulk of the informal economy of a country, have legal titles to their dwellings and small businesses. He argues that having a legal title to a property enables it to be used as collateral and one can avail of loans for business growth against it. This releases the capital locked up in these properties, which are in any case informally owned by those in physical possession of them. While his argument is logical, I wish to draw attention to the fact that having legal ownership of one's dwelling or other property also imparts a great sense of security and contentment. This happiness is further enhanced if the dwelling is treated by society and the government as inviolable, much like the Englishman's Castle. In the words of William Pitt or Pitt the Elder, Prime Minister of England in 1763: 'The poorest man may in his cottage bid defiance to all the forces of the crown. It may be frail—its roof may shake—the wind may blow through it—the storm may enter—the rain may enter but the King of England cannot enter.'[6]

5. Basic health care: With rising prosperity every nation will be able to afford more comprehensive health care. However, even before a society reaches a level of affluence some basic health care must be provided, especially to those who cannot afford to pay for it, firstly because it provides mental solace; secondly because it makes economic sense. Basic health care must include community-based health care like immunization programmes and hygiene-related aspects like safe drinking

water. These must be provided to every member of the community if they are to be effective. Diseases like smallpox and polio must be wiped out for all or not be wiped out at all. Basic health care must also provide emergency care until the patient can get back on his or her feet. The assurance that one will not be alone and helpless in times of distress is an important source of happiness.

6. Savings are safe in banks with little or no inflation: As we move through life, one of our prime objectives is security. Towards this end, we put away money, often in banks. We also put away money for our dreams. In a good year we tend to save more than in normal years. In a bad year we may dip into our savings. Every little bit that we manage to add to our savings, whatever the form of the savings, gives us an increased sense of security and brings us closer to our dreams. It is like climbing a mountain. Every little bit added to one's savings is another step up the mountain. While climbing a mountain, one can pause and tarry a while, secure in the knowledge that one will stay put at that height. If the mountain climb was on a slippery slope and one was constantly sliding back lower, whether one climbed or rested, it would greatly increase the unhappiness of the climber. Some mountains might appear too daunting to even attempt a climb. It is the same with savings. If our savings earn us less, by way of interest or other yields, than is taken away from our savings by way of inflation, taxes and in some bizarre cases a negative rate of interest offered by banks—or, in other words, we are required to pay banks for allowing them to use our money—we are on a slippery slope. Slippery slopes do not lead to happiness. Economic policies and government action must ensure close to a zero rate of inflation and a small but positive real rate of return on savings.

7. Expectation that a living can be earned: There is little to

be said about this. It is obvious that if we are confident of finding work when we need it we are happy. However, there are no easy palliatives for this. For jobs to be available, the entire economic engine with all its parts has to work with a considerable degree of efficiency.

8. An environment conducive to entrepreneurship, including the ease of setting up business: This in part is a continuation of the last point regarding availability of jobs, in the sense that if new business enterprises are easy to set up, it increases the likelihood of jobs being available. But it goes beyond that. Entrepreneurship is about taking your future into your own hands. It is about following your dreams. It is about not bemoaning the fact that a suitable job is not available but doing something about it and creating your own job and perhaps a few more in the process. The spirit of enterprise that entrepreneurs exhibit is one of the forces that drive economic growth. It is also an empowering and liberating spirit and conducive to happiness. Imagine a country, and many such exist in the world, where it is forbidden or extremely difficult to strike out on one's own and you will also imagine that its helpless citizenry cannot in any way be brimming over with happiness. There is a strong correlation among the countries that are at the top of the UN's ease of doing business index, the Legatam Institute's Happiness Index and the UN's Human Development Index.

The reader, I hope, will note that the requirements for increasing the chances of happiness are consistent with the view on economics espoused in this book. We may have evolved into homo sapien economicus, that is, humans wise about economics, and adapted so well to our economic environment that we have developed a feedback loop of happiness which gets activated when we do things that make economic sense.

REFERENCES

1. http://en.wikipedia.org/wiki/Gross_national_happiness. Accessed on 3 May 2016
2. http://www.prosperity.com/#!/methodology. Accessed on 3 May 2016
3. http://en.wikipedia.org/wiki/List_of_banks_acquired_or_bankrupted_during_the_Great_Recession. Accessed on 3 May 2016
4. http://en.wikipedia.org/wiki/Basel_II. Accessed on 3 May 2016
5. http://en.wikipedia.org/wiki/Gramm-Leach-Bliley_Act. Accessed on 3 May 2016
6. http://www.phrases.org.uk/meanings/an-englishmans-home-is-his-castle.html. Accessed on 3 May 2016

IN CONCLUSION

ONCE WE HAVE UNDERSTOOD THE WORKINGS OF THE ECONOMIC engine, with the analogy of a working nuclear power plant in mind, we realize that the economic engine is not as complicated a construct as it is sometimes made out to be. It has a few parts, and the function of each part is quite clear and follows a logical sequence. We need not be overawed by the terminology of economics. We do not need to value economic formulae over common sense. To be sure, the invaluable work done by many economics researchers has thrown sharper light on different aspects of the economic engine. They have been helped to a great extent by economics data that has been maintained since the nineteenth century, such as land revenue records, estate duty and income tax records. With the availability of data and statistical tools, economics researchers have been better able to understand many aspects of the economic engine and either validate or rebut various economic theories. Without such data, economics theories would have been just theories without any linkage to the real world. It would have been close to impossible without such data to know for certain even basic things like whether a country was getting richer or poorer and whether this was happening quickly or slowly. Or whether the rich were getting richer and the poor poorer or whether the gap between them was closing. Economics researchers with the help of the data available have been able to ferret out nuggets of truth about the economy and about ourselves and our behaviour patterns. It was up to the policymakers to use their findings wisely or unwisely.

While economics researchers have thrown sharper light on many aspects of the economic engine, these findings in no way invalidate the basic working of the economic engine as described in this book. The engine has worked splendidly at a few times and a few places but it often gets derailed. This happens when ever one of the parts of the engine is not functioning optimally. It also happens when the engine is asked to do things or perform functions it is not designed to do. For instance, the engine is not designed to foster get-rich-quick schemes or to dole out largesse from public finances. Get-rich-quick schemes always entail shifting money from one section of the people to another without involving the running of the engine which alone can create wealth and create more sound money.

The writing of this book has been a personally satisfying journey. The trigger that set me on this path was the serendipitous realization that the manner in which spontaneously emitted neutrons from a fissile atom caused other fissile atoms to emit neutrons of their own was very similar to the way ideas emitted by one person caused other individuals to generate more ideas. With this initial idea in place, one thought led to another. My great advantage was that I was not an economist locked into a particular school of economic thought and was therefore not constrained by preconceived thought processes. I believe that this book is based on first principles and evolves logically from them, without much reference to current theories or practices. As a result the book has come to some conclusions that are counter to current thoughts and practices.

This book is an attempt to delineate the workings of an economic engine, identifying its parts and the function of each. Just as it is not possible to remove a few parts from a well-designed automobile and expect the automobile to function superbly, it is not possible to eliminate parts of the economic engine and expect it to continue to function effectively.

This book may not be as detailed a manual as we might have preferred, but a rudimentary one is better than none and should enable a skilled technician to identify a malfunctioning part and attempt to rectify it. A rudimentary manual can be fleshed out and more details filled in with experience. Nevertheless, it is crucial for anyone tinkering with the engine to know its fundamentals. An automobile technician who is not aware of internal combustion is not one you would like to take your car to.

To recapitulate, I briefly enumerate the essential parts of the economic engine that lead to sustainable economic growth and increase the possibility of happiness.

1. Putting in place a universal compulsory education system which is free up to the high school level and oriented towards inculcating reason, critical thinking, innovation, ethical behaviour and the courage to stand up for one's rights along with the more traditional subjects.
2. Enabling easy access to information and knowledge along with an ability to share ideas. In today's world that means easy, cheap, untrammelled and as far as possible uncensored access to the internet as well as the ability to communicate with each other as cheaply as possible.
3. Developing a culture that does not suppress and punish ideas that are contrary to currently held beliefs and a culture that is respectful of other people's rights and properties.
4. Freeing businesses from overreaching laws and a bloated bureaucracy which hinders the conversion of ideas into business ventures and promotes corruption.
5. Preventing governments from deficit financing and printing

money. Deficit financing has three undesirable consequences as far as sustained growth is concerned. It enables the unlimited growth of government, decreasing personal liberty and stifling enterprise. It lowers interest rates, thereby disincentivizing savings and capital formation which is essential for growth. It promotes inflation and reduces the value of existing savings, reducing the ability of savings to buy goods, start ventures and promote growth.

6. Banning a core financial system from excessively risky speculative businesses, thereby promoting stability in the entire economic engine. This step also diminishes the likelihood of boom-and-bust cycles.

7. Establishing free and fair markets while curbing monopolistic behaviour and other restrictive trade practices among market participants. Certain subsidies can also amount to restrictive trade practices.

8. Eliminating or minimizing all taxes that are levied before profits or wages have been earned. Taxes such as sales tax or VAT, excise and high government licence fees to permit businesses reduce both demand and enterprise and prevent an economic engine from working to its full potential. These taxes also widen the gap between the rich and the poor, impacting social cohesion, reducing social capital and increasing transaction costs.

9. Promoting a strong, independent but answerable judiciary along with an efficient justice delivery system to ensure that individual and business rights are not trampled upon and there is security of life, liberty and property.

10. Above all, cultural courage to stand up for our collective rights and freedom, including those of women and suppressed groups. This could be inculcated in us by our education system and strengthened by an independent judiciary. If we let our liberties be usurped by a government or powerful elite it will

negatively impact economic growth. The economic engine can only function effectively against a backdrop of freedom of thought and action, provided our actions do not impinge upon the liberties of others.

The above ten parts of the economic engine all need to be in place before an economic engine can work to its full potential. Of the countries whose economic engines are not functioning optimally, different countries need to rectify different parts of the engine. No single prescription can cure all ailments.

However, the response of governments to slowing growth and economic crises is limited to a few areas. Governments appear to be unaware of the whole economic engine. Their responses are limited to printing more money or not printing more money and to increasing or lowering interest rates. I have never come across a government saying something to the effect that 'Our economy is in trouble, let us see how we can improve our education system'. I have heard leaders of Western nations bemoaning the fact that their young are no longer interested in mathematics and science but education is not just about mathematics and science. It is also about logical and critical thinking in every sphere of life, learning ethical behaviour and the need to stand up for one's rights. Among its more important goals, the aims of education must be to spur innovation, egalitarianism and, hopefully, happy coexistence. It is difficult to see how giving sanctity to creationism in America and other irrational beliefs in other countries can promote rational thinking. The role of leadership is to lead and mould public opinion rather than let policies be solely guided by public opinion. Nor have I heard any government saying, 'Our economy is stalling, let us strengthen our justice delivery system so that people may readily enter into contracts and their self and property are secure.' I have often heard of calls for judicial and justice delivery system reforms but have not heard of those reforms being linked to economic progress. In India, where hundreds of thousands of undertrials are locked up for years, even decades, it is viewed as a matter of human rights, which of course it is, but I have never heard it mentioned that speedy justice delivery is an essential ingredient of economic growth. I have not come across any government saying, 'Our economy is stalling because too many women and other disadvantaged groups appear to be excluded and we must try and fully liberate and educate them and treat them as equals.' Countries often have societal reform movements led by religious bodies, governments or other well-intentioned groups trying to change various aspects of their culture, but I have never heard of these efforts as being linked to economic progress or to aspects of culture that are needed for growth. I have never heard a government saying, 'Our economy is not doing well and our enterprise appears to be restricted so let us do away with a few government departments and some restrictive laws, which do little but hamper enterprise and growth.' In practice, all over the world, new laws that create more government departments are constantly being enacted. Indeed during times of slow growth, when life is becoming harder for all, it can hardly be expected that governments will impose new hardships upon themselves by trying to downsize. Their tendency will be to make themselves more secure with more laws, rules and regulations, to create more opportunities for themselves, whereas what their economies may need is fewer restrictions. Perhaps their moves are not ill-intentioned, but the imperative to survive is a very powerful incentive. If any downsizing of governments, laws or regulations is to happen, we must expect it to happen only at the initiation of non-governmental forces.

Every country needs to consider its unique set of circumstances and figure out its areas of weakness. It is to be expected that these areas will differ from country to country and so will remedial action. The examples that I have used in this book to highlight practices that lead to weakness in the economic engine are disproportionately about India. This does not imply that India has an inordinate number of weak areas or that the findings of this book are not equally applicable to all countries. The reason for giving many examples from India is that I live in India and am more aware of these practices.

Once a country has identified the parts of the economic engine that it considers to be its weak points, it must act to strengthen those parts. This is not always an easy task. While it may be relatively easy to take some steps, like axing unneeded laws or government departments that constrict the working of the economic engine, other steps will be more difficult and take far more time to implement. Any changes in education system may take years to take effect. Changes in the orientation of cultural aspects that matter to the working of the economic engine may take even longer. Today, considering that indirect tax collections partially contribute to the revenue of governments, governments will be loath to give up those revenues without being assured that the shortfall can be made up for by larger income tax collections. Perhaps they could start an inflation-protected savings scheme, the contributions to which are to be determined by the amount of taxes paid. Then if income tax collections rise, indirect taxes could be brought down progressively.

Whatever the means employed to transition to an efficiently running economic engine, the effort is worthwhile. This is the route to material wealth, fellowship, contentment and happiness.

ACKNOWLEDGEMENTS

These acknowledgements must start with my wife Vibha, for whom I often was an absentee partner while I was writing this book. I must thank the six people who read through my manuscript and gave both encouragement and constructive criticism: Vibha, my sons Varun and Viraj, and my friends Shankar Dey, Brig. Sandeep Bhalla and Leila Bohmer.

The first person to see this book outside my small circle of family and friends was literary agent Kanishka Gupta. He kindly introduced me to Dibakar Ghosh of Rupa Publications. I am indebted to Dibakar, whose insights into making a book more readable were a revelation to me.

Last but not least, my thanks to the entire team at Rupa Publications who made this book a reality.